FATAL
EXCHANGE

Books by Lisa Harris

SOUTHERN CRIMES

Dangerous Passage

Fatal Exchange

SOUTHERN CRIMES SERIES • BOOK 2

FATAL EXCHANGE

A NOVEL

LISA HARRIS

Revell

a division of Baker Publishing Group
Grand Rapids, Michigan

© 2014 by Lisa Harris

Published by Revell
a division of Baker Publishing Group
P.O. Box 6287, Grand Rapids, MI 49516-6287
www.revellbooks.com

Printed in the United States of America

Library of Congress Cataloging-in-Publication Data
Harris, Lisa, 1969–
    Fatal exchange : a novel / Lisa Harris.
        p.   cm. — (Southern crimes ; book 2)
    ISBN 978-0-8007-2191-6 (pbk.)
    1. Women teachers—Fiction. 2. Students—Fiction. 3. Drug traffic—Fiction.
I. Title.
PS3608.A78315F38 2014
813′.6—dc23   2013042560

Scriptures used in this book, whether quoted or paraphrased by the characters, are from the *Holy Bible*, New Living Translation, copyright © 1996, 2004, 2007 by Tyndale House Foundation. Used by permission of Tyndale House Publishers, Inc., Carol Stream, Illinois 60188. All rights reserved.

14   15   16   17   18   19   20   7   6   5   4   3   2   1

This story is dedicated to my three sweet children
who make my life complete.

CHAPTER 1

Mason Taylor shoved the airline ticket into the glove compartment of his single-cab pickup, then headed for the rear door of the police station. Guilt tore at him. He had been forced to choose between two impossible situations. The phone call from Denver two days ago had ripped through his world and left him reeling. But this morning's desperate call from Rafael, followed by photos of a brutally beaten young man, had become the deciding factor. Seventeen was too young to die. Denver, his dad, and everyone there would have to wait.

He pulled open the precinct door, his mind still spinning from Rafael's details of the setup. Drugs had slithered into Atlanta neighborhoods, both urban and suburban alike. They crossed boundaries of profession, class, and color, while leaving behind the ugly fallout by dealers, local gang members, and users. And more recently, cartel agents were being sent to cut out the middleman and bring in more profit.

The tug of duty pulled at him, but duty wasn't the only motivator that had tipped his decision to miss his flight. He'd seen firsthand how addictions destroyed families. His own father's habit had taken the man out of the picture for almost fifteen years.

For the moment Mason couldn't worry about the doctor's

report on his father's condition. His nine thirty flight was going to have to leave without him. Rafael had already faced enough tragedy and heartbreak in his lifetime. It was up to Mason to put an end to the situation and ensure Rafael didn't lose someone else he loved.

Inside the familiar walls of the precinct, Mason nodded at his fellow officers mingling in the hallway at the beginning of the morning shift. He paused in the doorway of Detective Avery North's office. Maneuvering to avoid the detective had become second nature on his part. Avery still believed that Mason was the leak who had put her brother Michael—his best friend—in an early grave. He'd finally come to realize that nothing he could say was going to change what she believed him capable of doing. The captain had him step in on a recent human trafficking case and help with a potential serial killer. Once they'd closed the case, Mason was happy to go back to another undercover gig away from Avery's watchful eyes. And he was certain she felt the same.

He pressed his hand against the doorframe of her office and drew in a slow breath before walking in.

Avery glanced up from the file she was working on, irritation clear in her expression. "Mason. This is a surprise." She pushed the file away and started twisting the engagement ring on her left hand.

Mason ignored the annoyance in her voice and closed the door behind him. "I need to talk to you about one of your current cases."

"I thought you were catching a flight to Denver this morning for some family reunion."

"News travels fast." A "reunion" certainly wasn't what Mason had called it, but he had no desire to add more grist to the rumor mill.

"It's a small precinct."

Mason shoved his hands into the pockets of his leather jacket and attempted to rein in his frustration. "I was supposed to go visit my father, but my plans have changed. I've got a problem."

She quirked a brow. "And you came to me?"

"We might not agree on everything, but like it or not, we are on the same side of the law."

"What is it?"

He hesitated, hoping he'd made the right decision. No matter what their personal feelings were toward each other, there was a boy's life at stake. "I understand your team has been working on the Torres case."

James Torres had been the first victim in an ongoing drug trafficking investigation. He'd been kidnapped by a local gang, held for ransom, then executed when the victim's family couldn't pay the ten thousand he owed the gang. Three more murders in the past four months, and they'd yet to find the men behind the brutal killings. All four victims had ended up with their throats slit—and those were the ones the department knew about. Rumors on the street had the murders tied to a new drug cartel from Mexico that was spreading through the streets of Atlanta like the bubonic plague. They made the Mafia look soft.

"You have something for me?" Avery asked. Even the possibility of a new lead hadn't erased the irritation from her face.

"I might."

"Okay." Her expression softened slightly. "Considering I've got four dead bodies and no solid leads on their murderers, I'm interested. What've you got?"

Mason handed Avery his smartphone. Eduardo Cerda stared into the camera in the first photo. Eyes wide open and bloodshot, blood trailing from his mouth beneath the gag, a bruise across his cheekbone . . . his nose clearly broken. Mason didn't need his ten years on the force learning to read people to know the boy was terrified. The only thing keeping him alive was the anticipation of the money the kidnappers were demanding. In the meantime, they'd torture him and wait to receive the ransom payout.

Avery studied the photos, her brow narrowed. "What are these?"

"Proof-of-life photos that came with a ransom note." Mason nodded toward the photos. "His name is Eduardo Cerda."

"Where did you get them?"

"From his brother, Rafael. The connections to your case are all there. Drug related, similar MO, including the ransom note tacked to the inside of their front door . . ." He had her attention now. "Could be your lucky break. This time we've got a witness and a live victim."

He'd discovered firsthand working undercover that a high percentage of drug-related kidnappings went unreported by victims' families who were afraid to call attention to their own involvement in the illegal drug trade. Which made it harder for the authorities to step in before it was too late. But this time, if they could find Eduardo before the deadline, they might be able to save his life.

"I can see you've studied up on my case files." Avery set the phone down on the desk between them. "You don't have to convince me to get involved in this."

Mason leaned forward, hands braced against the desk. "I'd like to take the lead on this case."

"Have you talked to the captain about this?"

"I decided to come see you first."

"Like I said, I agree this is worth following up on, but we've been working this case for four months, which means my team is more than capable of running point on this. Besides that, what about your time off?"

Mason caught her dismissive tone and bit back his own sharp response. "Denver can wait for now." Convincing Avery of his innocence was like proving there was sustainable life on the sun. "Listen, for just a second forget about Michael and everything you think about me, and try to be objective. There's a boy's life at stake here."

Her look pierced right through him. "Don't try and lay a guilt trip and turn this back around on me. I don't owe you anything."

"I never said you did."

Mason pushed away from the desk and clenched his fists. He'd been foolish to think he could convince her he needed to run this investigation. He could give her the information he had about the case and walk away. Except he knew Rafael, just like he'd known Michael. He couldn't—wouldn't—betray either of them. He'd lost Michael. He wasn't going to lose Rafael.

"Listen." Mason wasn't finished fighting. "I know this kid. His older brother sent me these photos. His name is Rafael Cerda. He's a straight-A student who's trying his best to stay out of trouble in a neighborhood filled with drugs and gangs. His mom and his brother are the only family he has, and he's scared of losing his brother. He came to me because he trusts me."

She drummed her fingers against her desk. "What do you know about Eduardo?"

"He's seventeen, no brushes with the law. An average student who has managed to stay out of trouble for the most part."

"What else? He's got to be a seller or at least a buyer for them to come after him this way."

"Rafael doesn't believe he's involved."

"And you believe that?"

"I believe that if Eduardo really is involved in selling, Rafael doesn't know."

"So we've got a drug-related ransom demand on a boy with no record, and a family with no clue of his involvement."

"It wouldn't be the first time an innocent victim ended up being held for ransom."

"Or the first time a kid was working the streets and fooling his family at the same time."

Innocent until proven guilty was supposed to be how it worked. Avery might be a good—even a great—cop, but her biases tended to run strong at times.

"I'm trying to be objective." Avery leaned back in her chair. "What else do you know about the Cerda family?"

"Father died when Rafael was twelve from a drug overdose. His mother cleans laundry at the Peachtree Hotel six days a week to keep food on the table. Rafael delivers newspapers and does odd jobs for his neighbors to earn extra money. And as I said, his brother's been pretty good to stay under the radar and out of trouble."

"Until now. You seem to know a lot about this Rafael. Where do you know him from?"

"He's part of a big brother program where I volunteer. He landed a full scholarship to Dogwood Academy a few years ago. Has dreams of college and becoming an engineer."

"Dogwood Academy?" Avery's chin tipped up and she caught his gaze. "That's where Tess goes to school and my sister teaches."

Mason nodded. He hadn't missed the connection. Avery's daughter was a student at the private school while her sister, Emily, taught history and coached girls' volleyball. Funny how things tended to go full circle. He'd fallen for Emily the first time they met, while she was still in college. Completely opposite from her sister, Emily had broken family tradition, opting for a career in teaching rather than law enforcement.

But despite the attraction, it hadn't taken him long to realize that she was everything he wasn't. Born into a well-off southern family, she had more charm in her little finger than he could hope to have in a lifetime. Not that his long-dormant feelings for Emily mattered at the moment. His eyes went back to the screen still displaying Eduardo's photo.

"What if Eduardo is selling?" Avery's question broke into his thoughts.

"Worst-case scenario is that he's working for some local drug lord and has an unpaid debt they're insisting he pay up." It was a scenario that even he couldn't ignore. Atlanta was nowhere near the Mexican border, but its highway system had become the perfect route in linking Mexico to the rest of the East Coast. "Best-case scenario is that Eduardo turns out to be a normal, law-abiding seventeen-year-old kid who happened to be at the wrong place at the wrong time. We rescue him, and you find out who's behind your latest string of murders."

Avery picked up a pen and tapped it against the table while he tried to read her expression. Irritated? Concerned? He wasn't sure.

"What about his mom?" she asked. "What does she think?"

"I haven't spoken to her, but Rafael said that if Eduardo is dealing, he's been able to hide it from both of them."

"Not too hard for a mom to miss something when working long hours six days a week."

Mason caught the flicker of understanding in Avery's eyes and felt his anger diminish slightly. Three years ago she'd lost her husband—a fellow officer—in a car accident. She knew firsthand what it was like to raise a child as a single mom.

"Where's Rafael now?"

"His mother can't afford any time off, so he drove her to work. I'm supposed to meet him at seven thirty. He's counting on me to find his brother."

"How's Rafael going to react if we end up having to put his brother on trial for selling drugs?"

"I'll help him deal with that when—and if—it happens."

Avery tugged on the end of her ponytail that had the same reddish highlights as both her sister and daughter. "How much do the kidnappers want?"

Mason tried to swallow the lump in his throat. "Two hundred and fifty thousand dollars."

Her gasp was audible, and he understood her reaction. He'd had the same one. A quarter-of-a-million-dollar ransom from a mom who barely made minimum wage?

"I know what you're thinking," Mason said, "but these kidnappers typically know where the money is and what their victims can afford to pay. There's money or drugs somewhere in this scenario. Even if it isn't Eduardo who's behind it, the kidnappers obviously believe he has access to it."

"Who else knows about this?"

"No one. They told Rafael not to tell anyone, but with time running out, he didn't know what else to do. You're the only one I've told."

"At least he did the right thing. How much time?"

Mason glanced at his watch. It was seven. "According to Rafael, we're down to just under seven hours."

CHAPTER
2

Emily punched the alarm button on her key fob, then started up the brick path toward Dogwood Academy's main entrance, wondering why she'd wasted a perfectly good weekend by agreeing to a blind date with a friend of a friend. The guy ended up being a psychologist who enjoyed long-winded monologues on dream interpretation. It might not have been so bad if he'd chosen a topic she knew something about. As it turned out, he'd almost put *her* to sleep.

Which was one reason she was looking forward to finishing the last week of the semester. Christmas break meant two weeks of sleeping in amid splurges of eggnog, shopping, and no blind dates.

A gust of wind whipped under her coat. Emily shivered. Rain was predicted, and if temperatures dropped enough, snow later in the day. But despite the dreariness of the weather this time of year, and the challenge teaching could be at times, she never let herself forget how much she loved her job.

Dogwood Academy's campus was a scattering of restored antebellum buildings from the 1800s along with modern-day structures and their ample conveniences. Beyond the refurbished main building were the music hall, athletic center, sports fields, and twenty-five acres of rolling hills and wooded running trails offering a glimpse into what Atlanta looked like a century ago.

"Emily, wait up!"

Emily paused along the manicured lawn scattered with uniformed students to let Grace Cowen catch up with her. In typical Grace fashion, she was running late, juggling armfuls of books and papers. Her dress was already somewhat disheveled, though she hadn't even made it yet to her first-period class. There were days when Emily wondered how her friend actually made it to school. But then again, Grace's inclination to be scatterbrained and tardy hadn't stopped her from winning Teacher of the Year three times in a row. Students loved her.

Grace caught up with her, out of breath. "Don't tell me you're running late too?"

"Got here forty-five minutes ago, actually." Emily held up her cell phone that had fallen under the passenger seat, then dropped it into her coat pocket. "Just ran out to the car to grab it. Can I help carry something?"

She reached for one of the bags that was slipping off Grace's shoulder. They might be polar opposites in almost everything, but Grace had still managed to be a steady anchor for her for as long as she could remember. In fact, she wasn't sure she'd still be teaching if it weren't for Grace's constant encouragement that had gotten her through her first couple of years.

"Take this one, actually. It's for you." Grace handed one of the bags to her.

Emily held up the black "Over-the-Hill Survival Kit" bag. "Are you serious?"

"Ignore the packaging. Mark made some of those to-die-for brownies you are always asking for and insisted I bring you some."

"Oh, I love your husband."

"You'd better watch it. He's taken." Grace's laugh was drowned out by a group of students rushing past them in the school's maroon and gray colors. "And by the way, please don't tell me that you picked up that outfit you're wearing at a secondhand shop."

Emily glanced down at the olive-green skirt peeking out from her open '60s-inspired coat. She'd matched the skirt with a white blouse and a pair of heeled boots. "You know I prefer the word 'vintage' to 'secondhand.'"

"Funny. Call it what you want, I still love the look, though I can only imagine what a pencil skirt would look like on these hips of mine."

Emily laughed this time. Leave it to Grace to tell it like it was while not caring she wasn't a size 4. "I can promise you, Mark will always love you no matter what you're wearing."

Grace blushed. "He did pick this outfit."

"Which I also love, by the way."

The multicolored maxi dress and denim jacket were perfect for Grace. But even more perfect was that after a year of marriage, she was still glowing. Who could have guessed that a bubbly English teacher and a highly focused industrial engineer could make such a perfect couple?

Grace nudged Emily with her elbow. "After all this time as friends, do you realize you still haven't taken me thrift store shopping and shared your secrets? I have a feeling that Mark would love me even more if I could find an alternative location for shopping that would make up for my expensive tastes."

Emily started walking again. "How about I do that when you stop trying to set me up on another blind date?"

"Okay. I know Saturday didn't go well with Greg, but I've actually found someone else for you."

Of course she had. "Forget it, Grace. No more blind dates. No more introducing me to lonely, desperate, single men who—"

"Just hear me out." Grace somehow managed to grab Emily's arm amongst all her bags. "Mark told me this morning about this new guy at his work that meets every one of your requirements.

Graphic designer, i.e., not a cop—check. Early thirties, check. Doesn't live in his parents' basement, check. Strong faith, check. He even plays in the worship band at his church."

Emily stopped to face Grace and shook her head. "The problem is, even if I could check everything off, in the end I still somehow always manage to strike out. Take Charlie, for example—the last guy I fell for and the reason for the reinstated 'not involved in any type of law enforcement' requirement. But having all the right boxes ticked is never enough in the end, which means clearly I'm missing something. That certain spark I've never been able to quantify on a checklist. So for the moment, the only thing I'm looking for is a house."

Emily started again for the front of the school. She might not currently fall in the "doesn't live with parents" category, but her stint back home was only until she saved up enough money for a down payment.

"I just hope you enjoy cuddling up with an electric bill and a stack of frozen dinners at night," Grace said.

Ouch. "What happened to you being my support system?"

"I always will be, and you know it. I just want you to have what Mark and I have."

Which was one of the things that got her into trouble in the first place. Wanting to get married for the sake of getting married. That was never a good idea.

"I refuse to approach thirty in the overt, desperate manner some single women do. I'm embracing who I am, along with the fact that whether I'm twenty-five or thirty-five, I can still be happy *and* single. That is why I'm buying my own house in the suburbs, complete with a fenced-in backyard, spa tub, and adopting this adorable German shepherd puppy I found online over the weekend."

Grace's gaze narrowed. "If you say so."

"I do say so, which means that for now—besides house

hunting—I'm looking forward to finishing up the semester and swinging into Christmas break, when I can spend uninterrupted hours soaking in the tub, reading, shopping, and eating as much of my mama's cooking as I want without an ounce of guilt."

Her Zumba classes would have to make up for the extra calories she planned to indulge in, but she'd take the class for herself, not to catch herself a man.

Grace's high heels clicked on the sidewalk beside her as they started for the main hall. "Maybe it's just too soon after your breaking things off with Charlie."

Emily frowned at her friend's comment. The fact that she'd been the one who broke things off hadn't stopped everyone from worrying about her. "If you want to worry about someone, worry about Charlie. But the bottom line is that it's been almost six months, and this has nothing to do with Charlie, or me, or our past relationship. It has to do with me learning to be happy being me whether I'm a part of a couple or not."

Which was true. She'd mistaken that biological clock ticking for love, along with her mother's nagging that made her feel as if in a few more years she'd somehow expire and get pulled from the shelf. How she'd decided Charlie was the perfect answer, she wasn't quite sure. On the outside, he'd been a decorated officer, attentive, and above average in the looks department. But after a whirlwind romance, there had been other issues that had played in her final decision. And while she might not be ready to stop looking, neither was she ready to throw herself back into the game.

"I just was so hoping there would be a spark between you and Greg."

"Any spark was one-sided and quickly died out. He only knows how to talk about one thing." Her phone sounded, and Emily stopped to pull it out of her pocket. "Case in point. Greg has called me a total of seven times since Saturday night to make sure I had a good time on our date and to ask me if I had a dream that I needed interpreted. Seven times, Grace."

"Okay, even I admit that's creepy."

She checked the caller ID on the still-ringing phone. Unavailable. The guy was persistent. It was time to put an end to things. "Listen, Greg. Apparently I didn't make myself clear the last time—"

"Emily?"

"Who's this?'"

"Mason Taylor."

"Mason?"

She stopped midstride. Students continued toward the crowded entrance of the school, anticipating the first bell of the day. Mason Taylor was the last person she'd expected to hear from. No matter what she thought about Avery's investigation into her brother Michael's death, Mason wasn't exactly a favorite guest at the Hunt dinner table. At least when her sister was around.

"Listen, I know you're probably getting ready to start school," he said, "but I wonder if I could talk to you for a couple minutes. It's something serious that involves one of your students."

Her stomach twisted. Becoming a teacher had helped fulfill a desire to not only educate but also inspire a future generation. The thought that one of them could be in trouble left her feeling uneasy.

"Of course." Emily glanced at her watch. She had fifteen minutes until the first bell rang. She hated being late, but not as much as she worried about one of her students getting in trouble with the law. "Where are you?"

"I'm coming up the front sidewalk right now."

Emily turned back toward the parking lot and saw Mason walking toward her. The last time she'd seen Mason Taylor had been at her brother's funeral. He'd changed little. He'd always been lean, muscular, and good-looking. Funny, the memories that surfaced at the most inappropriate times. In college, she'd had a crush on Mason, with his longish, dark-blond hair and soft brown eyes, despite the fact that he was five years older than she was, one of her brother's buddies, and not a believer. That last reason—along with the fact he was a cop—was why she'd ended up saying no the one time he'd asked her out. After that, he'd never done more than shoot her one of his heart-pounding smiles in passing.

Grace took a step closer to Emily and whispered, "Who is that?"

"He's a detective who's worked some with my sister." There wasn't time to share the rest of the family saga.

"What does he want with you?"

"I don't know. He just said it was something urgent that had to do with one of my students."

"Is he single?"

"Single?" Grace's question threw Emily off. "Seriously? Every man who comes along isn't a potential date, and this one certainly isn't for me."

"So you're not going to introduce me?"

"You're married."

"Funny. Say what you want, I'm just trying to help you find the bit of happiness I found."

Emily forced a smile and motioned for Grace to go on. The last thing she needed was for this to turn awkward. "No introductions today, but I promise I'll meet you for lunch."

"Fine. I'll be there."

Emily ignored the knowing look Grace shot her. She might not be convinced of Mason's guilt like her sister was, but neither did she plan to add another cop to her list of failed relationships.

She drew in a deep breath and smiled as he walked up to her. "Mason Taylor. It's been a long time."

CHAPTER
3

Mason shoved his hands into his pockets, suddenly feeling out of place in his jeans, T-shirt, and leather jacket next to the uniformed students walking past them. And next to Emily. She looked ready to take on the world in her tailored skirt, shirt, and fashionable winter coat. She'd pulled her auburn hair back in some sophisticated twist that framed her face. She was still just as pretty as he remembered her.

The last time he'd seen her had been at Michael's funeral, but even that memory didn't stand out as much as the first time he'd met her. He'd been invited to the Hunt home for Thanksgiving dinner a couple of months after his aunt died. He was new on the force, and he and Michael had quickly become close friends. Emily had been home from college. He'd found her sweet, smart, and classy, and he hadn't been able to stop staring at her across the table filled with the turkey and trimmings.

Michael had noticed Mason's interest in his younger sister, teasing that she was way out of his league, but Mason hadn't cared. Instead, after the last piece of pumpkin pie, he'd pressed Michael with a dozen questions. What was she studying? What did she do for fun? Was she dating anyone? Michael had told him right off that she wouldn't be interested. He already had three strikes against him. He was a cop, didn't share her faith, and she was *way* out of his league.

Turned out Michael had been right. She'd politely declined his invitation in an awkward exchange he still preferred to forget. And at the end of the break, she'd gone off to school without giving him a second glance.

He'd seen her periodically throughout the next few years when he hung out at the Hunt home for family dinners and summer barbecues, but always from a distance. She'd been friendly, but had never done anything to encourage him, and because he respected her beliefs, he'd never pursued her. Before he knew it, she was engaged to Charlie, and he'd realized it was time to forget her. That had been just over a year ago, the Thanksgiving before Michael was killed.

Despite his determination to forget the woman now standing in front of him, clearly those old feelings hadn't completely died. In fact, he was certain he had more courage to talk to a murder suspect while undercover than Michael's little sister, who somehow managed to raise his heart rate even after all these years. So much for keeping things strictly business.

He turned his attention across the lawn to the parking lot where parents were dropping off students, before forcing himself to look back at those deep blue eyes of hers.

He cleared his throat. "Listen, I'm sorry to drop by unexpectedly. I'm sure you have a lot to do at the beginning of the school day."

"That's okay." She glanced at her watch. "I have a few free minutes until school starts." She nodded toward a cast-iron and wooden bench paid for by one of the school's donors. "Out here is probably the quietest. The hallways are filled up with students hitting their lockers before school starts."

"Okay."

She sat down beside him, concern clearly etched in her

expression. "You said there was something wrong with one of my students."

"It's Rafael Cerda. He told me you know him."

Emily's concern turned to surprise. "Rafael? Of course I know him. Not only do I have him in class, but I tutor him as well. He's one of my best students and honestly the last person I'd imagine in trouble with the law."

"He's not in trouble, but his brother is."

She shook her head. "What's going on?"

"Early yesterday morning, three armed men broke into their apartment. They held Rafael and his mother at gunpoint and kidnapped Eduardo."

Emily's face paled. "Kidnapped him? Why would they do that?"

"Rafael is convinced they grabbed the wrong person, but what we are sure of from the ransom note is that this is drug related. We think it's connected to a rash of recent kidnappings for ransom and murders."

"And you? What do you think? That Eduardo is mixed up with drugs?"

"That's what I'm trying to find out. What do you know about Eduardo?"

She shrugged a shoulder. "He doesn't go to school here, so honestly, not a lot. I've spoken to him a few times, when Rafael has brought him to a football game or some other school activity. He's always been quiet and polite. Rafael told me once that Eduardo could do better in school if he'd apply himself, but he's never mentioned him being in any kind of trouble."

"Anything else?"

"They're close, and I know Rafael worries about him, especially since they go to different schools. That makes it harder for Rafael to keep an eye on him, but I think he's a good kid. Rafael's never mentioned any brushes with the law, or drugs for that matter."

"Rafael told me the same thing."

"So what's your connection to Rafael? I thought you were still working undercover."

"I am, but I've asked to be involved because I know Rafael." He wrapped his fingers around the cold metal bench. "Met him a couple years ago at a youth center where I volunteer, so this has become . . . personal."

"He's mentioned going there," she said. "Told me how much the center changed his life."

"I'm glad. I came from a broken family a lot like Rafael's, so I know what it's like to grow up without a father." He stopped. Emily didn't need to hear about the sordid details from his past. "I need to know if you've seen Rafael this morning."

"No, not yet. He usually comes in to see me three or four mornings a week for extra tutoring or college prep work, but he didn't come in today. Why? Don't you know where he is?"

Worry began to gnaw his gut. "I spoke with him this morning. He was supposed to meet me at seven thirty, after dropping his mother off at work. He didn't show up."

Emily's expression mirrored his own concern. "That isn't like Rafael. He's always very dependable. Serious about everything he does."

"I've noticed the same thing about him. What do you know about his family life?"

"Enough to know it's not easy for him. Father left years ago. I think he eventually died from an overdose. I've met his mother once or twice. She works a lot of hours and isn't around much. I know Rafael worries about Eduardo. Feels like it's his responsibility to keep him off the streets." Emily laced her fingers together, then quickly unfolded them to grasp the edge of the bench. "What are the kidnappers demanding?"

He hesitated before pulling out his phone and handing it to

her. "Rafael received these yesterday. They're demanding two hundred and fifty thousand dollars."

———

Emily sucked in a breath and pressed her hand against her mouth as she stared at the photos. Her stomach lurched. Growing up with most of her family on the police force had guaranteed she'd seen her fair share of the ugly realities of this world, but while she was used to hearing stories around the dinner table of what happened out on the streets, this was different. This was someone she knew.

"You can't be serious?" She shook her head. "None of this makes any sense. Rafael goes to school here on a scholarship. His mother works at a hotel. Who in the world would think Eduardo has that kind of money?"

"That's why Rafael is convinced this is a case of mistaken identity. He believes they picked up the wrong person."

"Is that possible?"

"It happens."

She gauged his expression. "But you don't think that's what happened in this case."

"Honestly, I don't know. Eduardo could be innocent, but we can't dismiss the possibility he is involved. If he's selling to his friends at school, kids in the neighborhood, and even throughout the school district, he could be bringing in some very serious income. And a seventeen-year-old wouldn't necessarily realize fully who he's dealing with and the consequences of crossing the higher-ups."

"I still don't understand." Emily felt her emotions swing from shock to anger to a sick burning sensation in the bottom of her stomach. "Say he is working as a dealer. Why kidnap a source of income?"

"Typically the reason's an overdue drug debt."

She tried to absorb the information. "Tell me everything. Exactly what happened?"

"Eduardo was kidnapped early Sunday morning at his house. The note said they have thirty-six hours to come up with the money—that's by two o'clock this afternoon."

Which meant time was quickly running out.

"And if they don't get the money? What happens then?"

"There's a chance they'll kill him."

Emily handed the phone back to him, stood up, and started pacing in front of the bench. She'd never fit into this world of police and criminals. It was why she knew she'd never marry a cop. She didn't want to spend her time worrying if her husband was coming home. Her sister, her father, her brother before he died . . . they all seemed to be able to dig deep inside themselves and come up with what they needed to handle situations they faced on the streets. But separating her heart from her work was something she'd never been able to do. Rafael wasn't just another kid to check off the attendance list when he came into her class every morning. He was the reason she did what she did.

She turned back to Mason. "If Rafael and his mother can't give them what they want, what do they think they're going to get out of this?" Emily bit the edge of her lip. "He's only seventeen."

"Too young in most people's minds to be involved, but certainly not impossible. It happens more often than you'd think."

Emily shifted her attention back toward the front steps of the school where students were making their way into the main hall. They came dressed in the smart uniforms—plaid skirts or gray dress pants, crisp white shirts, and maroon blazers. But she knew that even beneath the prep school image of money and prestige, they didn't all fit into that pristine world. Coming from a family of privilege might not be as challenging as growing up on the streets, but she knew that money didn't fix problems.

Sometimes money made everything worse. If that was what had happened to Eduardo . . .

Mason stood up beside her, slipping the phone back in his pocket. "Eduardo isn't the only person I'm worried about. I'm worried something might have happened to Rafael."

Emily felt her eyes water. She hadn't worked with Rafael all this time to have his life ruined by someone else's foolishness.

She looked up and caught Mason's gaze. She knew her sister believed Mason had been behind her brother's death. But was that the truth?

What she did know for sure was that Mason knew what life was like on the streets and had contacts across the city. If anyone could find Rafael, he could. "What can I do to help?"

"If he comes to school today, I need you to call me immediately and let me know."

"Of course." She brought up the list of received calls on her phone and added him to her contacts.

Michael had trusted Mason. She was going to have to do the same, because teenagers shouldn't have to deal with the dark realities of the world before even leaving home. Which was why a part of her wished she had the courage to step into her sister's shoes so she could help stop people like those behind Eduardo's kidnapping.

"You okay?"

"I will be." She looked up and caught those mesmerizing eyes she'd noticed the first time they'd met. She dropped her gaze. "Rafael's one of my success stories. He's been accepted to the University of Georgia on a scholarship. He has plans to make a better life for himself and his family. He deserves that chance."

"I know."

She brushed a tear from her cheek. "Thanks for letting me know what's going on. I'll be praying."

"I know you will. I'll be praying too. I still struggle justifying the evil that I see around me every day, but the older I get, the more I believe—have to believe—that no matter what happens, God is still in control."

Her father had told her about Mason's recent decision to follow Christ, making her wonder what might have happened if he'd been a believer when he'd asked her out all those years ago. Maybe she would have said yes . . .

Emily reined her thoughts back in. "I know you'll do everything you possibly can to find both boys—and get Eduardo out alive."

Mason nodded, then reached out and ran his fingers loosely down her sleeve. "I promise I'll do my best."

CHAPTER
4

Emily watched Mason turn away and head for the parking lot. No matter what her sister believed regarding Mason's involvement in their brother's death, Emily had always seen him as capable and skilled. And until the day he died, Michael had trusted Mason with his life. Whether Mason had actually betrayed Michael before the explosion at the warehouse that had taken his life, none of them might ever know, but she'd never forgotten the expression she'd caught on his face as he'd helped carry the casket out of the chapel after Michael's funeral. The haunting mixture of sadness, loss, even defeat had been clear. It was the same expression she'd seen on his face today.

But to Mason, this case was personal.

She headed for the main entrance and shivered despite the warm morning sun trying to penetrate the scattering of clouds overhead. The photos of Eduardo resurfaced in her mind. No one had been surprised when she opted for a future with a private academy instead of the police academy. And while the school with its manicured lawns and trimmed hedges was far from problem free, she'd much rather face off with a parent or student over a bad history grade than enter her sister's world of cops and robbers. Today had pushed her past the edges of her comfort zone.

Inside the main entry of Dogwood Academy, she started down the long hall. The pale blue walls held neat rows of gray lockers, classroom doors, and dozens of smartly uniformed students. The sound of her boots, clicking against the tiled floor with every step she took, was barely audible above the low roar of the students chatting about their weekend and upcoming holiday plans as they waited for the last minute before rushing off to their homeroom class once the first warning bell rang.

Snippets of conversations fluttered around her, but her mind was elsewhere. Students blurred past as she tried to shake the unease seeping through her. She might not know Eduardo well, but she did know Rafael and how seriously he took his role as the older brother. He'd mentioned more than once that it was his responsibility to not only keep his family together but to keep Eduardo out of trouble.

Emily paused to pull a flyer off the bulletin board of last week's senior debate she'd moderated. Nausea spread through her stomach. Whether or not Eduardo was guilty of dealing drugs didn't matter to the kidnappers anymore. His life hung in the balance, and whatever the outcome, it was going to take Rafael a long time to shake the guilt that he hadn't been able to stop this from happening in the first place.

She crumpled the flyer and tossed it into the trash. She was going to have to find a way to focus on the day ahead without obsessing over what was happening with Rafael and his brother. At least she now had Mason's number. Even if she didn't see Rafael, she could still call for an update.

"Aunt Emily?"

Emily paused beside the drinking fountain. "Morning, Tess." She glanced at her niece, then at her watch. "It'll take you a couple of minutes to get all the way to your class. Do I need to write you a pass?"

"I'll hurry." Tess sniffled. "Did you remember to bring my

English book? Mrs. Masters isn't going to be happy if I forget it again."

"No worries, it's on my desk." They started back down the hall at a quick pace toward her classroom, weaving their way through the sea of high school students. One day, she wanted two or three kids of her own, but in the meantime, being an aunt filled that maternal void. "How's your cold?"

"I wanted to stay home, but Mom insisted I was fine."

"She knows about your science exam?"

"Yes, but not how terrified I am to take it." Tess's frown deepened. "Mom and I got into a big fight this morning. It was all stupid stuff. She got mad. I got mad. I said things I shouldn't've."

"Over what?"

Tess dropped her gaze. "Jackson mainly."

Emily stopped to face Tess, ignoring the slamming locker doors and rowdy voices around her. "I thought you were happy your mom was getting remarried."

"I am . . . I was. I don't know." She shrugged. "Last night, Mom and I were supposed to go out for dinner. Just the two of us."

"And that didn't happen?"

"She worked late, then Jackson called and needed to talk about his grandfather. He might have to put him in an old people's home, or something."

"So dinner got canceled." Emily caught the hurt in Tess's eyes. After three years of widowhood, her sister had finally found the perfect match. But even a second chance was made complicated when there was a teen involved.

Tess let out a deep sigh. "I know I shouldn't feel so angry, and I know he makes my mom happy, but everything's changing, and sometimes . . . sometimes I hate it. I wish things could go back the way they were with Mom and me. Is that crazy?"

"No." Emily put her arm around Tess's shoulder and started

walking again toward her classroom. "I know it's been rough for you, losing your dad, but everything you're feeling is normal. Jackson's a good man, and I think he'll make a great stepfather for you, but it's going to take time. For all three of you."

"That's what my mom keeps saying. That it's going to take time for all of us to adjust to being a family. I just . . . I miss my dad."

Emily felt her own heart break. Her niece had been ten when her father died. She was old enough to remember holidays spent together, Braves games, and family meals around the dinner table. And she was old enough now to realize that while Jackson might make her mom happy, things were going to be different.

"Jackson's not in your life to come between you and your mom. Give both of them time to find that balance."

"I'm trying."

Emily walked into her classroom with Tess still beside her. There were already a half-dozen students talking in the back of the room. Emily set the bag of brownies Grace had given her on her desk, picked up Tess's forgotten English book, then turned back to her niece.

"Just remember that Jackson doesn't want to take your dad's place. That's something he can't and won't ever do. Your dad will always be a part of who you are—not just his DNA, but everything he did. What Jackson can do is help fill that emptiness in your heart, both your mother's and yours. He'll be there to help you get your driver's license, meet your date for senior prom, and one day . . . walk you down the aisle."

"You're not helping." A blush crept across Tess's face.

Emily nudged her shoulder. "You know what I mean."

Tess's blush spread as she ducked her head and nodded. "I guess."

Emily looked up as Rafael stepped through the doorway across the room, wearing his familiar green sweatshirt paired with a ball cap. A sigh of relief swam through her. At least he was okay.

Emily turned back to Tess. "Let me go ahead and write you a pass. The warning bell's about to ring."

Emily pulled out her cell phone and brought up Mason's number while she searched the top drawer of her desk for a pen to write the pass. He would be relieved to know Rafael was okay. He'd probably just got held up in traffic. She'd heard on the radio this morning that there had been an accident on the freeway that was slowing the morning commute.

Mason answered on the first ring.

"Mason, this is Emily. Rafael just showed up. If you'd like to speak to him—"

The warning bell rang, drowning out the wave of kids scurrying into the classroom at the last minute.

Emily signaled at Tess to wait a second, then called out Rafael's name.

He hesitated before turning to face her. His normal smile was gone. His eyes red. He took a step backward and shut the door.

"Rafael, wait. I need to—"

Rafael pulled a gun out of his sweatshirt, crossed the room, then grabbed Tess's arm. "I'm sorry, Miss Hunt, but I need you to give me your phone, then lock the door with your key."

"Emily?" Mason's voice sounded from the phone.

Emily fought to put Rafael's demands into focus. The blank face, the gun, the demands . . . She shook her head. "I don't understand."

"It's simple. Give me your phone and lock the door."

She stumbled forward with the phone, still trying to take in the numbing reality of what was happening. Tess's eyes were wide with horror. One of her students sobbed in the back of the room.

Emily fished for the key in her pocket, then glanced at the

phone. She had to let Mason know what was happening. "He's got a gun."

"Don't move!" Rafael yelled as he let go of Tess and knocked the phone from Emily's hand onto the tiled floor. He grabbed Tess's arm again, his other hand still gripping the gun out in front of him. Emily forced her mind not to shut down in panic. The school's—and her—priority was to keep the students safe.

Words like *lockdown*, *procedures*, and *minimizing the target* swam through her head. But in this situation, there was no place to hide from the shooter's attention. No way to provide 911 with the information they would need to help the police neutralize the situation. Because the potential shooter was standing right in front of her.

Rafael's got a gun?

Mason shouted Emily's name into his phone, but the connection was already lost. He'd heard enough, though, to realize that a drug-related kidnapping had somehow twisted into a school hostage situation. He hurried down the hallway toward Avery's office while redialing Emily's number. It rang a half-dozen times before her voice mail clicked on.

Rafael . . . what are you doing?

Mentally, he ran through their phone conversation this morning, struggling to figure out what he'd missed. Somewhere between telling him about the ransom demands and now, Rafael had decided to take things into his own hands.

Mason's heart pounded at the ugly truth. He'd been here before. A no-win situation where you realize that no matter how hard you try, there is no way out. But while Rafael's voice had sounded worried, Mason hadn't gotten the impression he was desperate. So how had he gone from trying to save his brother to committing a felony? Panic, guilt, feelings of responsibility? At some point, something inside that boy had snapped and pushed him over the edge.

Mason dialed a second number and gave his call sign and location before explaining to the dispatcher what he knew. Gunman at school, at least one weapon, Dogwood Academy, probable hostage situation . . .

A sick feeling flooded through him as he answered the dispatcher's questions. No matter how things played out, it wasn't going to end well for Rafael. And if the situation wasn't contained quickly, Rafael might not be the only person caught in the crossfire.

Avery was still at her desk, going through paperwork, by the time he'd hung up with dispatch and entered her office out of breath.

"Did you find your friend?"

"Yes . . . I . . . " Mason paused in the doorway. How did he tell her that he'd made a mistake in reading someone and her sister was now being held at gunpoint? If anything happened to Emily, he'd once again be the person to blame. But that wasn't the issue here. Emily's life—and the students in that room—were at stake.

"Mason." Avery set her pen down. "What's wrong?"

"When I spoke with Rafael this morning, I missed something."

Her expression darkened. "What do you mean?"

"I thought Rafael wanted us to help him. He called me because he trusted me, but instead of letting the police handle things, he . . . he showed up at the school a few minutes ago with a gun."

"You're telling me he's at my daughter's school with a gun?" Avery shoved her chair back from her desk, knocking it against the back wall, and jumped up. "If there's been a school shooting—"

"We don't know that. I've called dispatch. By now officers are heading to the scene, and the school will have already initiated their emergency procedures."

Mason watched Avery's face pale. She dug her keys out of

the side pocket of her pinstriped blazer. "Tell me exactly what happened."

"Rafael didn't meet me at seven thirty like he promised."

Her eyes narrowed. "So you went to the school?"

"Rafael told me he knew Emily. That she'd gone out of her way over the past few years to help him. I was hoping I could find him there. That she might have seen him this morning,"

"But he never showed up?"

"Not by the time I arrived, so I left and asked her to let me know if she heard from him. She called me just now, told me that he showed up for class. Then I heard her say he had a gun. He told her to lock the door. After that, we lost the connection."

Avery grabbed her phone and started dialing.

"I've tried to call Emily back. She's not answering her phone."

"So either she's still in the classroom and he's holding students hostage, or he's shooting up the school."

Avery let the phone ring. Emily still wasn't answering.

He knew her sister wasn't the only person Avery was worrying about. He tried to choose his words carefully. "Is Tess in Emily's classroom?"

"No." Mason caught a sliver of relief in Avery's eyes. "Emily teaches high school. Tess's classes are in the middle school, which is located in a completely separate wing."

"That's good."

Avery replaced the phone in her back pocket. "Give me a minute to brief my team, then I'll meet you at the school."

Mason nodded, then walked through the precinct bullpen where her team was working. No matter what he might think about Avery on a personal level, she and her team were good at what they did. Time in the marines had trained Carlos Dias in the art of interrogation. Tory Lambert might not look the part with her exotic model looks, but Mason had seen her work firsthand and knew that the computer geek and white-collar crime expert was not only diligent but smart. Eight weeks ago, the captain had assigned Levi Griffin—a former marine—to Avery's team, taking the place of her former partner who was killed in the line of duty. From what he'd heard, the detective had an exemplary record, including a stint in North Africa as a land mine disposal expert.

They worked beside a crime board where photos of the four murdered men in the Torres case were plastered across the top. James Torres. Ivan Cruz. Dante Ortiz. Adan Luna. Today they had to ensure Eduardo didn't become number five.

Heading for the parking lot, he redialed Rafael's number on the off chance he might answer. Still nothing. He was used to cases that fed on one's adrenaline, but when they became personal, it always felt like an extra blow.

Mason's phone rang as he unlocked his truck with the click of a button. If it were Rafael or Emily . . . He glanced at the caller ID, then hesitated.

Calvin.

He slid into the driver's seat, his stress level rising another notch. Whatever his baby brother had to say, it wasn't likely going to be good news.

"Calvin?"

"Hey, bro. Just got your message. Please don't tell me you're really not coming."

"I can't. Not now anyway." He'd used work as an excuse for years, but this time was legitimate. "I know it's bad timing, but it's a hostage situation and I can't just walk away."

"You might have to. I just finished talking to the doctor about Dad." Calvin's voice cracked. "Hospice is coming to the house this afternoon. They're only giving him a few more days."

Mason eased into the eastbound traffic, searching for the right response. Calvin would never completely understand why he wasn't ready to reenter the door their father had firmly closed so many years ago. His brother had been too young to remember the drunken brawls along with the seizures, hallucinations, and severe depression Mason had been forced to cope with. It had changed their relationship from father and son to Mason being the caregiver. Continuing the charade of having a relationship with the man he'd eventually rescued his brothers from had long ceased to be a priority.

But if nothing else, he needed to be there for Calvin and Craig.

"I'll be there as soon as I can. I promise."

Because he did care. But facing a man who had walked out of his life years ago and was suddenly acting on his deathbed as if nothing had ever gone wrong between them tore at his gut and left him feeling vulnerable.

Mason's stomach clenched as he hung up.

He punched in Rafael's number again. He needed to focus on the crisis at hand and deal with his father later. His father might be dying, but it was too late to develop the relationship he'd once craved. As for Rafael, he knew how hostage situations worked. The captain wouldn't hesitate to give the order to take him out if given the opportunity. Both situations he faced were losing battles.

The room spun in slow motion. Emily watched Rafael hold the gun against Tess's temple and dug for courage to take control of her emotions. Her niece stood frozen in front of him, her head tilted back, eyes wide in terror. No matter what he did, she felt like she was gambling with her niece's life.

Emily took a deep breath, looking from Tess to Rafael. "Tess, I want you to do exactly what he says. Rafael, I know about your brother. I know you're afraid, but this isn't the way to fix things. Let go of Tess. She's no threat to you. She's not going anywhere."

Rafael's phone started ringing again. Mason was probably calling, wondering why they'd lost the connection. Emily pressed her palm against her chest as fear closed in, threatening to strangle her. Saying the wrong thing could push Rafael over the edge, but not saying anything didn't seem to be an option. As soon as she'd locked the door, Rafael had ordered one of the students to close the blinds. Which meant they couldn't see what was going on outside the school.

God, I know you're here, but I don't know what to do. Please . . . please resolve this before someone gets hurt . . . or worse.

"You're going to have to answer the phone eventually," she continued. "They're going to want to know your demands."

He stared at her for a few seconds. "I'll talk to them when I'm ready." Rafael turned toward the other students, forcing Tess to move with him. "For now, I want all of you to move to the back of the room and be quiet."

Emily hesitated. Like Mason, she too had missed something. Rafael had always been her prize pupil. One she thought she knew. But now . . . His reaction didn't make sense.

"I spoke with Mason Taylor this morning," she began. "He was looking for you. Said you hadn't shown up for your meeting with him."

"Mr. Taylor can't help me. Now move to the back of the room and sit down. All of you."

He swung the gun upward until it was pointing at Emily, then let Tess join the other students. Besides the sound of someone whimpering in the back of the room, the only thing Emily could hear was the pounding of her heart in her ears.

Emily walked slowly in front of Rafael to where the students sat, fighting to keep her mind clear. A few months ago, all the teachers had been required to take a class on the school's emergency procedures, including a discussion of gunman scenarios. *Evaluate the situation, determine how many are involved, what kinds of weapons, don't try to play the role of hero, try to call for help, and most of all, remain calm . . .*

Calm? Right.

She'd memorized the school's emergency procedures. An all-school lockdown would now be in effect. Entrances would be sealed, no one allowed outside the classrooms until the "All Clear" was announced. Classroom doors would be locked, lights turned off, blinds and windows shut. Students and staff would sit against an interior wall. Status cards placed in the windows. Green for okay. Red for emergency assistance needed.

Emily tried to slow her breathing. It had been easy going over a scenario in a classroom with a PowerPoint lesson, catered barbecue on the back table, and a room full of her colleagues. Dealing with a gun pointed at her niece—and a dozen of her students—changed everything.

The problem was, she knew more about the American Revolution and the Italian Renaissance than how to negotiate a hostage situation. But until the police were able to take over, negotiating with Rafael might end up being their only way out. She glanced around her orderly classroom, searching for the right words. Desks and chairs were lined up in neat rows the way she liked it. Enlarged photos depicting scenes from ancient Greece to current events in the Middle East hung on the wall above history books she'd collected over the past few years. But details of the room weren't what she saw at the moment.

Instead, she saw Tess, sharing a seat in the back with one of her senior girls, Izzie Johnson, who had a protective arm around her younger niece. Philip Marx, a basketball player, sat beside them, his jaw tense. Amie Wright, sobbing quietly, sat to his left. She'd been through more than her fair share of trauma over the past few months after losing her best friend in a car accident. Shani Wells, Kevin Hunter, Lexi Valentine . . . She'd known some of them for years.

She lifted up another short prayer, then turned back to Rafael. "Mason told me about your brother, Rafael. He told me that they grabbed him from your house and are holding him for ransom. I'm so, so sorry."

"I am too, but being sorry won't keep him alive."

Emily tried to read his expression. He looked in control, but also clearly scared. As if he were fighting with his emotions. Which might be good. If he was hesitant at all about what he was doing, she might be able to gain the advantage and convince him to stand down. "Tell me what you want, Rafael."

"It's simple. They have my brother. If I don't get them what they want, they're going to kill him."

"Who are they?"

He tugged on the bill of his baseball cap. "Someone working with the Mexican cartel or maybe a local gang . . . Does it really matter? They've made their demands, and now I'm going to make mine."

Emily forced herself to keep her voice calm. "Mason mentioned you thought it was a case of mistaken identity."

"I know my brother. He might not be perfect, but he's not in debt to some drug lord. Which means there's no hidden stash of cash laying around my house."

"That might be true, but you know this isn't the way to get what they want. You can put a stop to this right now before it's too late. Before someone gets hurt."

"You're wrong." Rafael shook his head, his voice rising in volume. "What would you do if they took your sister or your niece and threatened to kill them? What choice would you have?"

"You always have a choice, Rafael—"

"That's easy to say in your position, but because I don't have what they want, my brother is as good as dead." His gaze narrowed. "Tell me honestly what you would do."

All the pat answers people had thrown at her after Michael

died came flying back at Emily. *Everything happens for a reason . . . I know exactly how you feel . . . You're going to have to move on and put his death behind you . . .* Most had left her angry enough to scream. And as much as she wanted to find an easy fix to Rafael's dilemma, she knew it wasn't possible. There was no pat answer she could give him.

"I don't know what I would do, but not this. You have your whole life ahead of you. Don't throw it away by panicking and doing something you'll regret. Think about it, Rafael. You already know there are people willing to help you."

Rafael blinked and she caught a hint of conflict in his eyes. If she could convince him to walk away . . .

"Rafael?"

"You're wrong." He shook his head slowly before answering. "Do you really think the police are going to hand over a bunch of money so they'll let my brother go?"

"No, but they might be able to find him—"

"And if they don't?"

Emily pressed her lips together. Sirens blared in the background. Communications would be set up by now, with negotiators and snipers moving into place . . . and they'd all be there with one goal in mind. To end the situation before any innocent students got hurt. And if Rafael went down in the process, that loss would be considered acceptable.

CHAPTER 6

Mason hurried across the Dogwood Academy parking lot toward the outer barrier the local uniforms had established to keep onlookers at bay beyond the police safety line. The information he'd passed on to the dispatcher would have already been evaluated at the scene to determine the number of students involved and the actual threat they were facing.

Guilt resurfaced as he replayed his conversation with Rafael earlier that morning. He'd missed something. After years of experience in reading people, he'd never imagined Rafael to be one who'd snap. If he'd caught something—anything—he might have been able to stop what was happening right now.

Captain Quinton Peterson exited his unmarked vehicle a dozen yards from them, clearly in charge as he approached the on-scene commander. With twenty-plus years on the force, Captain Peterson knew exactly what he was doing. Which somehow managed to make up for his brusque personality.

Lieutenant Green, blond crew cut, midthirties, stepped forward to shake the older man's hand. "Captain Peterson. It's good to see you."

"You as well, Lieutenant Green. I'll be taking over as the Incident Commander in this situation." The captain was direct and unapologetic for it. "This case is going to become high profile as soon as the media runs the story, which means while we might not be able to stop the press, we are going to need to wrap this up quickly and without any incidents."

"Yes sir."

Mason could feel the tension in the air. The last thing they needed right now was another Newtown. Maybe the fact that Rafael wanted something more than simply revenge would play in their favor.

Captain Peterson took off his sunglasses and rested them atop his kinky salt-and-pepper hair. "Tell me what you've done so far."

Lieutenant Green nodded at an older man who looked as if he'd just downed too much caffeine. "This is Vice Principal Tuttle. Principal Farley gave the order to lock down the school. We've just given the all clear to send the middle school students to the gym, which will be used as the designated reunification site where parents will be told to pick them up using the separate parking lot."

"And our gunman, Mr. Tuttle?"

"Unfortunately we have little information. We understand that senior Rafael Cerda is currently holed up in the east wing of the campus inside a high school classroom with an undisclosed number of students and the school's history teacher, Emily Hunt."

"Captain Hunt's daughter?"

"Yes sir."

The captain turned back to the officer. "Who do you have for the negotiator?"

"Charlie Bain's already been called in and should be here in the next . . ." The officer glanced at his watch. "Five, ten minutes tops. He's the best we've got."

Mason stared at a narrow crack in the parking lot where he stood while the lieutenant continued the brief.

"A command post is being set up in the main office, and the tactical team is being situated outside the classroom in case negotiations fail, making a forced entry necessary."

Mason drew in a breath of frustration along with the sweet smell of alyssum that always brought back memories of his aunt's garden. Beads of perspiration formed across his forehead despite the cool weather. Rafael was an eighteen-year-old kid who knew nothing about drug dealers, let alone a ransom situation.

"Captain?" Mason stepped forward.

Captain Peterson scowled at the interruption. "What is it?"

"I know Rafael."

The captain stopped and caught Mason's gaze. "You know the target?"

"He's not a target." Mason moved in front of the captain and handed him his phone with the photos of Rafael's brother. "What he is doing is inexcusable, but he's an eighteen-year-old boy in a panic over his brother being held for ransom. He's not a criminal."

Captain Peterson studied the photos. "Where did you get these?"

"Rafael sent them to me this morning. They're proof-of-life photos. They're demanding two hundred and fifty thousand dollars by two o'clock this afternoon to pay back a drug debt."

"So this is tied to the cartel?"

"Cartel or maybe someone on a lower level. Rafael's convinced his brother's kidnapping is a result of mistaken identity."

"Do you think he's capable of hurting the kids in that classroom?"

Mason caught the skepticism in the captain's voice. "No sir, I don't. When I spoke to Rafael this morning, he was agitated, but there were no signs of him being out of control. Clearly, I missed something, but that doesn't change the fact that I don't believe he is capable of shooting anyone."

Captain Peterson looked at the photos of Eduardo as a car pulled up, and Charlie Bains exited the vehicle. Even today, Bains looked like he'd be more at home in a country club than a precinct. It was easy even for Mason to see why Emily had once agreed to marry Charlie.

"I want you to put together a profile of him," the captain said. "I want to know everything there is to know about him, from what toothpaste he uses to what he likes to eat for dinner. And get his mother in here."

Captain Peterson turned to Charlie to begin the briefing, but Mason wasn't finished. Anyone could come up with a profile of Rafael. Charlie wasn't going to be able to connect with him the way he could.

"Captain, excuse me, but if you let me talk to him, I think I can convince him to end this peacefully." Mason tried to ignore the gnawing feeling that his insistence was trying to make up for his failure earlier that morning. But even if he'd missed something, he was still the best person for the job. "I know Rafael and could establish contact with him now without waiting for time on briefings and research. He trusts me, which could give us a huge step forward in the negotiations."

Charlie frowned. "From what I've been told, there are a bunch of scared teenagers locked in a classroom with a student in possession of a weapon. Just because you know Rafael doesn't mean you know anything about tactical intervention, psychological strategies, or crisis resolution. You could get everyone in there killed."

"Really? I've met with drug dealers face-to-face and negotiated my way out of dozens of hostile situations, which means I've had to learn to read people. I know how to negotiate with my own life on the line. There's no reason why I can't do the same here. Rafael knows and trusts me."

"We don't have time to argue this. Mason, you just got your

wish." Captain Peterson turned back to them, hands locked behind him, feet spread slightly apart. "Keep trying to get ahold of him. Charlie and I will be here to run the secondary roles, but this is your game now. Our goal is to convince Rafael to end this on his own."

The captain turned back to Lieutenant Green. "Call Detective North and have her team find out whatever connections they can between the kidnapping of Eduardo Cerda and the Torres case they've been working on. I want this boy's mother brought in, and search his house, in case finding where the brother is ends up being the only way out of this."

Mason dialed Rafael's number and let it ring. Still no answer. He stared out across the perfectly landscaped lawn to where Rafael was holed up inside a classroom with a gun in his hand and a bunch of scared kids. Rafael, no doubt, was feeling that same, overwhelming frustration. Not that that excused his actions, but at least he could understand the boy's desperation to save his brother.

Memories of his own brother swam through his mind afresh. Sometimes life didn't play favorites. Sometimes evil gained the upper hand. He might not have been able to save his brother, but he could do everything he could to save Emily and the students in that room.

God, the lives of these kids are on the line as well as Emily's. I need the right words to say to him . . .

Mason took in a deep breath. Michael's death had forced him to look at life—and death—differently, which was why praying was a new habit he was trying to form. Funny how the older he got, the more his aunt's words had come back to haunt him. He'd spent his life running from any structure and authority, and religion fell smack-dab in the middle of them both.

When he'd showed up on her porch with his two younger brothers, she agreed they could stay, as long as they followed her rules. She'd insisted on church three times a week, no drinking or swearing, and piano lessons for the three of them. Despite his rebellious tendencies, her unconditional love and bottomless bowls of peach cobbler had managed to make up for the altar calls and music recitals he couldn't avoid.

But somehow all of that had changed in the last six months. He still had a long way to go, but he was learning that following Christ wasn't about religion; it was an intimacy with his Creator that had him constantly hungering for more. Moments like this made him thankful he didn't have to forge ahead on his own strength.

Mason shifted his thoughts back to the issue at hand. He knew enough about hostage situations to realize that the initial forty-five minutes were the most dangerous. There was a good chance that more than one of the students was panicking. Emily's role as an authority figure was going to be key. While he'd never spent a lot of time with her despite his friendship with her brother, he had seen her confidence, sincerity, and heart to make the world a better place—particularly through her job.

She would need to get past the fear in order to realize the importance of her position, draw on any emergency training she'd taken, and do what she could to ensure Rafael—and the hostages—stayed calm. The fact that she knew Rafael should play to her advantage.

He took another deep breath and redialed the number.

He might never have handled formal negotiations, but his instincts had brought him through dozens of "unofficial" negotiations, and there was no reason why he couldn't do the same here.

The phone rang five times before Rafael finally answered.

Mason nodded at the captain. "Rafael, it's Mason Taylor. I know about the gun and the hostages. I want to help put an end to this, so no one is hurt. Tell me how you're doing."

"Me? I . . . I'm fine."

"Good. Is there anyone who needs medical attention?"

There was a long pause on the line. "No."

"I'm glad to hear that. I know it's been an emotional morning and you're worried about your brother, but I've asked to work as the negotiator so I can help you get through this without anyone getting hurt."

Mason was greeted again by silence. He glanced up at the captain. He needed to make some progress to prove both to him—and Charlie—that he was capable of doing this.

"Talk to me, Rafael. This morning you seemed resolved to let me help you. There are other ways to get your brother back without resorting to a hostage situation. You know I'll help in any way I can if you give me the chance, but this way . . . this isn't the answer."

"Things changed. I can't get the money they want, which means they'll kill Eduardo, and time is running out."

"I know you're worried about your brother, but I promised my help earlier, and I have no intention of backing out. We've already got a team trying to find out where he's being held. If you put an end to this before someone gets hurt, it will be easier for me to help you."

"It's too late. I brought a weapon to school, and I'm holding a bunch of students hostage. What do you think I'm already looking at? Twenty-five . . . fifty . . . life?"

"I don't know, but I do know that if we can put a stop to this now, things will work out better for you, which is what we both want." Mason's jaw tensed. Any idea he'd had that it would be easy to talk Rafael down had been completely wrong. The boy was clearly determined to go through with this despite the consequences. "If you won't walk away, what's your plan? Tell me what you need to put an end to this."

Rafael hesitated. "First of all, nothing heroic. Don't send anyone in, or I'll shoot one of the hostages."

Hostages, not students. Not friends or fellow classmates.

"What else do you need for this to be over?" Mason continued.

"Two million dollars."

"Two million? That's a lot of money, Rafael. The ransom's gone up quite substantially since we spoke this morning. You told me they're demanding two hundred and fifty thousand for your brother."

There was a long pause on the line. "The only way to get out of this is with enough money to not just pay off the ransom, but to give my brother, my mom, and me a second chance somewhere else."

Mason frowned. For an intelligent boy, he wasn't thinking clearly. It was going to be virtually impossible for him to escape this without facing serious repercussions. To think he was going to somehow disappear and sidestep the law was foolish.

"Stop for one moment," Mason said. "Do you really think that's going to happen? You don't want to spend the rest of your life running. And even if you could initially escape, where are you going to go to avoid the authorities breathing down your necks?"

"That isn't your problem." Rafael's pause added to the tension. "I need you to help me get the money . . . If I don't get what I want . . . I will shoot someone. I've got eleven students . . . Their parents won't miss a couple hundred grand out of their fat bank accounts . . . especially when it'll save the lives of their children."

Mason tried to swallow his irritation. He'd never heard Rafael sound so cold and aloof. "I'm going to need a list of the names of everyone in the room with you so we can contact the parents."

"Fine . . . Miss Hunt will do that."

The captain shoved a note in front of Mason. *Sign of good faith from his side.*

Mason nodded. "You also need to realize, Rafael, that it's going to take some time to get the money together. Give me a sign of good faith, and I'll see what I can do about your demands."

"Like what?"

"First of all, let me talk to Miss Hunt."

There was another long pause on the line, before she answered. "Mason?"

"Emily. Are you okay?'

"Yeah. For now."

"What about your students?"

"I've just got one girl . . . her heart is pounding, she's shaking . . . can't breathe."

"Asthma?"

"No. Panic attack. I'm worried about her. She's been through a lot this year and isn't coping well with this."

Her voice was even, in control, with just a slight hint of fear. She hadn't fallen apart like a lot of people would have, which was a good sign. Because she was going to need a lot of courage to get through the next few hours.

"I'm going to do everything I can to get her released. What's his mood at the moment?"

"That's enough." Rafael was back on the line. "I told you she was okay. That they're all okay. I don't want to hurt anyone, but I will if I don't get what I want."

"Emily said there's a girl who's having trouble breathing." If he could convince Rafael to let one person go, it would be a first step.

"She's fine. She's just . . . scared."

"Miss Hunt doesn't think she's fine. If you would send the girl out, it would go a long way with my boss."

"I can't do that."

"Rafael, I've known you for a long time. You're a good kid—"

"Maybe I haven't made myself clear. I'm not making any

deals. Things have changed since we spoke this morning. I'm not going to let anything happen to my brother, and this is the only way to save him. You saw the photos of my brother. If I don't get the money they're demanding, they'll kill him. Which means you've got just over five hours or I start shooting hostages."

CHAPTER
7

Emily paced the back corner of the room. Rafael might have let her speak to Mason, but nothing either of them had said had been enough to persuade Rafael to stand down. She'd prayed fervently that one of them would be able to talk some sense into the boy, but clearly he had his mind made up.

She tried to sort through her limited list of options. She could try to find a new approach that might convince him to change his mind, or she could simply stay quiet. She took a deep breath and willed her tensed jaw to unclench. Trying to reason with him could quickly backfire. But staying quiet wasn't going to get them anywhere either.

She looked up and tried to read Rafael's expression. The stress was clear in his eyes. They were red rimmed and marked with fatigue. But the intensity and resolve was there as well. She rubbed the back of her neck, wishing she could get rid of the knots the morning had produced. She'd known Rafael for a long time. Had always thought he valued her insight. Trusted her. Surely all of that hadn't changed overnight.

"Rafael?"

His head jerked up, and she caught the flicker of fear in his eyes. No matter what had happened the past few hours, he was still just a boy in way over his head.

"What?"

"I was just . . . thinking. We've known each other for three . . . four years now. I've always admired your determination. You've worked hard to get to where you are in school. And I thought you trusted me. The bottom line is that I'm worried about you."

Rafael stood at the edge of her desk at the front of the classroom. "I've thought about the consequences. If I don't do this, my brother will die. Those are my consequences. My mother's already lost one child, and I'm not going to let it happen again."

"You never told me about that." Emily's brow furrowed as she took in the new information. She knew a lot about Rafael and his family, but not this. If she could get him to talk more, maybe he'd be able to see that what was happening to his brother was no different than what he was doing to the students. "What happened?"

Rafael looked away for a moment. His chin quivered as he fought to control the emotion. "It happened a long time ago. Jose was shot and killed."

"I'm sorry."

"Me too. I was twelve when he died. I remember . . ." He paused as if debating whether or not to open up the old wounds.

"What do you remember, Rafael?"

"I remember him lying on the driveway outside our apartment. He was dead . . . there was blood . . . everywhere. After that, my mother cried all the time." He shook his head. "I won't let her go through that again."

Emily took a few steps toward him, then stopped to sit on the edge of one of the student desks. "He was in a gang?"

"Yeah." He stared at the floor. "I'd actually planned on joining one too."

"What stopped you?"

He looked up at her. "Mason Taylor."

Mason?

Mason had mentioned he'd met Rafael through a big brother program. Clearly, whatever Mason had done, it had been enough to help turn Rafael's life around. She'd seen the compassion in Mason's eyes while they'd talked. He was worried about Rafael. Concerned. Determined to help. And his concern went far beyond the normal parameters of professionalism. This really had become personal.

She dropped her head to study the floor tile with its patterns of tiny black and gray specks and drew in a deep breath. "If you trust Mason, then maybe you need to trust him with how to deal with this problem."

Rafael tightened his grip on the gun. "I can't, even if I wanted to. Mason can't fix this. My brother doesn't deserve to die."

"No he doesn't. But neither do these kids deserve to be held at gunpoint." Emily felt her lungs tighten within her chest. It was up to her to find a way to protect them.

"I need you to trust us, Rafael," she continued, this time moving a step closer to him. They were going in circles. "Give me the gun. I'll talk to them and make them understand. No jury is going to condemn you for trying to save your brother's life."

"No." He shook his head and caught her gaze. "It's too late."

Emily stopped midstride, wishing her sister were here. Avery would know what to do. She'd know how to look him in the eye and tell him to turn over the gun and end this now. "If you won't put an end to this, then at least let the students go. You can keep me."

"Miss Hunt?"

Emily turned around at the panicked voice. Izzie knelt in front of Amie, who sat bent over, head between her legs, her back heaving.

"Amie can't breathe." Tears collected in Izzie's eyes. "I don't know what to do."

Emily started for the back of the room. "Amie—"

"Wait." Rafael held up the gun. "Nobody moves without my permission."

"I'm just going to go talk to her." This time Emily shook her head. "I need to find out what's wrong."

Ignoring his command, Emily continued walking toward the back of the room. She could feel his stare. Knew his gun was pointed at her. She was betting he wouldn't shoot her, but either way, she'd had enough of taking orders from an eighteen-year-old who was out of control. Her heart pounded in her throat as she rubbed her sweaty hands against her skirt. Scared or not, she had a responsibility to the kids in this room.

Izzie scooted over so Emily could squat down in front of Amie. She placed her hands against Amie's shoulders, still ignoring Rafael. "What's wrong, Amie?"

"I . . . I can't . . . breathe." Her legs were trembling. Sweat glistened on her forehead. Her chest heaved at every labored breath.

"Are you scared, Amie?"

She nodded.

Three months ago, Amie had survived a hit-and-run accident that had killed her best friend. The faint, jagged scar across her forehead was the only remaining outward sign of the tragedy. But inside, Emily knew Amie struggled with the emotional impact of survivor's guilt. Not all the kids here had parents with hefty bank accounts. Amie's parents worked long hours to pay the school's tuition fees.

"It's okay to be scared, Amie. We're all scared. But I'm here with you, and I'm going to help you. I want you to try to take one slow, deep breath."

"I . . . can't."

"Yes, you can. Just one slow breath, then another."

"I can't—"

"Make her stop!" Rafael slammed his fist against her desk in the front of the room. "Please. Make her stop."

Emily stood up and faced Rafael. "Screaming at her isn't going to help, Rafael. She has to relax. She's scared. Just let me handle this."

His jaw clenched, he nodded. "Fine."

Emily turned back to Amie and knelt down in front of her. "I know you're scared, Amie, but you're going to be okay. I want you to look at me."

Amie's face rose slowly until she caught Emily's gaze.

"I want you to do exactly what I tell you."

Amie heaved another ragged breath, but nodded.

"I need you to close your eyes and slow down your breathing. That means taking deep, unhurried breaths." Emily closed her own eyes, trying to forget they were sitting in the middle of a hostage situation. That Rafael had a gun pointed at them. And that there was a very strong possibility that at least one of them would get shot before this was all over. She let out a deep breath. Even if they all got out of there alive, Rafael would probably spend the rest of his life in prison. There was no scenario that had this ending well.

God, I need you to help me stay calm and focused. To find a way to end this before someone gets hurt.

"Amie. I want you to focus on me and my voice. Nothing else. I want you to pretend you're blowing out a candle while you're breathing . . . good." Emily shook off the panic creeping up her spine. "You're doing fine, Amie. Izzie, I want you to help keep her breathing like this. We're going to get out of this and all of you are going to be okay."

Emily stood up slowly and let Izzie take her place. The calm expression she was used to seeing on Rafael's face had been replaced with one she didn't recognize. How long was it going to take for things to completely spiral out of control?

"So what happens now?" Philip, one of the school's basketball players, leaned against the back wall. Arms folded across his chest.

Emily addressed the lanky senior. "Philip, not now."

"Then when?" Philip kicked his foot against the wall. "He's demanding money from our parents, expecting them to hand it over, and then what? We all walk away from this and forget it ever happened? He's crazy—"

"Stop it." Rafael's jaw tensed.

"Enough, Philip." Emily held up her hand. "I need you to sit back down and wait. The police will handle things."

"You don't have the guts to shoot one of us." Philip took another step forward. "So I'm not going to sit down. Not going to play your stupid games anymore."

"Philip." Emily tried again. "All you have to do is sit and wait. The police are handling this, and it will all be over soon."

She knew how Philip felt. Restless. Caged. He was a senior, captain of the basketball team, and used to being in charge. Not taking orders from others.

But today everything had changed.

Emily felt the tension in the room close in around her. She'd had Philip in a few of her classes, but had never really connected with him. He was popular, athletic, and came from a wealthy family, but from what she knew, he had a rough home life and bad temper.

"Philip, please sit down," Emily said.

"Why?" Philip faced Rafael. "Have you stopped to think about how this is going to end? Do you think they'll just let you walk out of here with your suitcase full of cash?"

"Philip, I said that's enough—"

"As soon as they get tired of playing games with you, they'll come rushing in here with a cache of weapons and let their sniper take you out."

"You're not helping." She was losing ground quickly and didn't know how to retake it.

"Oh, and Miss Hunt, you've really helped by sitting here

and trying to sweet-talk your way out of this. Like that's really worked." Philip pushed past Emily, shoving her onto one of the desks.

Emily fought to catch her balance. *This situation is going to explode, God. I need a way out . . .*

She weighed her options. There was no way she could physically stop Philip if he decided to go after Rafael. He had at least six inches and sixty pounds on her. Emily's heart hammered. The only thing that could stop him was the loaded gun Rafael held.

"Don't you get it?" Philip hesitated a couple of feet from Rafael. "There won't be any money. No escape."

Emily grasped Philip's shoulder, but he pushed her hand off.

She glanced back at the other students. Amie was sobbing again. Izzie had her arm around Tess. If Rafael went through with his threat, one of them—including Tess—could be shot in the crossfire.

"I won't warn you again." Rafael held the gun out in front of him with both hands. "I will shoot you."

Emily swallowed her panic. "Rafael, let me talk to him. He's just scared."

"Scared? Don't talk about me like I'm not standing right here. I'm not scared, I'm mad." Philip clenched his fists and swore. "This whole hostage scenario is ridiculous. He's not trying to save his brother, he's just crazy."

Emily tried to edge her way back between them, but was blocked by Philip's solid form and the rows of desks on either side.

"Crazy?" Rafael asked. "The way I look at it, I'm the one with the gun, which means I'm in charge."

"Are you really?" Philip's taunting continued. "Move the blinds and look outside. The police always set up a perimeter. I bet it's full of enough squad cars, officers, and weapons to take down a small army. And they've got cops and snipers out there who'll be more than willing to blow your brains out if given the chance. And you know what else? Everyone will be glad they did."

Philip lunged forward. Before Emily could react, he grabbed Rafael's right arm, jerking it up.

The weapon went off mid motion. One of the girls screamed. Emily watched as Philip froze for one long, drawn-out moment before dropping and hitting the tiled floor.

"What have you done, Rafael?" Emily shoved aside the row of chairs between her and Philip's body, then knelt down on the floor beside him. "Philip, talk to me."

"He came at me." Panic laced Rafael's voice. "What did you expect me to do?"

"You didn't have to shoot him." Emily ignored Rafael for the moment, searching instead for the extent of Philip's injury. There was blood on the side of his head where he'd hit the desk as he fell. And a bullet wound in his shoulder.

Rafael walked to the back of the room, his expression a mixture of frustration, fear, and determination. He grabbed Tess, then dragged her with him to the front of the room. "You all thought I wasn't serious. Now you know the truth. No one else move."

Emily fought back tears. "I know you're serious, Rafael, but please. Let her go. This wasn't her fault."

Blood oozed onto the floor beneath Philip. Tess sobbed quietly. She needed to save her niece . . . needed to save Philip . . .

God, I don't know what to do. Show me how to put a stop to this before someone else gets hurt. Please . . .

"Philip . . . Philip, can you hear me?" Emily felt her throat constrict. "I need somebody's jacket. Something to help stop the bleeding."

Izzie brought her a faded gray sweatshirt. Emily pressed it

against Philip's shoulder. He was losing blood. Too much blood. If they didn't get help right away, they could lose him.

Rafael moved to the front of the room, his arm still wrapped around Tess's shoulders. "I warned him. I've warned all of you. If he just would've done what I told him and didn't interfere, this wouldn't have happened."

Emily heard someone sob at the back of the room, Amie's raspy breathing, the sound of a chair scraping against the tile floor. She felt the walls begin to close in on her. Blood covered her hands, her shirt, and the sweatshirt she was still pressing against Philip. She gasped for a lungful of air. She was responsible for these students, and she'd failed.

She was responsible.

She swallowed hard. She couldn't give in to the fear threatening to overwhelm her. She had to find a way to stop this.

"Izzie, I need you to help Amie relax like I showed her. Rafael, I need you to call Mason."

Rafael's phone began to ring before he had a chance to respond. They'd heard the shot.

"This wasn't supposed to happen." Rafael picked up the phone, but didn't answer the call. "He shouldn't have come at me like that."

"I don't care if you planned for this to happen or not. It did happen." Emily pressed harder against the wound with one hand while fumbling to find Philip's pulse with the other. "Only you can put a stop to this, Rafael, but now it might be too late." She rocked back on her heels to begin CPR. Her body shook. "I think Philip's dead."

CHAPTER
8

Pick up your cell phone, Rafael. Come on . . .

Mason pushed redial and listened to the phone ring. It had been an hour and a half since he'd heard Emily say *"He's got a gun."* Fifteen minutes since he last spoke with Rafael. Sixty seconds since they heard a shot fired.

He stared out the window of the school's main office where they'd set up the command post. The tension of the morning continued to close in around him like the heavy dark clouds moving in across the city carrying today's predicted rain. The weather mirrored his mood. Frustrated. Drained. Emotional.

He ended the unanswered call for a third time and turned to the captain. "He's not answering."

Mason pressed redial, then tugged at a loose thread on the bottom edge of his T-shirt. When he wasn't on the phone, Charlie and the captain had continued to prep him on a string of basics from Negotiation 101. Make the hostage taker work for what he wants. If you do give in to a demand, ensure you get something in return. And all of this while avoiding a violent confrontation. They'd been right when they said it was all about psychology. His role was to somehow convince Rafael to release his hostages without anyone getting hurt.

And now there was a possibility that someone had just been shot.

But when it came down to it, no hostage situation played out strictly by the book. Like in working undercover, he was going to have to go with his gut as well as with the so-called rules.

What's going on in there, Rafael?

While rushing negotiations in a hostage situation could prove costly, they were ready for an assault. He'd watched the other teams in action as they'd set up the command post. A team had swept the school for secondary shooters and had found nothing. Which meant everyone was focused on Rafael. The Special Response Team, the tactical team, the negotiation team. Men crouched behind ballistic riot shields, snipers waited for their orders—

"Call him again."

Mason nodded at the captain's order. Ten seconds later, Rafael picked up.

"I shot him."

"Okay. Tell me what happened." Mason felt adrenaline rush through him. If they had a dead body in there . . .

"It's Philip. I didn't want to shoot him, but he gave me no choice." Rafael's words came rapid and uneven. "He came at me. Grabbed my arm. The gun went off."

"Rafael, I need you to slow down." Mason knew it was crucial for Rafael to stay calm. Even if the shooting had been accidental, he was clearly agitated. That could, in turn, up the chances that someone else would get hurt. "I understand you didn't mean to shoot him. Is anyone else injured?"

"No. Just Philip."

"I know this is difficult, and sometimes things happen that none of us can anticipate, but I need you to let me help you. We need to ensure that no one else gets hurt. Tell me Philip's condition. Is he breathing?"

"I don't know. I think he's dead. He . . . he's not moving. He's just lying there . . ."

Rafael sounded like a scared little boy. Alone. Panicked. They needed to get him out of there.

"Are you sure?"

"I don't know."

There was a long pause on the line.

Mason signaled to the captain. "Get the paramedics in there with a gurney on standby outside the classroom and have them wait for the go ahead." He turned back to the phone. "Rafael? I'm going to send in some medical help for Philip."

"I know what'll happen if someone comes in here and takes him. There are snipers outside this room. If I let anyone in, they'll kill me."

"Rafael, you know I don't want that to happen, but Philip needs medical help. I'll do everything I can to help you as well. But I need your cooperation on this."

"Why? I told you I was serious. Maybe now you and the others will believe me."

"I understand your frustration, but I need you to do something for me. Let me speak to Emily, so I can find out how Philip is. Can you do that?"

Again silence.

"Rafael. Please. Let me speak to Emily. I need to understand how serious Philip's injury is. If you'll just let me speak to her for a moment."

"Fine. I'll put it on speakerphone, but don't . . . don't try to send any coded messages. I'm right here listening."

A moment later he heard her voice. "Mason?"

"Emily." Mason let out a slow breath of relief. "Rafael said Philip is dead."

"I thought he was, but he's not. His pulse is weak, and he's lost a lot of blood. He hit his head when he fell. I'm using a sweatshirt to put pressure where he was shot, but I don't know what else to do."

"You're doing fine, Emily. Stopping the bleeding is the first thing you have to do." He tethered in his own emotion, knowing the importance of keeping his voice calm. Feeling the strong desire to protect her and everyone in that classroom. "What about you and the other students? Is everyone else okay?"

"For the moment. The kids are scared but not hurt."

Mason caught the edge of alarm in her voice, but the determination was still there, which was good. She wasn't giving in to the fear or giving up.

The captain leaned against the office counter where he was listening in on the conversation and leveled his eyes on Mason. "You need to get that boy out of there."

"I know." Mason turned back to the phone. "Rafael, I need you to listen to me. I'm sending in a stretcher and two paramedics. If Philip doesn't get the medical help he needs, he could die. I know you don't want that to happen."

"No . . . I can't. No one is going anywhere."

"Rafael, listen to me. As a friend. I don't want Philip to die. You don't want him to die. Right now the DA can charge you with felony kidnapping. You don't need murder added to that. This isn't who you are."

Rafael's breathing sounded forced and rapid. "I didn't mean to shoot him. You have to understand that. I didn't mean to . . . but I will do whatever it takes to get the money and save my brother."

"I understand you didn't mean to shoot him, but you don't need to make things worse by letting him die."

"Fine . . . I'm willing to let Philip go so he can get help, but I expect some things in return."

"What do you want?"

"Anyone in the hallway needs to be moved outside so when I open the door no one rushes in."

"Okay."

"I'll have someone standing in front of me the whole time. If anyone tries to take over the classroom, I'll shoot them."

Mason's jaw clenched. If another shot was fired, they might not be so lucky this time. "I'm going to stay on the phone with you, okay? I've given the order for the medics to go in now. You need to unlock the door and let them in."

"There's another one of the girls," Emily broke in. "Amie. She needs medical attention."

"No. She isn't a part of the deal."

"Rafael. Please." Mason fought for control. "You know Amie's having trouble breathing. Let her go with Philip."

Another long pause. "No. I'll let Philip leave. No one else."

The captain gave the signal that the medics were ready to go in.

"The medics are at the door, Rafael. You need to let them in."

Mason swallowed his frustration at Rafael's refusal to let Amie go. As soon as the medics were out, they would be debriefed, along with Philip once he was able. Gaining valuable information about the situation inside the classroom would be crucial if they ended up having to launch a tactical assault in order to rescue those inside.

Ten minutes later, the medics were clear.

"I've held up my end of the deal and let Philip go," Rafael said through the speakerphone, "but just so you know I'm serious, I'm gonna make another demand."

"What do you mean?"

"I'm setting a new deadline. You've now got until noon to get me my money, or I'll shoot somebody else. I'm tired of playing games . . . of feeling like I'm getting the runaround."

"Rafael, you have to understand that it's taking time to get the money. Hurting someone else won't change that."

Rafael ignored his advice. "Make sure the captain and the rest of the negotiation team know that the new countdown starts now."

CHAPTER

9

Avery banged on the front door of the Cerdas' apartment, where she stood beside Griffin and Tory. Five miles south off of I-85, the complex was located in a fairly quiet neighborhood, surrounded by local businesses and dense groves of trees.

She took in a deep breath, wishing she could escape the reality that Tess had been on the list of hostages. Talking with Jackson on the phone had helped calm her fears, but separating her professional self from her personal life was proving to be impossible. Ten minutes ago, they'd received the call that one of the students had been shot. That student could have died. That student could have been Tess.

Staying busy was the only way she knew to keep going. In spite of not being able to track down Mrs. Cerda, they hadn't had any problems getting a search warrant. They needed answers, needed to find Eduardo and his mother along with anything that might tie Eduardo to the drug cartel.

Avery studied the signs of yesterday's break-in on the doorframe, then knocked again. No answer.

Where are you, Mrs. Cerda?

An older woman started up the open stairwell with a load of groceries. A second team was on its way now to canvass the apartments. Someone had to have seen something the night Eduardo had been kidnapped.

Avery turned to the apartment manager who'd come with them. "When was the last time you saw Mrs. Cerda, Ms. Odell?"

"You can call me Pepper." The bleached-blonde manager, who couldn't have been a day over twenty-five, grinned.

"Okay . . . Pepper. When did you last see her?"

"Saturday—no—Sunday. Last night. She was bringing a basket of laundry back to her apartment. Elaine is a sweet woman. She has a lot on her plate, but she pays her rent on time and never causes any problems."

"What about this morning?" Tory asked.

"This morning . . . I saw Rafael leave to drive her to work like he does every morning. Is she in trouble?"

"We just need to speak to her. What about the boys, any problems from them?"

"Not Rafael. He's a good kid. Never causes any trouble."

"And Eduardo?" Avery asked.

"A bit rougher around the edges than his brother. He's always coming and going at strange times. I don't think his mother knows about it."

"And you didn't think you should tell her?"

Pepper shrugged a shoulder. "Wasn't my business."

"Go ahead and open the door, please."

"Are you sure I won't get into any trouble? I mean, I watch those cop shows on TV, but—"

Avery held up the warrant. "You're not going to get into any trouble."

Pepper slid the key into the lock, turned the handle to open the door, then stepped aside.

"If you'll stay outside, ma'am, we'll take it from here." Avery stepped into the darkened apartment foyer with Tory and Griffin, then shut the door behind them. "Mrs. Cerda?"

Avery breathed in the smell of a vanilla candle as she moved from the entryway into the open dining, living, and kitchen area. An old leather couch with cracked armrests, a coffee table with a neat pile of magazines. Curtains half open. Beyond the living room was a bar that opened up to the kitchen.

"Spread out and check the place," Avery said.

She started for the second bedroom, Glock raised, senses on alert, while Griffin and Tory checked the rest of the apartment.

"Clear."

"Clear."

"Clear."

Thirty seconds later, they met back in the living room. A cat walked into the room and nudged its chin against Avery's leg. She reached down to stroke its back, wondering if someone had forgotten to feed it this morning. Tess loved animals. Strays in particular. Avery had lost count of how many she'd brought home to temporarily foster with their own eclectic collection of Tiger, their Birman cat; Mr. Whiskers, the hamster; three female mice; and an African clawed frog . . . Her eyes watered at the thought.

"Avery?"

She glanced up at Tory. "I'm okay." Or at least she would be when all this was over.

She drew in a deep breath and pushed aside her emotions for the moment. She'd have time to deal with them later. After Tess was safe and sound with her at home.

She shifted her thoughts back to the apartment. Before Ethan had died, she'd have seen the space as nothing more than low-income housing where the father had walked out and the mother was rarely home to raise her children.

Today, she saw signs of a woman who worked long hours and struggled to make enough to pay the bills and keep food on the table. She understood all too well the pressures of meeting the constant demands to ensure that her sons had what they needed.

LISA HARRIS

Avery tried to swallow the guilt that followed. Her last words to Tess had been in anger. Apparently Mrs. Cerda wasn't the only person finding it difficult to balance work and motherhood.

God, I can't get through this on my own. I need you to take the lead and show me what's here. Show me a way to get my daughter back . . .

She nodded at Tory and Griffin. "Tory and I will start with the boys' bedroom. Griffin, take the master bedroom."

Griffin glanced at Tory with a hint of amusement in his eyes. "Sure you ladies won't be needing my protection?"

"Right." Tory laughed. "I think we can handle ourselves."

In the boys' room, Avery started going through the large desk next to the window, picturing what had transpired the night the cartel had taken Eduardo out of the apartment. She'd conducted interviews in the Torres cases, with family members who'd experienced a similar terror as Rafael and his family had, and she knew the probable scenario. The intruders had broken in during the night wearing dark clothing and ski masks, and carrying assault rifles. They'd dragged Eduardo from his bed, duct taped his hands behind him, and beat him while Rafael and his mother watched and begged for them to spare Eduardo's life.

You've got thirty-six hours to come up with two hundred and fifty thousand dollars if you want to see him alive . . .

According to Mason, they might as well have asked for the moon. Avery shook her head. She needed a distraction from the images playing in her mind.

She glanced up at Tory. "You know he has a crush on you."

"Griffin?"

"Who else would I be talking about?"

Tory shook her head. "Crushes are for sixth graders, Avery."

"Maybe." Avery lowered her voice. "But I've seen the way he looks at you. Overly attentive and helpful. He brings you coffee most mornings, offers to buy you lunch at least once a

73

week, and is always trying to make you laugh. How else would you interpret it?"

"I don't." Tory closed the closet door with a little more force than necessary. "You're imagining things."

Avery pulled open the top drawer of one of the dressers. "Am I?"

"We work together. I find his company . . . entertaining. It's like working with one of my brothers. That's it."

"You've got four brothers. Somehow I don't think you need another one."

Tory chuckled as she opened the other closet door. "You've become a romantic, Avery."

Maybe she had, but Levi Griffin had an exemplary record as a cop and was the perfect southern gentleman when it came to the women in his life. Add to that his charming dark looks, boyish grin, and a hint of a mystery about his past that only the captain knew about, and she could see how he had women turning their heads.

Avery dug into the next drawer, jammed with socks and T-shirts. The routine nature of an initial search helped numb the worry and keep her mind off reality. The tech team would come in behind them and do a full sweep, taking computers and electronics back to the lab and dusting for fingerprints, followed by the K9 drug team that was on their way. But they needed something now.

A gnawing sense of guilt returned as she continued searching. She knew how hard it was to be a single mom, and she not only had a good-paying job but a family who was there to pick up the slack when she couldn't be.

From what she knew about Elaine Cerda, the woman had neither. No husband or boyfriend. Low-paying, minimum-wage jobs . . . Sometimes life simply wasn't fair. Ironic how they were now both facing similar situations with their children.

Avery glanced across the room at Tory. "I'm realizing how much we have in common, Elaine Cerda and I. Her son held for ransom, while her other son holds my daughter."

Both of them faced a mother's worst nightmare. Their children's lives were in danger. Avery felt the bottom of the drawer for anything hidden, then shoved it shut.

"I know this is hard on you—you don't have to do it." Tory stood up and rested her hands against her hips. "You can go back to the station, back to the school, to your parents' house, wherever would help you get through this. We'd all support your decision."

Avery shook her head. Nothing could help her get through this. "I need to be here. But what makes it even harder is that Tess and I had a fight this morning." She'd always prided herself for not bringing her personal problems to work—just like she tried not to bring her work problems home. "I never like to send her off to school mad, but I needed to get to the office early for a meeting and we were running late. My mom offered to take her to school."

"No matter what happened between the two of you, Tess loves you and knows you love her."

"I know." Avery twisted her hips, trying to relieve the ache in the small of her back. "But how does anyone handle the fact that your child is in danger, and there is nothing you can do to stop it?"

"I don't know, beyond trying to take one moment at a time without letting your mind settle on the worst possible outcome."

Avery finished going through the bottom drawer of the dresser, digging through contents, then feeling around the sides and top for anything that might be hidden. For now, staying focused on her job was better than sitting around worrying. At least she was doing something. If Mason couldn't convince Rafael to stand down, finding Eduardo was their only other option. She'd deal with her emotions once this was all over. And Tess was safe.

"Anything?" Tory interrupted her thoughts.

Avery shook her head. "Nothing."

No drugs, no cash, nothing that pointed to Eduardo's involvement with the cartel.

Griffin entered the room. "I just spoke to Carlos. He finished checking footage from the street cams around the hotel where Mrs. Cerda works."

"And?" Avery pressed.

"Rafael was telling the truth. They spotted his car dropping off his mother at the corner just after seven."

"Can they tell where she went after she got out?" Tory asked.

"She headed toward the service entrance of the hotel, but once Rafael drove away, she doubled back down the main road, then took a side street. After that, the camera loses her."

Avery tugged off one of the gloves she'd been wearing. "What was she doing?"

"It's impossible to say," Griffin said. "Maybe she was contacted by Eduardo's kidnappers with further instructions. Or maybe she decided to contact a rich relative."

"So all we really know is that she didn't go in to work this morning. What about her phone logs?" Avery asked. "Did someone call her this morning before Rafael dropped her off?"

"Carlos is checking that right now, but if it's the same person who called Rafael, they used a burn phone and the number will be impossible to trace."

Technology had its advantages, except when it ended up giving the bad guys the edge.

"So Rafael drops her off at work, and then what?" Tory leaned against the dresser. "Not only did she not go in to work, Rafael didn't meet Mason as planned. So between his talking to Mason at seven and his pulling a gun on a roomful of high school students an hour later, something had to have changed."

"Maybe not." Avery spoke her thoughts. "His brother is being held for ransom, and he knows he and his mom can't pay it. What would you do if you couldn't pay a ransom and knew your brother's life was on the line?"

"I wouldn't pull a gun at school," Griffin said.

"Rafael was threatened not to go to the police, so maybe he started to regret his decision to talk to Mason," Tory added. "In his mind, he was out of options."

Griffin shook his head, clearly not buying into the theory. "I can maybe understand the option of taking his class hostage crossing his mind, but most people wouldn't actually follow through with it. Certainly not a kid like Rafael."

Something crashed in the back of the apartment.

Avery pulled her Glock out from beneath her jacket. "Someone's in here." She headed out of the room. They couldn't have missed someone . . .

He came from the master bedroom, carrying a duffel bag, and sprinted toward the front door with Griffin right behind him.

"Freeze!"

The man turned and plowed into Griffin, knocking him down before running out the front door.

"Go . . . go . . . go!" Griffin yelled.

Avery flew out the front door behind the suspect, ducked beneath the stairwell to the cement steps leading outside. He was already a good ten yards ahead of her before he was forced to slow down to hurdle the shoulder-high chain-link fence on the other side of the sidewalk that surrounded the property. It was raining again, leaving the ground soft and slick.

She shoved all worried thoughts of Tess and Emily aside, leaving just enough to act as motivation to catch the guy. They needed to know why he'd been in the apartment and what he knew—if anything—about their case.

She jumped off the last step, holstering her gun as she crossed the sidewalk, then propelled herself over the fence, landing on all fours. Her knee skidded across the wet grass on the other side, ripping her pants, but she stood back up and started running after him down one of the wooded trails behind the apartment complex.

She had to stop this guy.

Her lungs burned, legs ached, but she pushed through the pain. She'd missed her run this morning and hadn't planned to make it up.

I don't know that I'm up for this today, Lord.

She was gaining. Ten yards, six . . .

He miscalculated the sharp curve in the trail and slipped in the mud. Avery landed on top of him, hard, then heard his body slam against the ground beneath them. His elbow jabbed into her ribs as momentum carried her forward. Shoving his shoulder against the ground, she ignored the throbbing pain in her side.

He tried to push her away, but she pressed her knee into his back to hold him down as Griffin pulled out his handcuffs.

"Don't even try to move!"

It was over.

"Guess you didn't need us, boss."

"It's about time the two of you showed up."

Avery looked down at her pants, now caked in mud, and frowned. At least she'd gotten him. "He could have picked a day when it wasn't raining outside."

Avery turned the guy over and pulled him up onto his feet. "What's your name?"

He turned away, jaw clenched.

"He was carrying this." Tory unzipped the bag. "Dropped it a few feet back."

Griffin let out a low whistle at the pile of cash inside.

"Not enough to pay off the ransom demand, but still, not a bad start." Avery turned back to their runner. "Apparently you had the same idea we had. Except you don't have a search warrant."

She pulled a wallet out of the man's back pocket and found his license. "Ben Jacobs?"

Avery's heart quickened at the memories the name evoked. This was the man she'd been looking for the past five months. The intruder who'd broken into her house. If it weren't for Jackson and her former partner, Mitch, who'd insisted on protection duty outside her house all night, she could have been seriously hurt. Ben Jacobs had escaped but had left DNA on a piece of broken glass—DNA that connected him with her brother Michael's case. And with the cover-up surrounding his death.

"Ben Jacobs." She looked at him. "What were you doing in the Cerda apartment?"

"I don't have anything to say."

"Oh, I think you have a lot to say. Starting with your connection to the Cerda family, a kidnapping—"

"Kidnapping? Wait a minute. I might admit to breaking into that apartment, but you've got it all wrong if you think I'm involved in a kidnapping."

"I don't think so, and I'm not even finished yet. Add to that ransom demands, drug dealings . . ." Avery gave him a penetrating look. "And the death of my brother, Michael Hunt."

CHAPTER
10

Emily glanced up at the clock on the classroom wall and watched the second hand move in slow motion. Each minute that passed felt more like a day. She slipped off the sweater she'd exchanged earlier for her coat, draping it over the back of the chair where she sat. Despite the cool weather outside, the room felt muggy. Humid. She wished she were out shopping with Grace. Drinking hot chocolate in front of the Christmas tree with her family . . . anywhere but here.

But like so many instances in life, there was no escaping this moment.

Or the feeling that she wasn't doing enough.

Her gaze shifted to the red-stained tile halfway down the row of desks where Philip had fallen. She squeezed her eyes shut, wishing she could ignore the reminder, but instead, the scene replayed again and again through her mind like it had over and over the past thirty minutes. She'd watched the medics walk cautiously through the door, while Rafael pressed the barrel of the gun against Tess's head. She'd seen the terror in her niece's eyes, while she sat helpless to do anything. The message was clear. Rafael might not have meant to shoot Philip, but he would shoot Tess if he had to.

She'd wanted to pass on information to the medics. Communicate something to Mason and the others that would help, but nothing she could think of was worth risking Tess's life.

All she'd done was watch.

How many times had she sat through a cop show on television or the movies and imagined how she might react? She'd always fantasized that she'd end up being the hero of the day, but reality was proving to be completely different. Forget brave and heroic. She was terrified. If it weren't for the students and the fact that she was the adult responsible for their safety, she'd have already lost it.

But she was out of options. Unless Mason and his team could find out who was behind Eduardo's kidnapping, bringing a resolution to this was completely out of her hands. All they could do now was wait for the demanded ransom money to be transferred and pray that things resolved without anyone else getting hurt.

God, I've never felt so out of control. Never felt so helpless. All I can do is sit and wait and pray that you somehow turn this mess around.

Izzie nudged Emily's shoulder from behind her, pulling her from her thoughts. "Miss Hunt?"

Emily nodded at her to continue.

"I meant what I said earlier to Rafael. This isn't like him." Izzie hesitated before lowering her voice. "Something seems . . . off."

Emily shifted around in her chair to face Izzie. She'd felt the same thing all morning, but had finally decided she was trying too hard to make excuses for Rafael. She wanted to believe that somehow he was an innocent player in all of this. It certainly wasn't true. Still . . . "What do you mean?"

"Rafael has always been nice, Miss Hunt. He smiles at everyone. Says hi to me in the hall . . . I don't understand how he could do this."

"I don't either, but he is. And as much as I'd like to think there's somehow another explanation, he's ultimately responsible for what's happening in this classroom right now."

Izzie played varsity volleyball, ran track, and had been on the homecoming court this fall. Nothing in life prepared you for something like this.

"I know, but he's not like the loners you see on the news who end up blowing up all the kids who ignored them."

Izzie was right. Emily had been racking her brain for the past couple of hours, trying to remember anything in Rafael's past behavior that would explain his snapping like this. His going to Mason had proved that he had started off in the right direction. But something had happened to make him believe that this was his only option. The question was, what?

"Last week these boys from my third-period class were bothering me," Izzie continued. "Rafael stood up for me. That's not the kind of person who threatens to shoot you."

Emily looked back at Rafael, who was on the phone again with Mason. Every fifteen minutes the detective called in an attempt to make headway in the negotiations and give Rafael an update.

She turned back to Izzie. "Sometimes stress does things to people. Sometimes when people feel trapped, they do things they wouldn't normally do. He's scared and not thinking properly." Emily listened to her own explanation, not wanting to justify Rafael's actions, but simply trying to make sense of what was happening.

"I noticed something else," Izzie continued. "Maybe I'm imagining things, but . . ." She lowered her voice again. "Have you noticed how he pauses before saying something?"

"Yes, but he's scared."

"What if it is more than that? What if someone is telling him what to say?"

Emily felt her heart skip a beat. Izzie was speaking out loud the same thing that had been running through her mind. Except she'd dismissed the idea, thinking it was too outlandish to be true.

But if it were true, what kind of leverage would it take to have made him do something like this?

She turned to watch Rafael. His reactions, his mannerisms, his expressions. He shifted the hat on his head and continued to pace, jaw tensed. What had they missed?

"Maybe it's just my imagination," Izzie said, "but what if someone is forcing him to do this?"

Rafael hung up the phone and walked toward them, interrupting their conversation. "What are you talking about?"

"I'm just making sure everyone is okay and stays calm." Emily kept her voice steady. If Izzie was right, there had to be a way to find out the truth. "They're scared, Rafael. You know that. I don't want anyone to get upset and panic like Philip did."

He shoved his phone into his pocket. "As soon as I get the money, all of this will be over."

Emily stood slowly, weighing her options. There had to be a way to test their theory. "What did Mason say?"

"He asked if everyone was okay. Told me they're working on getting the money. That I need to be patient. That it was going to take more time. Nothing has changed. I reminded him he was running out of time."

"It takes awhile to get that kind of money. You're asking for a lot." She moved down the aisle between the desks, closer to him. "I'm worried about you. This isn't like you at all."

"We've gone over this before. It's too late to stop this."

"I'm not talking about that right now. I know you're worried about your brother. You know I'm here to help."

"Go back and sit down with the rest of the class." The

irritation was back in his voice. "As soon as I know that the money's been transferred, this will all be over."

Emily hesitated. The kids sat silent, tears on the faces of some of the girls, worry mixed with fear on the boys'. If there was an outside person, they would need a way to communicate with Rafael. Could they hear him? See what was going on in the classroom?

The room was wired to communicate between her classroom and the office, but she'd know if they were using that. The school administration had discussed putting in video monitors as extra security but in the end had felt it wasn't necessary. Still, there were definitely other options. The technology was readily available. She knew Avery wore a wireless earphone in certain cases. A video camera could easily be placed in a hat.

She looked back at Rafael. No. The anger and defiance were clear in his expression. She had to be imagining things. She'd had students in the past who she'd believed would make it until they'd gotten involved with drugs or the wrong crowd. Rafael wasn't any different. They all wanted to believe he couldn't do something like this, but it wasn't true. With his brother's life on the line, he'd made the decision to save him at any cost. Even if it meant losing everything he'd worked for. As much as she wanted to believe he was somehow innocent, deep down she knew it couldn't be true.

But if there was any chance Izzie—and her gut—were right, she couldn't let fear stop her from helping him.

"Rafael?"

He shook his head. "Stop talking."

"Why?"

"Because you're only going to make things worse. Why can't you just accept that I'm going through with this and nothing you can say will change my mind?"

"I just want to help."

"You always think you can fix things. After-school job openings . . . a scholarship to Penn State . . . Do you think any of that is really going to make a difference in the long run?"

A scholarship to Penn State?

She must have heard him wrong. Rafael had been offered a scholarship from the University of Georgia. She caught the intensity of his gaze, the slight shake of his head, the tensing of his jaw. She blinked. Was he trying to tell her something?

She shifted her eyes to the desk in the front of the room where Rafael had left her phone when all of this started. If she was reading him right, she needed to get a message to Mason. If she was wrong, any attempt to communicate would get her—or one of her students—shot. Avery would know what to do. She, on the other hand, was a schoolteacher trained to prepare students for tests on medieval history, not in psychological profiling or how to handle a ransom situation.

God, so much is at stake here. Show me what to do . . .

She cleared her throat. Her students were depending on her. Tess was depending on her. Her sister . . . "Rafael, there's a box of tissues on my desk. Do you mind if I get some? Some of the girls could use them."

"Fine." He caught her gaze. "Just remember that I'm watching and listening to everything you say. Because everyone in this classroom—and I mean everyone—will die if the money isn't transferred on time."

Watching . . . listening . . . everyone in this classroom.

Everyone including Rafael?

The words gnawed at her as she walked toward the front of the room. What if he was trying to tell her something? What if someone else *was* listening? Watching. What kind of leverage were they using?

Whatever it was, they were threatening the lives of everyone in this classroom. And if they were, she had to get a message to Mason. All she had to do was get her phone.

Emily slowly slid the box of tissues toward her, her eyes locked on the phone. If she was right, this might be her only chance. With the tissue box hiding her movements, she palmed the phone and slipped it into her pocket.

CHAPTER
11

Mason rapped his fingers against the office counter and watched Charlie, whose worry was evident even from across the room. He might not particularly like the man, but he couldn't help but respect him. Charlie knew how to run a negotiation and would be in charge now if the situation were different. And that wasn't all. Mason hadn't missed the fear in his eyes.

Mason bridged the gap between them and lowered his voice. "You're still in love with her, aren't you?"

"With Emily?"

"Yeah."

"Things have been over between Emily and me for a long time."

"Still, this must be difficult for you."

Charlie's gaze flickered as he shoved his hands into his pockets. "I didn't say I didn't still care about her. Sometimes . . . sometimes it's hard not to regret how things turn out."

The captain strode into the room, interrupting their conversation. "I just spoke with Avery. There was no sign of Mrs. Cerda at the apartment. Drug dogs are searching right now, but so far they haven't found anything. They've already started questioning the neighbors and, interestingly enough, a burglar they caught trying to leave the premises with fifty-thousand dollars in cash."

Someone let out a low whistle from the back of the room.

"Fifty-thousand dollars?" Charlie asked.

"We'll know more soon, but I'm going to assume there is a connection here with Eduardo's involvement in the drug scene."

"Who's the guy they caught?" Mason asked.

"An ex-con by the name of Ben Jacobs," the captain answered. "And if this case weren't complicated enough, he was also the one who broke into Avery's house four months ago and stole her brother's file. As most of you know, Michael was working undercover when he died. They're interrogating Jacobs now to figure out how this all fits together."

Mason processed the information. They'd taken Eduardo. Mrs. Cerda had disappeared. The deadline was approaching, and the kidnappers still didn't have their money. They needed extra leverage . . .

Extra leverage.

"What if Eduardo's kidnappers found a way to use his mother to control Rafael?" The thought streaked through Mason like the lightning illuminating the Atlanta skyline. Saying it out loud reinforced the idea. It made sense. Finding out his mother's life was in danger could have been the motivation for Rafael to believe he had no choice but to walk into that school and demand the money.

"What are you saying?" Charlie asked.

"Think about it," Mason continued. "Eduardo's kidnappers realize that Rafael and his mother aren't going to come up with the money. Killing Eduardo would cut off any leverage they had, but if they take the mother—"

"They've just doubled their advantage." Charlie finished his sentence, then turned to the captain for his reaction.

"I don't know. Seems extreme, but if Rafael knew they had

his mother as well, it could have given him the motivation to walk into a classroom with a gun."

"The other possibility is that Rafael doesn't know his mother's missing, and the leverage is for Eduardo," Charlie threw out. "They took his mother to get Eduardo to tell them where the money is."

"What we can confirm is that there was a call made to Elaine Cerda's cell phone this morning from a burn phone," the captain said. "The same number that called Rafael."

"That would have been right after I spoke with him," Mason added. "What do you suggest, Captain?"

"We focus on finding Eduardo and his mother while moving forward with the negotiations. We can't assume that Rafael won't follow through with his threats. We need to convince him it's time he gave us something."

"Like what?" Mason asked.

Charlie grabbed a foam stress ball from one of the desks and started working it between his fingers. "Start by finding a way to convince him to release Amie as a sign of good faith."

"I tried that . . ." Mason clamped his jaw shut midsentence and nodded. "I'll try again."

As much as he didn't want to admit it, Charlie was right. So far they hadn't made much, if any, progress.

"I'll need an update to give Rafael." Mason stepped away from the window to address the captain, feeling the pressure of his responsibilities mounting. Saving the lives of everyone in the classroom was their priority. And that included Rafael. "What about the parents? Have they all been contacted?"

The captain nodded to the principal. "Mr. Farley?"

"Going from the list of names we were given, all but two of the students' parents are here. Chad Valentine flew to Savannah on business yesterday. Mrs. Johnson is visiting her elderly parents in Marietta. Both should be arriving soon."

"What about the ransom money?" Mason winced at the question. It felt cold when said out loud. "Can we make the deadline if he insists on it?"

"They're working with their banks, but coming up with that kind of cash isn't easy."

Mason glanced out the front window of the school. On the other side of the campus, parents of the students inside that classroom were facing their worst nightmares. And so far his strategy to get them released hadn't worked. He needed to step away, clear his head, and pray.

"Something wrong, Taylor?"

Mason waved his hand at the captain. "I need five minutes."

"Be back in five, then make that phone call."

"Yes sir."

Mason stepped out in front of the school and took in a gulp of fresh air. Rain pounded across the parking lot and lightning flashed in the distance. The weatherman had predicted snow in Colorado. He should be there right now, sitting in some small, dark room with his brothers nearby and hospice hovering in the background. At the very least, he should call. Get an update on his father. That was the least he owed his brothers. And he would, as soon as this was over.

On the other side of the campus at the gym parking lot, parents were escorting their children to waiting cars. He could only imagine their relief in realizing that their children weren't the ones being held hostage.

But eleven others hadn't been so fortunate. Tess, Emily . . . He knew their faces and stories. Knew their family and their love for God. And even those he didn't know, they had families—moms, dads, brothers and sisters . . .

God, this one is hitting far too close. I need some perspective.

He struggled for words. Learning how to pray had become a sequence of baby steps as his faith grew. Letting go and depending on someone else to lead his life had been an even bigger challenge. But lately he'd found a deeper peace as he sought to let God become his biggest source of strength. He was tired of depending on himself.

Because after his years on the force, the evil in the world still managed to surprise him sometimes. And in his weakness, God's power seemed magnified. But even that realization didn't make days like today easy. He'd seen so much evil and hurt that if the desire to fight for justice wasn't so strong, he'd have jumped ship years ago for some eight-hour shift in a monotonous downtown office. Life was full of evil men who made evil choices. That was a fact of a fallen world. A fact that had prompted him to finally put his trust in a Savior.

But now Emily was caught up in the fallout of some of those evil choices. He shook off the urge to rush in there and rescue her himself. For some crazy reason, he wanted—needed—to protect her. But Emily Hunt wasn't that twenty-year-old college student anymore, or just his best friend's baby sister. Too much had happened since then. Michael's death, Avery's accusations, and the department's investigation into his role in the incident. He might have come out clean to the higher-ups, but Avery had yet to drop her investigation. And Emily was a Hunt.

There was also the issue of Emily's former relationship with Charlie. Mason had been at the Hunts' house to see Michael the day she'd announced her engagement to Charlie. He'd finally dug up the courage and was going to ask her out again that day, not realizing that Charlie had gone from first date to a serious relationship in a matter of weeks.

He'd stood in the Hunt living room, watching her show off her engagement ring that was the size of a Georgia peach. She was wearing something vintage. Something completely Emily. He'd walked out the door, leaving his feelings for Emily behind. Or at least he thought he had until today. But whatever he felt—or didn't feel—toward Emily didn't really matter right now.

His phone beeped with a message and he pulled it out of his pocket to read the text.

Rafael's being manipulated.

Mason felt the punch to his gut as he read Emily's message. He stared out across the grassy slopes, soggy from the rain, the words replaying in his mind. He'd considered his mother's disappearance as leverage, but manipulation?

He typed in a new message.

Tell me what you know.

———

Emily hesitated with her response. If she'd somehow read Rafael wrong, she could be putting the lives of all of the students on the line by communicating with Mason. Rafael had let Tess go and was now pacing the front of the room, like he'd done most of the morning, quietly focused. Nothing had changed, except now he was keeping his head turned away from her.

On purpose?

Her gut told her yes. Because being wrong wasn't an option. Someone could die if she'd misread the situation. He was turned away from her on purpose. Giving her a chance to do something to help put a stop to this.

At this point, though, she had no idea how any of them could stop what was happening without someone else getting hurt. And if someone was watching Rafael, watching all of them . . .

Tell me what you know.

Emily read over Mason's message again. She'd contemplated contacting her sister or her father, but the only person who made sense was Mason. Especially if she only had a few minutes to communicate. He was the negotiator. He knew Rafael and Rafael trusted him.

But she still wasn't sure what to tell him. The medics who had taken Philip out would have already been debriefed by Mason's team. Her mind had walked through the probable timeline over and over. Somehow, between the moment Mason had first talked with Rafael this morning and the time he showed up with a gun at the school, someone had gotten to him. But who? And what had they said to convince him to take a classroom of students hostage?

Someone is communicating with him.

Emily waited for Mason's response while old memories surfaced. She remembered him so clearly in his smart blue uniform before he'd become a detective. For her, he'd been—like her father, brother, and sister—a symbol of protection in a world far too prone to injustice. She'd daydreamed of him coming to her rescue and saving the day. Funny. She'd never expected that day to really come.

Who?

She squeezed her eyes closed, wondering what her sister would do in this situation. Tess sat in the desk beside her, her head resting in her arms, eyes closed. Besides the clicking of the clock and the occasional fidgeting of the students, the room was quiet.

But she had no idea who was behind this and didn't know how to get an answer out of Rafael. She mulled over his words, wondering if he'd given her some sort of clue. He'd said that someone was watching. Listening. Whoever had kidnapped Eduardo was the obvious answer, but a useless one. Their original monetary demands had seemed crazy. Taking a class hostage for two million even crazier. As far as she knew at this point, Mason and his team knew a lot more than she did.

Don't know. Can't talk to Rafael. They're listening. Watching.

She waited for his response, needing some kind of assurance that she wasn't the crazy one. That none of this was simply because she couldn't believe Rafael capable of this.

What else?

She hesitated before typing in her response.

No money, all will die.

Not going to happen, Emily.

She wanted to believe him, but how much control did he have? Another message.

How many weapons?

Emily took in a deep breath. He was wanting to verify the information the medics had given. She needed to stay clear-minded and focused.

1 semi-auto handgun

She might not be an officer, but her father had taught her about weapons. Had taken her shooting dozens of times as a child. Her stomach clenched. She knew why Mason was asking these questions. If things couldn't be resolved peacefully, they needed to know what kind of firepower they were up against. Whether or not someone was behind this, they needed to know the best way to take Rafael down.

Where are you & the students?

She forced her mind back on the question.

Back NE corner of room

Rafael?

Front

How is he emotionally?

Emily looked back up at Rafael. Jaw clenched. Deep frown. Constant pacing. He'd made it clear he was determined to save his brother. Even if it cost him everything. And with the way things were going, his actions *were* going to cost him everything.

Scared. Intense. Determined.

Tears burned her eyes. She trusted Mason. She had to. But she sure wished they were chatting over a cup of coffee right now. Listening to something mellow in the background. Laughing over something that didn't really matter. Anything but this.

Mrs. Cerda missing. Possible motivation.

Emily sucked in a lungful of air as she read the text, then glanced up at Rafael. That was it. Motivation for him to walk into this room this morning. He had to know they'd taken her.

A second message from Mason came through.

We find Eduardo & Mrs. Cerda & this will be over.

She reread the last phrase. *This will be over.* But would it really? While she wanted this hostage situation to be over, she knew the moment Rafael walked out the door, his trouble would just be beginning. Even if someone was behind this, he was still responsible for his actions.

And what were the odds of finding Eduardo in the next couple of hours? As wrong as Philip had been in his approach, he'd been right about one thing. Even if the money was transferred, there wasn't going to be a happily ever after in this situation. Rafael wasn't going to be able to just walk away from this.

Which is what whoever was behind this was counting on. She felt a chill race up her spine. The moment Rafael had stepped into this room and grabbed Tess, he'd sealed his fate, but he didn't care. This wasn't about the money or his escaping. It was about getting Eduardo's captors what they were demanding so he and his mother could be set free.

Her fingers fumbled on the keypad.

Find them.

She wanted him to promise he would, but knew he couldn't. How many unsolved cases still sat on her sister's desk, including their brother's? They might never discover who had orchestrated this.

She refused to give in to the fears lurking in the back of her mind, but nothing seemed certain anymore. She looked at the gun Rafael held. If this was bigger than Rafael, if someone really was somehow manipulating him, and they knew what was going on in this classroom, then this situation was no longer in the control of an inexperienced eighteen-year-old, but of drug dealers. Who would have no qualms in ending Rafael's life—or anyone else's.

Mason's text interrupted her turbulent thoughts.

Need to inform captain.

Tess's quiet sobbing in the desk beside her jerked Emily back to reality. Her niece had been held at gunpoint, watched a fellow student shot . . . Even with all of Mason's promises, for the moment, there was no escape. Nowhere to run to.

Tess needed her. Emily slipped the phone into her pocket, then went and knelt down beside Tess. They had to find a way out of this, because time was running out.

———

As soon as Mason sent the last text, he hurried back into the school. Key players from negotiation had taken over the office with its rows of file cabinets, trophies, and a familiar blue-and-white bobcat mascot hanging on the wall, transforming the room into their command station. Computers, surveillance equipment, live video footage of the hallway outside the classroom. The captain and Charlie sat in the middle of it, poring over a set of blueprints.

The captain rubbed the back of his head. "We need eyes in that classroom—"

"Maybe we have them." Mason addressed the captain, but he had the attention of the entire room. "I just received a text message from Emily."

"From Emily?" Charlie took a step forward. "How?"

"She's using her phone. She believes Rafael's being manipulated."

While he knew Emily believed this to be true, he knew they also couldn't dismiss the possibility that Rafael could be, for whatever reason, manipulating *her*.

Lieutenant Green took a step forward. "So this whole ransom scenario being played out right now wasn't the brainchild of Rafael. He was set up?"

Mason wished he could be certain. "Emily can't communicate directly with Rafael, but apparently he found a way to give her some clues and he's letting her text. She believes someone else has eyes and ears in the room."

Charlie shook his head. "How is that possible?"

Mason shrugged a shoulder. They needed answers, not more questions. "I don't know, but clearly the technology is readily available. We use earbuds and cameras in surveillance all the time."

"Maybe, but just like Mason's theory that Mrs. Cerda is being used as leverage, this doesn't follow the cartel's typical pattern." The captain dropped the blueprints onto the table. "Why take school kids hostage? This story is being played on every mainstream and internet media outlet. The local drug lords don't usually play that way."

"They might for two million dollars." Mason tried to work through his own train of thought. "I know Rafael. I've never felt that he could do something like this on his own. I think Emily could be right—this was someone else's idea, and that someone is telling him what to do and say."

"And what if Emily is wrong?" the captain asked.

The same question plagued him. Emily wanted Rafael to be innocent as much as he did, but if he was nothing more than a pawn, then they had to find out exactly who was calling the shots.

Mason rubbed the back of his neck, trying to help alleviate the headache that was starting to spread. "Like some of you, I've known Emily and her family for years. And while Emily might not have the experience we do, she's smart. She wouldn't have taken the risk to contact us if she wasn't certain she was right about this."

The captain nodded. "For the moment, I think we have to move forward, believing Emily is right."

"So at some point," Charlie said, "something happened to change the game."

"Then maybe we need to change it again," Mason said.

Once again, he had the captain's full attention.

"How?"

"Let me go in there."

"In the classroom?" The captain shook his head. "Not an option."

"I have to agree," Charlie said. "The risk is far too great. We still have no idea what Rafael is capable of doing."

"If Rafael is being manipulated, he's not going to shoot me. And even if he isn't, I still don't believe he would hurt me."

"You can't know that," the captain said.

"The bottom line is that I can only make so much progress talking on the phone with him," Mason said. "I need to be in that room with him. Face-to-face."

"You got a plan?"

Mason hesitated. He hadn't thought that far ahead. There was just a gut feeling that going in there was the right thing to do.

"They've got to be hungry," he said. "We order pizza."

"And you go in as the delivery boy?"

"Yeah."

The captain's eyes narrowed. "It might just work."

"I disagree." Charlie shook his head. "This is a mistake, Captain. Going in there could get those kids killed."

Mason could tell from the captain's expression he'd already made his decision. "Is it a risk? Yes. But a face-to-face conversation just might work. Mason, grab your bulletproof vest. You're going in there."

"I still say this is a mistake, Captain," Charlie repeated.

"Noted." The captain dismissed Charlie and started barking out orders to the tech team. "If Rafael is wearing an earbud to communicate, the range will be limited. Set up a frequency scan. We're going to find who's out there trying to play God."

CHAPTER
12

Mason took a sip of the coffee someone handed him earlier and frowned. It was lukewarm and bitter, but he could use the caffeine. The rain had finally stopped, but according to the weatherman, snow was predicted for later this afternoon. Which meant they'd probably end up with an inch or two of powder that by morning would melt into a nasty slush, making a dreary week even more dreary.

It was cold outside, but he needed a couple of minutes to clear his head while they waited for the pizza to be delivered. He hadn't expected the captain to grant him permission to go in. If they'd made the wrong decision . . . if he ended up doing or saying something that got someone killed, he'd never forgive himself.

"Now isn't the time to question your abilities."

Mason turned around to face his former captain. "Captain Hunt."

"I'm not a captain anymore."

"You always will be to me, sir."

And more. Thomas Hunt had become the father he'd never had over the past few years. Mentor, spiritual advisor, and counselor . . . He'd helped him in his new relationship with Christ that in turn had brought a peace into his life he'd never experienced before.

"So I managed to read your mind?"

"Yeah."

Mason took another sip of his coffee, then looked away. He'd always felt confident in his abilities as a cop, as an undercover agent, investigative detective, wherever the cases took him. Gut instincts, that had saved him more than once, helped him face the adrenaline rush and brain games he was forced to play in order to stay alive.

But today, he was afraid he'd make the wrong move and, like a row of falling dominoes, everything around him would come crashing down.

"I find myself questioning everything. Every word, every decision. So much hangs in the balance. We need to find Eduardo and his mother. We need to know who is manipulating Rafael. We need the parents to come up with the ransom money if all else fails."

"And you're asking yourself, what if everything in this house of cards collapses."

"Exactly." Mason tossed the empty coffee cup in the trash can beside him, then tugged on the bottom of his bulletproof vest. "Despite the stress of what I do, when I'm undercover, all I have to do is remind myself that when I walk out on those streets, I'm a part of helping make this world a better place. But this . . . this is different. It's not just taking down some drug lord who deserves what he gets in the end. It's a kid who I know doesn't deserve any of this. A kid who more than likely is being manipulated to do the crazy thing he's doing."

"Things are never straightforward in this business, are they?"

Mason looked up at the captain. "No, but somehow I thought I could jump into this situation, take the lead, and convince Rafael to stand down, but I've not made any progress. And

I'm not sure that talking face-to-face is going to make a difference, unless he really is being manipulated as Emily believes. Unless he really is trying to find a way to ask for help. If we're wrong about this, time is quickly running out and Rafael has threatened to kill everyone in that room if he doesn't get what he's demanding."

Mason looked to him, knowing he needed the older man's advice. "Do you think I should go in there?"

"Normally, no, but this case is different. I think this is the right decision, and a face-to-face talk might be the only way to find out the truth. Rafael knows you, so his initial response to seeing you shouldn't be violent, especially if he is being manipulated."

"That's what I'm counting on. I appreciate your input, sir."

Captain Hunt took off his police cap and grasped it between his fingers. "I was twenty-nine when I negotiated my first hostage case. I was thrown into a situation with a young mother, her nine-month-old son, and the elderly grandfather, all barricaded in a house with her ex, who was holding them captive with a gun."

"What happened?" Mason asked.

"The mother and baby made it fine, but the grandfather was shot and killed. I blamed myself for weeks for his death. Couldn't stop going over what I could have done to save all of them. Maybe if I'd been a better negotiator, or insisted the tactical assault be delayed."

"I guess it's impossible not to feel that way."

"Yes, but my point is that this job's never easy. Walking into this, you knew this wasn't going to be easy."

"You're right." Mason felt as if he were trying to fix something that couldn't be fixed. Change something he had no control over.

"If Rafael is being manipulated, as Emily believes," Captain Hunt said, "that adds another layer of risk to the situation that isn't going to be easy to manage."

Hearing Emily's name reminded Mason that he wasn't the only one with an eye on the stakes. "As for you, sir. I'm sorry about your family. Emily . . . Tess. I can't imagine what you must be feeling right now."

The older man's brow narrowed. "I've always tried not to make my cases personal, but here there's no way around it."

"I've always thought of Rafael like a little brother."

"None of us are completely immune."

It was those personal cases that were always the hardest.

"There is something I wanted to ask you before you go in," Captain Hunt continued.

"Anything."

"They gave me an update and told me you've been in contact with Emily. How does she sound?"

"Scared, but strong. She seems to be making levelheaded choices. For one, it had to have taken a lot of courage to grab that phone and text me."

"She never thought she had what it took to become a cop, but if you ask me, dealing with a classroom of high school students five days a week takes an enormous amount of courage."

"I'm sure you're right." Mason laughed. "I've always admired her for her passion for kids."

"If I remember correctly, you asked her out one summer she was home from college."

Mason shoved his hands into his jacket pockets. How had they stumbled onto such an awkward subject? "Yeah, she turned me down."

"I also seem to remember her mother telling me she had a crush on you back then."

"Really?" The statement surprised him. There'd always been something about Emily that stood out. Something that told him she was the kind of woman he wanted to spend the rest of his life with.

"What about Tess?" Captain Hunt's question interrupted his thoughts. "Do you know how she is?"

He pushed his own straying feelings aside. "All I know is that no one else has been hurt."

Mason glanced at his watch. The captain was going to call him any minute now. "I'd appreciate any further advice before I go in there, sir. I might be a cop through and through, but you've been in my place before. I've got to do this right."

"No one is ever completely ready, and textbook procedures don't cover everything. This is real life, where people don't follow a script. That being said, you know Rafael better than any of us, which gives you an advantage. I have every confidence in the world you can find a way to bring Emily, Tess, and the other students safely out of there."

"What if something goes wrong and this blows up?"

"Then you deal with that when—and if—it happens. You've done a good job so far. Don't let them pressure you into trying to pull off a tactical incursion unless absolutely necessary. The chances of someone getting hurt will greatly increase."

"Yes sir."

"One last thing." Captain Hunt caught his gaze. "I thought you were supposed to fly to Colorado today."

Mason felt the familiar surge of frustration. "I was getting ready to leave until Rafael called me."

"And your father?"

"He's dying."

"Can I give you a piece of advice on that situation?"

"Yeah."

"Forgive him. And as soon as all of this is over, go see him. The pulls of this job never end, and family has to come first. No matter what has gone on between the two of you in the past, don't live with the regret of not telling him you forgive him. Once he's gone, you'll never be able to change that."

The pizza delivery car pulled up in the circular drive in front of the school. It was time to go.

Captain Peterson called out to him from the entrance of the school. "You're on, Taylor."

Emily's father nodded at Mason. "I'm praying for you, son. I know you've got a lot of pressure coming at you from all sides to make sure we get those kids out of there alive, but you *can* do this."

"I have no intention of failing, sir."

Three minutes later, Mason stepped slowly into the classroom, pizza boxes in hand, as he assessed the situation. Students huddled in the back of the classroom, sitting on chairs or leaning against the back wall, fear clearly written across their faces.

Emily sat in a chair in front of Rafael, gun pressed against her temple, her expression tense, but still in control. Rafael wasn't taking any chances.

"Rafael, I've got six large pizzas. Just like I promised. Can I come in now?"

"Mr. Taylor, I . . ." Rafael fumbled with his words, clearly taken by surprise.

Mason kept his voice even. "I am the negotiator. I thought it would be better if we talked face-to-face rather than over the phone."

"No. This . . . this isn't what I agreed to. I didn't mean you could come in here. I was expecting a delivery boy."

"They didn't want a civilian involved."

Rafael looked confused. Scared.

What have you gotten yourself into, Rafael?

"Talking face-to-face isn't going to change anything," he said.

"Maybe, maybe not." Mason set the pizzas on Emily's desk at the front of the room.

Rafael held the gun steady, avoiding eye contact with Mason. "I will shoot her if you try to pull anything."

"I'm not trying to pull anything on you, Rafael." Mason held up his hands. "I just want to ensure that you and the students and Miss Hunt are safe."

"You can see that they're all fine. And you need to leave. Now."

Mason took a step forward. "You used to trust me, Rafael. I can still help you, but I need you to trust me again."

"No."

"Why not?" Mason chose his words carefully, knowing he needed to find a balance of authority and understanding. "I'm here because I can help, Rafael. I'm going to stay."

Rafael hesitated before speaking again. "Fine. Close the door behind you and lock it."

"Okay." Mason moved toward the door and locked it before turning back to Rafael. "The door's locked. Why don't you let Emily go?"

"In a minute." Rafael nodded at one of the boys in the back. "Search him. Make sure he doesn't have a weapon, a cell phone, or a wire."

"I'm clean, Rafael. I just want to talk." Mason held up his hands and let the boy search him. He'd come in clean, counting on Emily's phone to communicate. "Why don't you let Emily help pass out the pizza to the kids. I got your favorite."

"I'm not hungry."

"Pepperoni, olives, and jalapeños."

"I said I'm not hungry."

"Okay. That's fine."

Rafael stepped back from Emily and nodded at her to hand out the pizza. He stood at the front of the room, seemingly more remote than he'd been this morning when they'd talked. If someone were manipulating him, they'd found a way to completely control him.

Mason handed Emily a couple of the boxes. "You hanging in there?"

She looked up and shot him a half smile. "Yeah."

She looked tired, but determined. Which was good. If they were going to get out of this, he was going to need her. No doubt she felt as if she were responsible for the kids in this room. Seeing Philip shot had to have been terrifying. And it was proof that Rafael—or whoever was behind this— wasn't here to play games.

"What about the students?"

"I'm still worried about Amie." Emily set the pizza boxes on a couple of the desks near the back and opened them. She nodded toward one of the students. The girl's eyes were red from crying, breathing clearly labored. They needed to get her out of there.

"Why don't you let Amie go, Rafael? I brought food so I could do something to help. This would help."

"I already let Philip leave. She'll be fine."

"I appreciate what you did for Philip, but Amie needs to see a doctor."

"No." Rafael stuck out his gun and shook his head. "I'm not letting anyone else leave this room."

"I've been working to get you the money you asked for. This would be a sign of good faith to the parents that you aren't going to harm their children. It will go a long way."

Rafael's face reddened. "I'm still in charge, and I said no."

"Okay." Mason held up his hands and took a step backward. "No one is disputing that you're in charge. What I want to do is get this over with as quickly as possible without anyone getting hurt."

"It's clearly too late for that. I want my money, and then it will be over. Not before."

Mason studied Rafael's expression and caught the fatigue in his eyes. His emotions were draining him. As soon as this was over he was going to crash.

Mason needed a new approach. "Have you thought about

what happens when you get the cash? We need to talk about that."

Rafael shook his head. "What happens to me really doesn't matter. They'll kill my brother if I don't get the money."

The tension in Mason's gut tightened at the obvious implications. Rafael didn't expect to leave this room alive a free man. Apparently, the cartel—if they were the ones behind this—had come up with the perfect plan. They'd gain access to the money while Rafael took the fall.

Or a bullet if it came to that.

"You're wrong, Rafael. What happens to you does matter."

"You know what . . . I've had enough of your talk. You never should have come in here."

"Rafael—"

"No." Rafael held up the gun and pointed it at Mason, shaking his head. "I don't want you as my negotiator. Go sit down in the back of the room. I'm finished talking to you."

CHAPTER
13

I don't want you as my negotiator . . .

Rafael's sharp words to Mason echoed through Emily's mind. She shoved her uneaten pizza aside as Mason walked down the aisle toward her. She'd watched his interaction with Rafael. Voice even. Temper in check. But clearly nothing he'd said made a difference. Rafael had made it clear he was finished talking. That meant that whoever was behind this had found a way to completely control Rafael.

Mason slid into the seat in front of her. No matter what Rafael's reaction had been, Mason's presence helped take the edge off the panic she'd felt all morning. With him in the room, she could almost believe they were all going to be okay.

"How are you doing?" he asked.

She managed a smile. "I'm fine, considering my day."

"*I'm fine* aside, how are you really doing?"

She shivered and reached for her sweater from the back of the chair. He leaned forward to help wrap it around her back. His hand brushed against the back of her neck. Prickles ran down her spine—having nothing to do with the dropping temperature of the room. And everything to do with the man sitting in the desk in front of her. Emily slid her arms into the sleeves. This wasn't the time or the place to let her imagination—or her heart, for that matter—distract her. But while the girlhood crush she'd had on him in college had faded years ago, what she was feeling now was something brand new.

She focused on his question as she rubbed her finger across someone's pencil doodle of a unicorn on the top of the desk. "My stomach is knotted, and I'm cold, except for my hands, which are sweaty. But we're all still alive, so I feel as if I have something to be thankful for. And . . ." She hesitated again. "Having you in the room helps a lot."

"Being here clearly isn't making a difference with Rafael." He kept his voice low, but his frustration was obvious. "You should eat. Keep up your strength."

She looked at the slice of pizza on her desk. "I can't eat."

"I understand. I was certain that if I could just get in here, I could find a way to convince him to turn himself in, but now . . . I'm not sure there is a way out short of finding Eduardo or handing over the money."

"Then that's what we wait for. Because he's determined to see this through." Emily glanced up at Rafael, not knowing if she and Mason should be talking. For the moment, though, he was letting them. Just like he'd allowed her to continue to walk around and check on each of the students every few minutes. "You texted that they took Rafael's mother."

Mason nodded. "At this point we're assuming she's with Eduardo."

Rafael had worked hard to keep his family together. Knowing his mother's life was on the line would have been enough to push him over the edge.

Emily lowered her voice. "Any leads on their whereabouts?"

"Your sister's team is working on finding him. Jackson and the lab are trying to narrow down a location." Mason glanced back at Rafael. "Do you still have the phone? I need to send the captain a text."

She nodded, then slipped him the cell phone under the desk.

The clock ticked in the background while Mason wrote a text to the captain. Rafael had started pacing again in the front of the room. Fatigue showed on his face.

The kids sat quiet. Waiting. Pizza boxes lay open at the back of the room, half empty. A couple of the kids were still eating. Some hadn't eaten at all. Emily tapped her fingers against the desk. She couldn't blame them. Having your life threatened with a bullet tended to erase your appetite.

A moment later, Mason finished typing, then slid the phone under his leg. How could he be so focused and alert and calm?

"Do you ever get scared?" she asked.

He touched the dark stubble on his face. With his hair brushing the collar of his leather jacket, he had a look of rugged charm about him. Complete opposite from Charlie, who preferred suits and ties to jeans and T-shirts.

Not that she was comparing.

"I've learned to cope with fear, but yeah, I get scared. I remember one of my first assignments as a rookie cop. We were called out to handle a domestic dispute with weapons and ended up walking into a shooting match. Before we could arrest the couple, I was certain I was going to get killed. I don't think I've ever been so scared in my life."

"I guess we know the outcome to that one." She caught a brief flicker of a smile at her response and grasped onto the small sliver of hope that this day would also end without anyone dying. "What did you do?"

"I ran."

Emily's eyes widened. "You ran?"

"It was either that or get shot. Turns out the weapons they had were assault rifles, and they were shooting at anyone who came near them."

"You were lucky."

"Nope." He smiled at her, and she noted the dimple in his right cheek. And the fact that his eyes weren't just plain brown, but a half-dozen shades of the color. She looked away. She was clearly losing it. "I've learned God had something else in mind for me. It's taken me a long time to realize that though. As for you, you've held up under a lot of pressure today."

She felt her stomach flip at the compliment. It'd been a long time since she'd let a man affect her this way . . . since Charlie. For some crazy reason there was something about Mason that was managing to rekindle feelings she'd thought were long buried.

Or maybe it was just the fact that she'd been thrust into a terrifying situation, and he'd suddenly become her hero.

She pushed the thoughts away. "I just wish I'd been able to convince Rafael that what he's doing isn't going to work."

"You can't beat yourself up either, Emily. I've known him for a long time as well and couldn't get him to step down. You've done a great job in not allowing a bad situation to get worse."

"I don't know how it could get worse. A boy was shot and almost killed in front of all these kids. Amie's still having trouble breathing, he held a gun to my niece's head . . ."

"Your quick response helped save Philip's life."

"Maybe, but I didn't have a choice. No matter how scared I am, these kids are my responsibility." She glanced back at Rafael, surprised he was still allowing them to talk. He lifted the blinds a fraction, peaked outside, then started pacing again. No matter what had happened or what he had said or done, he was nothing more than a scared boy. "What about my texts? I know someone is manipulating him, and there has to be a way to figure out who is behind this."

Mason lowered his voice. "There's a team scanning for a signal. If he's wearing an earbud—and if someone's out there—they'll find them."

"Do you believe someone's manipulating him?"

"Yes, but only because I don't want to believe he was able to orchestrate this on his own. But no matter what I think, we can't rule out the possibility that he's playing us."

"Playing us?" Emily leaned forward. "Why would he do that?"

"If he can't find a way out of this, blaming someone else would be a viable option for him."

"So he finds a way to make me believe someone else is out there controlling him, so when this is over, he can walk away?" Emily shook her head. She didn't buy it. "If he's doing this on his own, wouldn't he want me to think he's in complete control? Otherwise, he'd appear vulnerable and weak."

"I don't know. I spoke with him this morning. He sent me the photos of his brother, and I heard the fear in his voice. I don't think there's any way he could do this on his own, but that doesn't mean the captain doesn't have a point. We have to consider all the options."

"And in the meantime?"

"I'm going to give him a few minutes more to cool off, then try and talk with him again."

Feelings of vulnerability she'd tried to bury all morning resurfaced. "Odd how all the scenarios we went over in our teacher training tried to prepare us for what to *do*, but not for the emotional impact."

"Sometimes nothing can fully prepare you."

Like Avery. Even with all of her sister's experience in dealing with tragedy, knowing her daughter's life was on the line was going to affect her. "What about Avery? I'm assuming she knows Tess is here?"

"Yes."

"How's she handling it?"

"You of all people know that your sister's strong, but I know this has to be tough on her. The captain sent her back to the precinct to run intelligence and search the Cerdas' apartment."

"Ouch. I'm sure that didn't go over well. I know she's wishing she could barge into this classroom with the SWAT team, grab all the kids, and run."

Mason chuckled softly. "I'm sure she's thought of that idea once or twice."

Emily tapped her fingers on the desk and looked at Tess. She sat in the next desk over, head down, eyes squeezed shut. "Avery and Tess fought this morning before school. I know it has to be weighing heavily on both of them."

He paused for a moment, a shadow crossing his expression. "I'm sure she's also not happy that I'm the one in this room trying to negotiate your and Tess's release."

Emily shook her head. "I wouldn't worry about that. I'm pretty capable of forming my own opinions of people."

"So her feelings toward me haven't affected your trusting me to head up this negotiation?"

"I learned a long time ago to let Avery have her own opinions. I might look up to my sister, but that doesn't mean she's always right."

"She's completely wrong in this case." The hint of amusement on Mason's face vanished. "I didn't have anything to do with Michael's death, Emily. He was my best friend. I never would have done anything to betray him."

"You don't have to explain—"

"Maybe not, but I feel like I do." He shook his head. "I need you to believe me."

She ran her finger across the doodled unicorn again. "Avery was hit hard when Michael died, and we've both seen how his death has affected my mother. Add to that, Avery's the kind of person who wants to fix everything. There are some things that simply can't be fixed."

"And you?"

"It's been a hard few months. Michael and I were close. But

so were you. I haven't forgotten that you lost your best friend and, really, lost a family too."

"Your family always was the family I could only dream of having. Mine . . . well. Let's just say I love my brothers, but beyond that, it was your typical broken, dysfunctional unit."

She could read the disappointment and longing in his eyes. She knew enough about him to know that his home life had been difficult. He hadn't experienced the healthy family she'd been blessed with.

Mason grabbed the phone from under his leg, then glanced up at Rafael, who was slouched against the teacher's desk.

She felt her heart pound. "Another message?"

"From the captain. This might be over sooner than we thought." Mason squeezed her hand. "They think they've found where the cartel is keeping Eduardo and his mother."

CHAPTER
14

Avery felt the familiar punch of adrenaline rush through her as she and her team burst through the doors of Graceland Funeral Home with a warrant from Judge Atlas. Tory had taken Jackson's discovery of glutaraldehyde—a chemical used to embalm bodies—on three of the four victims in the Torres case, cross-referenced it to suspected cartel involvement, and found one probable match. Which at the moment gave them one shot at finding Eduardo and his mother.

The strong scent of flowers engulfed her inside the pale-blue reception room. It was exquisitely decorated in order to make a grieving family feel comfortable when they walked through the door. For her, though, it only managed to dredge up unwanted memories connected to Ethan's and her brother's deaths. The pungent scent of flowers. The casket and burial vault display room. Why was everything bringing on a slew of unwanted emotions today?

A woman walked into the reception room. She looked to be in her late twenties, with a red-highlighted black ponytail, jeans, and a pink Mickey Mouse T-shirt. "I'm sorry, but we're closed . . ."

Her voice faded as she caught sight of the uniformed officers behind Avery.

Avery held up her badge. "Who else is in the building?"

"No one . . . just . . . the janitors." She tugged on the end of her ponytail. "We're closed on Mondays. I'm just here to finish some paperwork."

"We have a warrant to search the premises."

The girl pulled out a phone from her back pocket. "I'll need to call my boss—"

"You can hold off on making that phone call for now," Avery ordered.

The girl's face paled. "I don't understand."

"Where is the room where all the documents and files are kept?"

"Downstairs."

"Which room?"

The girl hesitated.

Avery's patience was gone. They'd noted the edge of a file cabinet in Eduardo's ransom photos, and since many funeral homes had a windowless, concrete room so records and files would be preserved in the case of a fire, that's where she planned to look first. "I have a warrant. Which room is it?"

"It's at the end of the hallway, but I can't let you in there. Diego would kill me if he found out—"

"You don't have a choice."

"Even if I wanted to, I don't have the key."

"That's not a problem." Avery nodded at one of the uniformed officers. "Stay with her. Griffin, Tory, and I will check out the records room. The rest of you spread out and search the building."

Ignoring the girl's protests, Avery started down the dimly lit staircase in front of Griffin and Tory. At the bottom of the stairs was a long hallway with a couple of naked bulbs hanging from the ceiling and casting eerie shadows along unfinished cement walls. She grabbed her flashlight as they started down the hall and shone it down the line of doors, a stark difference from the polished decor upstairs.

Lord, they have to be here . . .

A guard sat in front of a door at the end of the narrow corridor, chair tilted back, earphones plugged in, eyes closed.

Avery kicked the chair onto all fours. The guard grabbed for his gun but didn't react fast enough.

"This is an interesting place for an armed guard." Avery pointed her gun at him. "Set your weapon on the ground, stand up, and put your hands behind your head."

He yanked the earphones out of his ears, set his weapon beside him, then stood up slowly.

"Where are they?" she asked.

"Who?" He shook his head. "I'm just the janitor. Taking a break. I don't know what you're talking about."

"Right."

Griffin pulled a set of keys from the guard's back pocket and started fishing for a match for the doorknob. "Got it."

Avery stepped into the room while Tory cuffed the guard. She switched on the light and felt the air in her lungs escape. She recognized the boy sitting in the corner from the photos. The same bloodshot eyes, bruised cheekbone, crooked nose . . . How many others had sat in this room trying to prepare themselves for a horrible death?

He glanced up at them, his eyes squinting at the light. He started pulling against the pipe where his hands had been secured with duct tape, unable to speak with the gag in his mouth. Avery knelt down beside him and untied the bandana. Her stomach quivered. A few more hours, and he might have been another victim for her to find with his throat slit.

"Eduardo. We're the police. It's over."

He gasped for air. "They said they were going to kill me."

"Who are *they*?"

"I don't know. I never saw them before."

Avery glanced behind a row of filing cabinets for the boy's mother, but there was no sign that Elaine Cerda had even been there.

"Where's your mother?"

"My mother?"

She helped Eduardo to his feet, grasping his arm tighter when the boy stumbled. She'd make sure he got the medical care he needed, but there were questions she needed answers to first.

"We thought she was being held here with you."

"Why would she be here? They grabbed me from our house. They didn't take her."

"Someone did. Early this morning from outside the hotel where she works. Your mother's missing, Eduardo."

"No." He struggled to keep his balance. Avery caught the hint of panic in his eyes. Or maybe it was guilt. "Where is she?"

"I wouldn't be asking you if I knew, now would I?"

"If they have her, they'll kill her."

"Maybe you should have thought about that before you got involved with the wrong people." She nodded to Griffin. "Cuff him and take him back to the precinct."

"Wait." Eduardo tried to pull away from Griffin's grip. "You can't arrest me. I was kidnapped. I'm not the one who's supposed to go to jail."

"Really?" Avery caught his gaze, her anger mounting. He might be a kid, but how many lives had his bad choices affected, including his own? His mother. Rafael. Emily. Tess . . . "The police dogs found drugs hidden under the carpet beneath your bed, and then there's a little matter of fifty-thousand dollars in cash. If you can find a way to talk your way out of both of those, you might get lucky, but I have a feeling the DA's not going to be very helpful."

"It's not what you think."

"So you're not dealing drugs?"

Eduardo looked down.

An officer entered the room. "The rest of the building is clear."

Avery nodded. They'd take the receptionist in for questioning to see what she knew, but more than likely she was a part of the legitimate front who was purposely kept in the dark.

They headed up the stairs for the front door. One piece of the puzzle was still missing. Mrs. Cerda should have been here.

"Where's the woman?" Avery asked the guard at the top of the stairs.

The man's brow wrinkled. "The only person I saw was the boy."

She shook her head, uninterested in playing games. Until they found Rafael's mother, Tess was still in danger. Avery took a step forward until she was less than six inches from the man's face. "Tell me where the woman is."

"I said, I don't know."

"You're already facing charges of kidnapping for ransom, and now you're too stupid to cooperate—"

"I swear, it was only the boy." He made eye contact and kept it. "No one else has been here, and they don't tell me nothin'."

Avery backed off. More than likely the man was telling the truth. But why hold Mrs. Cerda at a separate location? It didn't make sense.

"She has to be here somewhere," Avery said.

Tory shook her head. "There isn't any sign that there was anyone here besides Eduardo."

Avery turned back to the guard. "Tell me who you're working for."

"They pay me to sit and guard this room. I don't ask questions. And like I said. They don't tell me nothin'."

"When do you expect them to return?"

"They usually bring food once a day, along with a replacement for me. Not exactly a lot of traffic down here."

Avery turned to their backup team. She didn't believe him, but a few rounds in the interrogation room with Carlos would change things. "I want you to keep this building under surveillance. If anyone comes in or goes out, I want them brought in for questioning."

"Yes ma'am."

Avery started for the door with Eduardo at her side, in step with Tory and Griffin, as the front door of the funeral home burst open.

One of the officers walking out with them shouted—"Gun!"

A shot echoed across the reception area, shattering a plate of glass behind Avery. She pulled out her weapon, then jerked Eduardo with her behind the receptionist desk.

"How many?" she shouted at Tory.

"Two. One bald, the other with a tattoo across his left forearm."

If they were out to silence their only witnesses, then Eduardo knew something.

Avery turned to the young man. "What do you know?"

"Nothing."

"Tell me the truth, Eduardo."

Two more shots were fired.

She'd had enough surprises for today. Enough bad guys. All she wanted was to snuggle with Tess on the couch and for this to all be over.

She fought to focus. Emotions she'd held on to the past few hours were beginning to unravel. After today, the captain was going to throw her off the case, and for once she'd have to agree that he was correct.

"They're using your brother to get the money they believe you owe, Eduardo. What are you involved in?"

The boy's face paled.

"They took your mother as well." What was it going to take to convince him to talk?

"I'm a seller."

"How much do you bring in?"

"A couple hundred thousand a year."

A couple hundred thousand?

"Partly earned . . . partly stolen."

"And they want it back."

Eduardo nodded. "But I don't have what they want."

He'd been trying to play the cartel.

"And your mother doesn't know?"

"She's too busy."

"Who do you work for?"

"He'll kill me."

"They're going to kill your brother and mom. Who is it?"

One of the men moved into her line of sight on the far side of the counter. She pulled the trigger. No boom. Just a click. Avery tapped the bottom of the magazine, racked the slide, then flipped the gun to the right, and let the empty shell fall out. The magazine dropped, leaving her defenseless, but he'd seen her. She—and Eduardo—were pinned in. She needed a way to get him out that wasn't in the line of the gunman. And he was making his way toward her.

The man in a black knit cap rounded the corner . . . dark hair, scar on his left cheek, gun aimed straight at her. Avery grabbed her backup pistol from her ankle holster.

He fired off two shots, seconds before she did. The first bullet hit Eduardo. The second slammed into her like a baseball bat as it ripped through her thigh. Her breath caught. Adrenaline flooded her system. She waited for the pain, but all she felt was a hot burning sensation and a strange numbness.

The room tilted diagonally as the gunman fell to the ground. Someone had hit him. Tory and Griffin shouted in the background, their words mumbled and garbled. Her mind tried to grasp what was happening as they moved in slow motion toward her. She tried to focus, but all she wanted to do was close her eyes.

The diagonal room tilted further as she dropped to her knees. Blood dripped onto the floor. Red. Sticky. Her blood. If the bullet had hit her femoral artery, she could bleed out in a matter of minutes.

She tried to shout. Tried to think. But all she could focus on was that they had to save Eduardo. He was the only link they had to finding who was behind this. If he was a dealer, he had to know who was behind the kidnappings . . .

"Eduardo . . . We can't lose him."

Tory knelt in front of her. "Avery, you're going to be okay. We're going to get both of you to the hospital. Paramedics are on their way now. Just hang in there."

She groaned. Memories blurred. She'd been there when her partner Mitch had been shot. He'd died, leaving behind a fiancée who loved him. Parents who hadn't expected to bury their child. She wasn't ready to die. Wasn't ready to say goodbye to Tess and Jackson. Needed to tell them she was sorry. So sorry . . .

She tried to open her eyes. Tory was pressing against her with something hot. Avery tried to push it away. She needed to get up. If they didn't find his mother, Rafael would have no reason to let the students go. And Tess . . .

"Don't get up, Avery. You need to be still."

"Have to get up." Her head swam. "Eduardo—"

"Eduardo was shot. One of the shooters is dead. The other's in custody."

"No. He can't die. We have to find his mother."

"We'll find her, but in the meantime, you're off the case. You're going to the hospital."

Sirens wailed in the background. Tory's voice drifted away until Avery couldn't hear her anymore.

CHAPTER
15

Mason tapped his foot against the tiled floor while he waited for an update from the captain. Until Avery and her team were able to locate Eduardo and his mother, his only option seemed to be to wait.

He glanced across the room where Emily had knelt down next to one of the desks to talk to a student at eye level. She'd spent the past few minutes making her way from student to student, something she'd apparently been doing since the ordeal had begun. She kept her voice low and soothing as she asked them how they were coping and assured them that this was all going to be over soon.

While Rafael was still refusing to speak to him, he had seemed to accept Emily's decision to take charge in this small way and hadn't made any attempts to stop her. Even though she might think his presence helped to take the edge off her panic, in his opinion, she was the calming factor in this room. Even for him.

He was struggling to keep his heart from taking the lead. Although he might have had feelings toward her in the past, what he felt today was something new. But he also knew that when dealing with emotional situations, feelings quickly grew out of proportion. He'd worked enough cases over the past decade to understand the strong emotional link that was often felt by the victim for their rescuers. And sometimes it happened the other way around. Emily was strong, yet vulnerable. He was the hero who'd come to save her. Any positive reaction he'd sensed from her had probably been just an emotional response that would disappear as quickly as it had surfaced. He wasn't really her hero. And when all of this was over, along with the tension of the day, she'd probably walk away from the situation—and him—without ever looking back.

Because there was also the fact that the rift between him and her family—with the exception of her father—simply ran too deep.

Emily's phone vibrated again under his leg. He pulled it into his lap, out of view from Rafael, and read the text from the captain.

Get Amie released.

Mason's mind snapped back to the present as he reread the text. Ten minutes ago, he'd tried to approach Rafael again, but Rafael was still refusing to talk to him.

Rafael's phone rang. Mason felt his muscles tense. The captain clearly had a plan.

Rafael spoke to the caller for a few moments, frowned, then nodded at Mason. "It's the captain. He wants to talk . . . to both of us."

Mason walked to the front of the room while Rafael switched his cell to speakerphone. He set the phone on the desk, then stepped back, leaving a good three feet between them.

"Mason?"

"I'm here, Captain."

"We should have the money in about an hour. Rafael, we need to know where to send it."

Rafael gripped his weapon tighter. "I have an account."

"Why don't you give the number to me now?"

Rafael shoved his hand into his front pocket, pulled out a crumpled piece of paper, then tossed it onto the desk.

Mason picked up the paper and glanced over the numbers. He didn't know a lot about banking—any more than Rafael likely did. Which only served to add to the questions he wanted to ask the boy. Where did he get the account, and the gun? And did he really think he was going to simply walk away from here when this was over?

He read the numbers to the captain, then turned back to Rafael. "What about after the money is transferred?"

"I'll need to check to ensure a transfer has been made to the proper bank account."

"And then?"

"Have a car waiting for me at the back east entrance . . . keys in the ignition. A tank full of gas." Rafael stared past him, hesitating briefly. "I'll take Tess with me and won't hesitate to shoot her . . . If I see anyone in the hallway, I'll shoot her. Anyone outside the building, I'll shoot her . . . If no one gets in my way, and no one follows me, I'll drop her off somewhere safe."

Rafael's words came out like a rehearsed speech. Any lingering uncertainties over whether or not he was being manipulated began to dissolve. Someone was feeding him the information, and they had to find out who. If they were listening, anything Mason said could put Rafael's mother's life in danger. Which meant that for the moment, his hands were tied.

"One last question," the captain said. "Does anyone in the room need medical attention?"

Get Amie released.

"Amie," Mason said. "She's still struggling to breathe. She needs to see a doctor."

"No—"

"Mason's right." Emily stood up, interrupting Rafael's objections. "Please, just let her go. All of this will be over soon, but she needs to go, and her staying won't change anything. You'll still get your money."

Mason hid his relief as she backed him up. Smart girl.

"We've been over this before." Rafael shook his head. "She's fine."

"She's not, and you know it. Just think about it, Rafael," Mason continued. "This is all going to be over soon. The money's almost here. Let her go."

"What if this is a trap?"

"Do you really believe that?" Mason chose his words carefully. "My job is to keep you safe, along with the lives of everyone in this room. Let her go. The money will be ready to transfer within the hour. You'll be safe as well. I promise."

Rafael chewed the side of his lip. "Fine."

The captain spoke again. "I'm sending someone to the door to escort her out of the classroom. All you have to do is unlock the door and let her walk out as soon as you hear them knock. I'll call you back as soon as the money transfer has been finalized."

The captain disconnected the call.

Mason looked up at Rafael. "What happens after you leave here?"

"I make sure Eduardo's kidnappers get their money. They'll let my brother go."

"And your mother? What about her? She's missing. How is she involved in all of this?"

"I don't know."

Rafael avoided his gaze. He knew something. Something he couldn't or wouldn't tell him?

"And you think this will really all be over when they get their money?"

"It has to be."

Someone knocked at the door. Rafael nodded at Emily. "Take her to the door, unlock it, then lock it again once she's out."

Relief mixed with fear as Emily walked to the back of the room to get Amie. Relief that this was almost over. Fear because so much could still go wrong. Her heart pounded, lungs about to burst, until she realized she was holding her breath. She let out the air slowly as she forced a smile at Amie, who was wheezing again.

She wrapped her arm around Amie's waist and started for the door. "It's going to be okay, Amie. You're almost out of here."

"Wait." Rafael signaled for Izzie to move in front of him, then settled the gun against the back of her head. He wasn't taking any chances.

Emily tightened her arm around Amie as they approached the door.

Please, Jesus, let her get out of here okay—

The moment she unlocked the door, they burst into the room. Someone pulled them into the hallway. Amie screamed.

They were all around her. Running. Shouting orders. Men in black with official logos on their backs and caps, weapons drawn as they swarmed the room behind her. Someone grabbed Amie and hurried her down the hall, assuring her she would be okay.

Emily pressed her back against the wall as her brain tried to register what was happening. Amie's release had been a setup. The students began to exit the room. Faces ashen. Crying.

Her mind clicked into teacher mode. These were her students and she had to make sure each one got out of the classroom alive . . . even Rafael. The effects of the panic she was feeling would have to be dealt with later.

A uniformed officer stepped in front of her. "Miss Hunt. I need you to come with me."

"Not yet." She was counting them as they went by. Six . . . seven . . . Mason was still in there . . . and Rafael. "I need to make sure they all get out okay."

"Ma'am, we will ensure they all get out—"

"Emily?" Mason exited behind the last two hostages. "Are you okay?"

She pulled away from the officer and ran into Mason's arms. "What just happened?"

"I don't know. The situation had to have changed, necessitating their going in there."

"He could have shot Izzie."

"But he didn't."

The reality of the situation and all the emotions that came with it flooded through her. Relief. Fear. Anger. Her stomach heaved. "Where's Rafael?"

"The captain will bring him out." He shoved aside a stray lock of hair that had slipped across her forehead. "All that matters right now is that the students are safe—"

A gun fired.

Emily jerked away from Mason and bolted toward the classroom. If they'd shot Rafael . . .

One of the officers lunged toward her. "Get her out of here!"

Mason grabbed her waist to hold her back.

She tried to pull away. "You promised he'd be okay."

The captain emerged from the classroom with another officer. "Mason, take Miss Hunt to the front office to be debriefed, then I want you to report back to me immediately."

"Who was shot? Where's Rafael?" Emily pulled away from Mason's grip and stopped in the middle of the hallway in front of the captain. His hands were covered with blood. "You shot him."

"I didn't have a choice."

She bolted for the open classroom door, but Mason's grip on her arm stopped her. "You can't go in there, Emily."

"He didn't do this on his own," she shouted. "I told you someone was using him."

"He lunged at my officers with his weapon," the captain said. "I had no choice but to stop him. We tried to revive him . . . I'm sorry, Miss Hunt, but Rafael is dead."

CHAPTER
16

Rafael is dead.

Emily walked away from the uniformed officer outside the front of the school, still trying to process everything that had just happened. Nothing seemed real, even after giving a detailed statement, which had forced her to replay today's events. Instead, it was as if she were trying to wake up from a nightmare where everything had gone horribly wrong.

And no one would tell her why.

The officer had assured her that he understood she'd been through something traumatic, but that anything she could tell them would be helpful in wrapping up the case. What was her relationship with Mr. Cerda? Had he seemed upset lately? On edge? They wanted answers, and she wasn't sure why it mattered. With Rafael dead, the hostage situation was over.

A streak of sunlight broke through the dark clouds, but did nothing to take away the early afternoon chill. Emily fumbled with the top buttons of her coat. She should be relieved. She was safe. Her students—and Tess—were all going to be okay, including Philip. She crossed the parking lot in search of her father and Tess, but all she could think about were the final moments in that classroom.

God, I didn't want it to end this way. There had to have been another way.

But nothing they'd done had made a difference. She'd tried talking to Rafael, begging with him to put the gun down and end it. Mason had tried to fix the problem. Tried to negotiate an end to the situation. But nothing had worked.

She'd tried to read Mason's expression as he'd hurried her down the hallway, but whatever he'd been thinking at that moment had stayed hidden behind those piercing eyes of his.

A sick feeling spread through her as she stared at the row of ambulances along the school driveway, where medics were treating her students. Jackson had arrived to take Rafael's body for autopsy while forensics swept her classroom, now cordoned off with yellow crime-scene tape. No matter what they found, they'd never find all the answers.

She hunched over, a dozen yards from Jackson's vehicle, hands braced against her thighs. Forgetting was impossible. The sound of the gun going off, the closed body bag when they'd wheeled Rafael past her . . .

She tried to steady her breathing. Her students were reconnecting with their parents and siblings. Did anyone care that their freedom had cost a life? To them it might be worth the loss, but not to her. Rafael might have made bad choices by not getting the help he needed, but she still believed he hadn't gone into that classroom on his own.

And then there was Elaine Cerda. She couldn't imagine what Rafael's mother would feel when she discovered she'd lost not one, but two more sons. One to the cartel and the other to an early grave.

She stared down at the sidewalk, unsure of what she should do. She needed to talk to Mason. She needed him to help her understand what had happened in those last few minutes. How they'd gone from trusting in Rafael's safety to seeing him zipped up in a body bag. She needed someone to make sense out of what she'd witnessed. But maybe it was already too late for that. Maybe finding out the truth now really was going to prove to be impossible.

Emily straightened her back, looking for a familiar face. Security was still tight and police officers surrounded the school. She wanted to go home, but wasn't sure she was ready to be alone. Grace would drive her home, or any of her teacher friends if she asked, but that would mean facing a barrage of questions that she didn't have answers to. It was going to take a long time to process what just happened.

Mason stood near the school entrance, talking to the captain. She couldn't decipher what her heart was telling her. In the classroom, he'd provided that one link of sanity and protection she'd needed when her world had spun out of control, but now she didn't know what she felt about him. She started walking toward the parking lot again. She needed to find her niece, then get away from all of this.

"Miss Hunt?"

Emily turned around at her name and stumbled backward as a smartly dressed woman shoved a microphone in front of her face. She'd been so focused on getting away, she hadn't even noticed the growing crowd filled with media pushing against the edges of the barricade the police had set up.

"Miss Hunt, I understand that you are to be congratulated. You're being hailed a hero by many of the parents and staff for your bravery in a very difficult situation."

Hero?

Emily's mind spun at the word. She was no hero. "I . . . I'm just a teacher who did what I had to do. Anyone in my place would have done the same thing."

"But you are the daughter of the city's former police captain, Thomas Hunt. Isn't that correct?"

The camera hovered in front of her. The reporter waited for her answer. All she wanted to do was bolt. "Yes, he's my father."

"I understand as well that the gunman was one of the students you've been mentoring. Tell us how you felt, knowing that your life was being threatened by someone you'd given so much to."

Where did they dig up all this information?

"Miss Hunt. Tell us what happened inside that classroom."

"You'll have to speak with one of the officers." Emily backed away. Anything she said would be twisted on tonight's evening news. "I . . . I don't have anything else to say right now. I'm sorry."

She turned and spotted Tess standing with a group of students and rushed toward her across the wet grass. Emily had arrived at school today like any other day with little more than plans for house hunting, shopping with Grace, and Christmas vacation. Now all of that seemed frivolous.

"Tess?"

The girl turned and looked at her. It wasn't Tess. Where was she? There was no sign of her father or sister either. Just a blur of familiar faces, but no family. Her father had to be nearby . . .

"Emily?"

She turned around, ready to fight off another reporter, then let out an audible sigh. "Grace."

Her friend gathered her up into a big hug and held on tight. "Are you okay?"

"Numb."

"Come on, we're going to get you out of here." Grace grabbed Emily's bag, then slipped her arm around her shoulder. "They're all desperate for another angle on the story."

"They think I'm a hero. I'm not a hero." Emily sucked in a deep breath and tried to stop the flood of tears that was about to erupt. "Philip was shot . . . Rafael is dead . . . I couldn't stop any of it."

"Most people here agree you are a hero. You kept the kids calm and, according to Principal Farley, found a way to communicate with the police."

Emily's hands were shaking. She needed to sit down. Needed to pull herself together.

"Oh, sweetie, I'm sorry. So, so sorry this happened. I . . . I just don't know what to say." Grace pulled back and caught Emily's gaze. "It must have been absolutely terrifying."

She wasn't all right. She was shaking and unsure of exactly what she felt. "They shot him, Grace. They didn't have to do that. I just don't understand why they couldn't have waited until after the transfer was made. They could have let the students go, then arrested him . . . not kill him. Nothing makes sense."

"I know and I'm so sorry. I know how you cared about him. As a student and young man he'd come so far, but sometimes things just don't make sense and maybe never will. Sometimes people are thrust into situations and they make the wrong decisions. That's what happened today. And the captain did what he had to do."

Emily listened to Grace talk, feeling as if she were watching the scene through the eyes of a bystander. Not a key player in some shocking headliner that was about to show up on the evening news. Maybe she'd been wrong about Rafael. Maybe he'd simply found a way to manipulate her. He was smart. But she'd been so convinced he would never have done what he did on his own.

Emily pulled her coat closer. She wanted to defend him, but Grace was right. You couldn't ever really know someone.

She closed her eyes, not wanting to relive the last few moments in the school again. Wishing there was a way to erase the past few hours from her memory.

"Mark thought it might help to bring over some sandwiches and brownies for the officers and staff," Grace continued. "I

FATAL EXCHANGE

know the hostage situation is over, but it's going to take awhile for them to process the crime scene and get things back to normal."

Grace sounded like her sister. They were processing the crime scene. Her school. Her classroom. How long would it take before coming to school felt normal again? How long before she wouldn't think about what happened when she had to walk between the desks where one of her students had been shot, and another killed? How long would she worry that another student would decide to walk into the school and start shooting?

"I'm sorry . . . normal wasn't the right word."

"It's okay, Grace." Emily searched her memory for what they'd been talking about. Normal. Crime scene. Food. "I'm sure people will appreciate some of Mark's goodies."

"I could get you something. You need to eat."

Emily shook her head. She hadn't been able to eat the pizza in the room. There was no way she'd be able to eat now.

"Then why don't you let one of the medics check you out before you leave? They're looking at the students, and offering counseling—"

"I've already talked to someone."

"At least let us drive you home."

"I can't leave yet. I need to find Tess. And my father. He's supposed to be here somewhere, and I'm sure Avery is on her way as well now that this is over."

"I haven't seen Tess. Didn't she come out with you?"

"Yes, but then the police needed a statement, so I'm not sure where she is."

Emily heard the panic in her voice and tried to shake it. She scanned the edges of the school grounds again, trying to find her niece. Tess was safe. She had nothing more to worry about.

"I did see your dad a few minutes ago," Grace said. "Maybe she found him."

"There she is."

Emily let out a sharp sigh of relief and felt some of the tension in her neck release as she hurried across the sidewalk to where Tess was standing.

"Tess." She gathered her niece into a bear hug. "I've been looking everywhere for you. Are you okay?"

"Aunt Emily." Her face was red, and she'd been crying. "Someone told me to wait here for Grandpa. That he was coming to take me home."

"Good. And I'm sure your mother will be here soon as well."

"They told me Rafael was shot. He's dead, isn't he?"

Emily nodded.

"I've never known anyone who died like that except for Uncle Michael, but even then I wasn't right there. I can still hear the shot."

"They were just trying to keep you safe."

"I know." Tess's breath caught. "Grandpa."

Emily let her father gather them both into his arms. It didn't matter how old she was. Having him here made her want to disappear into his embrace forever.

"Emily . . . Tess."

"Have you heard from my mom?"

"Yes. She . . ." Her father hesitated.

"Daddy, what's wrong?"

"I just got a call from Carlos." He tightened his grip on them. "She's going to be okay, but she was injured during the raid to find Rafael's brother."

"Injured?" Emily felt the now familiar waves of panic sweep through her. "What happened?"

"They were able to track down Eduardo at a funeral home a few miles from here. While they were leaving, two men showed up and opened gunfire on the officers."

"But she's okay?"

Her father nodded. "Carlos said the bullet caused a deep graze across her thigh, so while she lost a lot of blood and is going to need to be patched up a bit, it didn't penetrate deep and thankfully didn't hit anything vital. They took her to the hospital, but knowing your mother, she'll be out before things are even wrapped up here. Eduardo was also shot, but I don't know his condition."

"So can we go see her?" Tess asked.

"You bet. We'll pick up your grandma, then go see your mom. Do you need a ride, Emily?"

"No, I'll drive my own car, but I'll be right behind you."

Her father didn't look convinced. "Are you sure?"

She nodded and forced a smile. "I'm sure."

Grace rested her hand on Emily's arm as her father and Tess walked off. "I really think you should let someone drive you."

She looked up to where she'd last seen Mason. He might not have all the answers, but at least it was a place to start. "I appreciate the offer, but there's someone I need to talk to before I leave."

———

Mason held the two steaming cups of coffee he'd snagged from the teachers' lounge and headed down the sidewalk to where he'd just seen Emily making her way toward the entrance of the school. He'd been surprised at the amount of relief he felt knowing she was safe. He wasn't sure what her reaction would be toward him. He'd promised to protect her, but he'd also promised to help protect Rafael.

As frustrated as he was with the way things had ended, that wasn't the only reason he needed to see her. Something had happened over the course of the past few hours that had managed to ignite a fire inside him toward Emily Hunt. Which was why he wanted . . . needed . . . to see her again, even if it were nothing more than to make sure she was okay.

"Emily." He stopped next to the bench where he'd showed her the photos of Eduardo a few hours ago, and held out one of the drinks. "I wanted to tell you how sorry I am. You know this isn't how I wanted things to end."

"I know. Me neither." She took the drink and nodded her thanks before taking a sip. "I still don't understand what happened in there, but I guess you were right."

"Right about what?"

He waited for her to take another sip of coffee and collect her thoughts. It was going to take awhile for her to work through everything that had happened in that classroom today, but talking about it was definitely the right step forward.

She looked up at him and caught his gaze. Her blue eyes were wide with question and hurt. "You were right about the fact that Rafael tried to play me. He played us both. I just . . . I just don't understand why. Even if someone else had manipulated him somehow into walking into that classroom, he could have walked away. You'd promised to help him. I'd promised." Tears framed her lashes, adding a layer of vulnerability to her expression. "I need answers, Mason. Whether or not he was guilty, why didn't the captain wait until the transfer was made? The kidnappers would have what they wanted, and maybe Rafael would welcome the protection of the police then. Why go in there if there was a chance that someone else was behind this?"

Mason wasn't sure how to respond, because he really didn't know much more than she did. "I wasn't in the room when Rafael was shot, so all I can guess is that Rafael's emotions were running high, and he panicked. There are also some who believe Rafael knew about his brother's drug dealing and might have even been involved."

"No. I'll never believe that." Anger seeped through her. Just like she'd never believe Rafael should have died. "Why go in there in the first place? What changed between arranging to wire the kidnappers the ransom money and bursting through the door?"

"I'll know more soon." He wished he could give her the answers she needed. "The captain is giving a briefing in fifteen minutes, but something had to have changed. Something that forced them to make a decision to go in."

Her hand shook, splashing coffee over the side of the cup. She reached down and set it on the bench next to them, then pressed her fingers against her temples. "I'm sorry. My head is killing me. I'm angry and frustrated . . ." She looked up at him. "But you don't need to hear this."

"You have nothing to be sorry about, and I don't mind listening. You need to talk about it."

"I just don't know who to be angry at. Myself for not convincing Rafael to give up. The captain for going in there . . . No matter what Rafael was involved in, he didn't have to die."

Mason understood her frustration, because he felt it himself. His job had been to ensure the situation ended with everyone alive. Nothing he could say or do could change the reality that Rafael was now lying in a zippered body bag.

"You can add me to the list of people to blame." Mason pressed his lips together. "I was convinced that I knew Rafael well enough. Believed he trusted me. None of it was enough."

She looked away. A tear slid down her check. He set his coffee beside hers, gathered her into his arms, and let her cry. She leaned into him, her head against his shoulder, her heart pounding against his chest. He shouldn't be the one holding her, but he was glad he was.

He wanted to tell her she had the most beautiful eyes. Even when she was crying. That being next to her did something crazy to his heart he hadn't expected. That he found her brave, strong, and captivating, and wanted to get to know her better.

Instead, he just held her.

He pulled back a few moments later to brush away the tears sliding down her cheeks. "I know it sounds trite, but you've got your family, your friends, your faith . . . you'll get through this. We both will."

"I know. I've just never been so scared. I hate guns." She looked up at him. "I hate the violence, and the fact that there can't be a happily ever after in this. I wanted to fix this situation and I couldn't."

"You have nothing to be sorry about. It's normal for a barrage of emotions to hit after the trauma is over."

"Maybe, but it still hurts so bad." She drew in a deep breath, then let it out slowly. "What happens next?"

"Carlos and Griffin are in the process of questioning the men who were holding Eduardo captive. Hopefully it won't be too long until we are able to track down Mrs. Cerda, along with whoever was behind all of this."

She was close enough that he could see the slight tremble of her lip and smell the lingering hint of jasmine from her perfume. His heart was falling fast, but he still couldn't help but wonder if some of his own feelings had been tainted by the situation. He knew how fear could manipulate emotions. Just because they'd gone through something traumatic together didn't mean she owed him anything, or that she was even interested in finding out more about him. But there was something in her eyes, beneath those long, dark lashes, that made him believe she was feeling some of the same emotions he was.

Her lips curved into a slight smile. "Thank you."

He resisted the urge to grasp her hands. "For what?"

"For being here for me."

"Anytime."

"I need to go see my sister. And I'm sure you've still got a lot of work ahead of you in wrapping everything up."

"Yeah. But first, do you need me to get you a ride to the hospital?"

"No, I'll be okay."

She still hadn't moved. Like she didn't want to go. He didn't want her to go either. If he had his way, he'd sweep her away to some quiet place far away from here where they could sit and talk. Where he could put his arms around her and tell her he had this crazy idea he was falling for her.

"But there is something you can do for me." Her smile faded as she looked up at him and caught his gaze. "Promise me you'll find out the truth as to why Rafael had to die."

CHAPTER
17

Emily took the last sip of her coffee as she headed toward her car. She knew exactly what her sister would say if she could read her mind right now. She'd tell her she was crazy to trust Mason, and even crazier to be thinking she'd love the chance to get to know him better. Avery would tell her to stay away from a man she was convinced had played a role in the death of their brother. Emily tossed the empty cup into the trash can at the edge of the parking lot. Even she knew that all her sister's evidence was only circumstantial. And today she'd seen the side of Mason she remembered. Compassion. Empathy. Concern.

That wasn't the kind of man who betrayed his best friend.

Emotions jumbled, she managed to make it to the staff parking lot without running into any reporters. All she wanted to do right now was ensure her sister was okay, then go home and collapse, though she still wasn't sure she wanted to be alone. Every time she closed her eyes she heard the gunshot that killed Rafael and saw the black body bag.

A voice called to her from behind. She stopped beside her car and turned around to see Charlie. Ex-fiancé . . . the man she'd once loved. Or at least thought she'd loved. He always managed to look perfect, even after working all day. Suits paired with expensive silk ties and high-end loafers. Never secondhand.

Charlie was the last person she felt like dealing with at the moment.

"Emily . . . hey." He jogged the short distance between them. "I know you've been through so much today. I wanted to check to see how you're doing. Are you okay?"

She felt her blood pressure rise. Why was everyone asking her if she was okay? She wasn't okay. She wasn't sure she'd ever be okay again. Or at least she'd never look at things the same. Charlie and her sister dealt with situations like this every day: dead bodies, criminals, arrests. But not her. Those were the things she watched on television—ironically as an escape. Not something she experienced in real life.

Charlie reached out to grasp her arm. She pulled away and took a step back. The gesture felt too intimate. Too personal.

"I'm sorry." Charlie cleared his throat. "I just . . . I know things are over between us, but that doesn't mean I don't still care about what happens to you." He leaned against the car parked beside hers and folded his arms across his chest, giving her the space she needed. "You know I still care, don't you? If anything would have happened to you today, I never would have been able to forgive myself for not having insisted on being the negotiator."

Charlie had always known what to say to get what he wanted. He was suave, confident, self-assured. But she'd gotten over that a long time ago.

"Nothing happened to me—physically anyway. I'm fine."

"When you were in there, I don't think I've ever been so scared in my entire life."

"I'm thankful to be alive, but there's a dead boy who should still be alive as well."

"I know." He cracked the knuckles of his left hand one at a time. "But he held your class hostage, shot a student, and tried to take out an officer. All you have to do is watch the news to see what can happen when someone brings a gun into a school. You could have died in there."

"But I didn't." She shook her head, wondering how long it took to shake the fear that had surrounded her the past few hours. How long would it take to forgive herself for not finding a way to save Rafael? How long would her heart hurt because things had ended this way? No matter what anyone said, Rafael died to save his family.

"I'm so sorry you had to go through all of this, but it's over and you're okay," he said. "That's what counts."

"Do you remember Rafael?"

"I . . . you talked about so many of your students."

Of course he wouldn't remember. Not that it mattered anymore.

"I've been working with him the past three years, since he was a freshman in high school. He was planning to go to college next year. He was bright and had plans."

"I know he was one of your students, but he gave up his right for freedom when he decided to take a class hostage. Maybe it shouldn't have ended the way it did, but according to the captain, they didn't have a choice."

"I was told the same thing."

"It's the downside of what we do, Emily. Sometimes there's a price in bringing justice to the world."

She studied his expression. Confident. Self-assured. He hadn't changed at all. His job had always come first and had always been more important than what she did. He might have loved her, but to Charlie, being a schoolteacher hadn't exactly fit the bill of saving the world. To her, though, the impact she tried to make on the students' lives mattered. And when she couldn't make that difference, it hurt.

"I was making progress with him . . . I honestly believe that he would have let everyone go if he hadn't been pushed."

"I wasn't there, but I do know that the captain wouldn't have shot him unless he knew he had to. Believe me when I say that I wish the situation would have ended differently. His death was an unfortunate ending to a very unfortunate situation."

"An unfortunate ending?" Emily shook her head. "Is that what you plan to tell his mother?"

Charlie shoved his hands into his pants pockets. "How did I get to be the bad guy here?"

"You're not . . . I'm sorry." He was right. She shouldn't take out her frustrations on him. "It's just that last week he was accepted to college. He had his entire life ahead of him."

"He held a bunch of students at gunpoint and shot one of them. There is no excuse for something like that." His expression softened. "Please, Emily. Don't be mad at me."

"I'm not mad at you." Emily pushed the button on her car fob and unlocked her vehicle. "I just want to go check on my sister, then find a way to put all of this behind me."

"I heard your sister's going to be okay?"

"Yeah. It could have been so much worse."

She started to open the car, but he grabbed her free hand. "Emily, wait."

"What is it?"

"Before you go, there's something else I need to say. I . . . I know you're going to think I'm crazy, but while you were in there with those students, it made me start thinking again about you . . . about us. This isn't the first time I've regretted us calling off the wedding. Today brought everything back and made me realize how much I need you back in my life."

She wasn't in the mood to argue the fact that it hadn't been a mutual decision. She'd been the one who'd called off the wedding, though she was certain the entire police force believed he was the one who'd dumped her. She'd never attempted to change anyone's perspective. It didn't make any difference to her. The only thing that did matter was the fact that all the feelings she'd once had for Charlie were gone.

"As soon as I'm finished," he continued, "we could go somewhere for dinner. You've been through a lot. I could listen. You're going to need someone to talk to."

He'd always been a charmer, but it just wasn't enough anymore. "I can't, Charlie. You know as well as I do that things are over between us, and that isn't ever going to change."

"I think you're wrong. I think you still care about me as much as I care about you."

She looked up at him, clean-cut, suave, and good looking. He'd swept her off her feet, but instead of falling in love with him, she'd been caught up with the idea of getting married—until the desire to get married had become more important than the person she was marrying. She'd finally realized she had to walk away.

Two weeks before they'd planned to send out the announcements and order the cake, she'd returned the engagement ring he'd given her. Most of her friends hadn't understood why she'd broken things off. Sometimes even she wasn't sure when she'd first realized her relationship with Charlie simply wasn't what she was looking for.

She wanted a marriage like her mother and father, who'd managed to make it through both the good and the bad, who had a marriage where Christ was the foundation, and where divorce wasn't an option. Maybe she was an old-fashioned optimist, but she was searching for the same thing.

Ultimately, Charlie didn't end up being the man she knew she wanted to spend the rest of her life with—even if she was pushing thirty and still dreamed of having a family. It was a choice she'd yet to regret.

"Neither of us were ready for marriage, Charlie, and you know that. I want the ring, a family, the house eventually, but—"

"Not with me? What if you're wrong? About us. Take me up on my offer. We'll go eat somewhere after I wrap things up here. No strings attached, just you and me. And if in the process we discover something is left between us—"

"There isn't anything left between us, Charlie. And while I appreciate your concern, I'll be fine."

Eventually.

She looked past Charlie to the school. Mason was standing on the front steps of the school, talking with another officer. He and Charlie were complete opposites. While both were focused on bringing justice to a messed-up world, Mason was far more laid back in his jeans and five o'clock shadow. Charlie was the polished one, always knowing what to say and when to say it.

Funny how it seemed that coming from a family of cops she was destined to fall for a cop, no matter how hard she tried to resist. First Charlie, now Mason . . . Emily's gaze dipped. No. She hadn't fallen for Mason. There was a difference between admiration and infatuation.

"Emily?"

She turned back to Charlie. "I'm sorry."

His eyes darkened. "So it's Mason now?"

"He's just a friend. My family has known him for years."

"What happened in there between the two of you? I saw you together a few minutes ago. You looked . . . cozy."

"There's nothing going on between Mason and me. He did a good job today. He handled things well, helped to keep the students calm—"

"And wasn't able to stop Rafael from getting shot."

She shook her head. "That wasn't his fault, and he saved the kids that were in there."

"Maybe, but he had no business trying to negotiate a hostage situation. He's an undercover cop, for goodness' sake. If I had been there, things would have ended differently."

"Would they? I don't think there's any way to know that." She frowned. He always had been so sure of himself. "I appreciate your concern, but I'm going now."

"Let me call you. Once this is behind us."

She shook her head. "Don't call me. We're through, Charlie."

A message beeped on her phone. She pulled it from her pocket, glanced at the message, and felt her chest heave.

This isn't over. We have Tess.

CHAPTER
18

No . . . no . . . no." Emily couldn't breathe.

She fumbled with her phone, dropping her bag onto the pavement in the process. One of her pens rolled out of the dumped-over bag. This had to be a mistake. Tess was safe, on her way to see her mother at the hospital.

Charlie picked up the pen and handed it to her. "Em . . . what's wrong?"

"It's a message from . . . from a blocked number." Emily handed him her phone, all the panic and alarm from the day returning. Except this time she felt as if she were stumbling in the dark. This time she had no idea who was behind the message. "I don't understand how, but it says they have Tess."

"Whoa. Slow down." Charlie turned her toward him, his hands on her shoulders. "You don't know what this means. Not yet. It could be nothing more than a prank. Someone's idea of a very bad practical joke."

"A prank?" Her eyes widened. "I don't believe that, and neither do you. Not after today."

Charlie pulled out his own phone. "I'm calling the captain."

This should have been over. The students had been released. They'd found Eduardo. So why the text? Why Tess?

Lingering hope that Charlie's first instincts had been right hovered at the edges of her thoughts. Maybe this wasn't anything more than someone's idea of a sick joke.

Charlie waited for the captain to answer as she tried to sort through the facts as she knew them. The cartel had kidnapped Eduardo and his mother. Demanded money owed them. Tried to manipulate Rafael . . .

They'd never gotten their money.

"They didn't get the money," she spouted.

"What?" Charlie ended his unanswered call and caught her gaze.

"The ransom money. Someone else has to be involved."

"But why Tess?"

She took her phone back from Charlie. "I don't know, but I need to find my father."

She pushed her father's number on speed dial, then started searching to see if his car was still in the parking lot. She found it halfway down the first row. He hadn't left yet. Where was Tess? She hung up the unanswered phone. And where was her father?

Panic sifted through her as Charlie stopped beside her. "They have to be here somewhere."

"Emily?"

She turned at Mason's voice. He must have seen her running across the parking lot.

"What's going on?" he asked.

She tried to catch her breath. "Someone's taken her. There has to be a connection to Eduardo and Rafael, but I don't know what it is."

"Wait a minute. Slow down. Taken who?"

"Tess." She showed him the message. "We need to find the captain and my father. We can't get ahold of either of them."

Mason took her phone. "Who did this come from?"

"I don't know. It's a blocked number."

"When's the last time you saw Tess?"

"Right before I spoke with you. Fifteen . . . maybe twenty minutes ago. She was with my father. They were leaving to go see my sister at the hospital."

"I just saw your father," Mason said. "The captain needed to speak with him about something in private."

"Was Tess with him?"

"No."

Something shiny flashed from under one of the bushes. Emily bent down and picked up her father's set of keys with the familiar inscribed key ring. A silver car with flashlights for headlights.

Her father's.

She looked up at Mason, the jingle of keys audible between her shaky fingers. "So what happened? He sent Tess to the car to wait for him?"

"Would she have gotten into a car with someone she didn't know?"

"Her mother is a police detective. She'd never get in a car with a stranger."

"And the school grounds are full of reporters and police officers," Charlie added. "If someone tried to grab her, there would be witnesses."

"Okay, then could it have been someone she knew?" Mason asked.

"Maybe."

Emily's head pounded. It hurt to think. All she could do was follow Mason and Charlie back toward the school. Mason started barking out instructions at the other officers.

"We've got a missing student. Another possible kidnapping. Tessica North, Captain Hunt's granddaughter. I want the grounds searched immediately. Everyone questioned . . ."

A few reporters still lingered at the edges of the parking lot. They were going to be all over this story, but she didn't care. Like them, she'd thought all the students were safe now. Thought the situation had been resolved, but now . . .

She watched Mason hand her phone to someone. She was impressed at how he'd automatically taken charge.

"Get this phone to Tory and have her trace the last text. Charlie, get an AMBER Alert out."

She caught the look that passed between them and expected Charlie to balk, but instead he just nodded.

She felt Mason's hand on her shoulder. "Emily?"

"We have to find her." She'd thought things couldn't get worse when Rafael had shown up with a gun in her classroom. They'd made it through that. They'd make it through this. They had to.

"We're going to find her," he assured her, "but right now I need to know an exact timeline leading up to her disappearance. You said you saw her about fifteen minutes ago."

"Yes." Emily's chest burned. She tried to breathe, but the air wasn't reaching her lungs. She tried to calm herself, knowing that panicking wasn't going to help Tess. "After talking with the police, I found Tess and my father. Daddy told us what happened to Avery and Eduardo. He headed to the parking lot with Tess, planning to drive her to the hospital to see her mom. That was right before we spoke."

"And Charlie?"

"I met him in the parking lot after talking with you. He wanted to make sure I was okay." She was having trouble staying focused. "I need to find my father, Mason."

"I've got someone trying to get ahold of him now."

She'd been scared in that classroom, but at least she'd known Rafael. Maybe she'd been wrong, but a part of her had never really believed he would do anything to hurt her or Tess. But now . . . Rafael was dead, and she had no way to know who was behind this.

Oh God . . . I'm trying to trust you in this situation. You know where she is. You know we have to find her.

She glanced up as her father came running toward her.

"Daddy." She let him gather her into his arms, trying not to remember that the last time she'd seen him, Tess had been with them.

He pulled back, his arms still around her. "What's going on? I was just told that Tess has been abducted?"

"I received a text message." She heard the sound of her own voice. No inflection. No emotion. She was running on autopilot. "Someone's taken her."

"What? Who?"

"I don't know."

Her father turned to Mason, the creases across his forehead pronounced. The gray more evident than she remembered. Her father was strong, but he'd already lost so much this year.

"Has the text been traced?" Thirty years of police experience snapped into play.

"I've got Tory working on it, but if it's a burn phone she won't be able to trace it."

"School surveillance footage needs to be gone over." Her father jutted his chin toward the school. "I'll speak to the principal about getting that set up, then make sure the captain's aware of what's going on. You ensure we've got teams out there looking for my granddaughter, starting with the school grounds. Question anyone who might have seen something."

Mason nodded. "One other thing, sir. We found the keys to your car in the bushes in the parking lot."

Emily glanced up at her father. "Where was Tess?"

Her father's eyebrows furrowed. "The captain called and told me he needed to speak to me in private. He offered to send one of his officers to wait with Tess at the car, because I didn't want her to be alone."

"Do you have the name of the officer?" Mason asked.

"One of the new recruits . . . Officer Reed."

"Good," Mason said. "I'll have someone track her down."

"We're going to find her. But please . . ." Emily grasped her father's arm as Mason rushed off. Standing around doing nothing would push her over the edge. "Let me help with the footage. I need something to do."

"You and me both." His frown deepened. "I can't believe I let Tess out of my sight—"

"You didn't know." She worked to match his long stride as he hurried toward the office. "None of us did. The danger was supposed to be over."

Now wasn't the time for either of them to allow guilt to cloud their vision. All that mattered was finding Tess.

"Emily, before we go in there . . ." Her father stopped just outside the entrance of the school. Dark clouds hovered overhead, bringing with them a light flurry of the predicted snow. But Emily's focus was on the worry in her father's expression. "I need you to listen carefully to me, sweetheart."

She shuddered at a gust of cold wind that seemed to blow right through her. "Daddy . . . what's wrong?"

"I don't know who's behind this, or what's going on, but I want you to stay here in the school offices until I get back."

"Okay, but—"

"There's one other thing. If I get delayed, I need you to know you can trust Mason."

"Mason?" His words caught her off guard. "Why?"

He squeezed her hand. "If I'm not here to keep you safe, he will."

"What do you know?" Fear was back. The nightmare still lingered. Emily shook her head. "Tell me what's going on. Please."

"I can't—"

Her father's phone went off, and he pulled it out of his jacket pocket.

His face paled. "Another text just came through. It's from the kidnappers."

"What do they want?"

"The two million dollars they didn't get the first time."

CHAPTER
19

We're missing something.

Mason stood for a moment, staring out across the school lawns that were now covered with a dusting of white, then pulled out his phone. He was cold, tired, and emotionally drained. He hadn't heard from the captain. Or Emily's dad, for that matter. And after twenty minutes of searching the school and its grounds, there was still no sign of Tess. If they didn't find her soon, they were going to have to extend their initial search radius. They needed a solid lead. Evidence from the surveillance footage, a witness who had seen what happened in that parking lot, a confession from the men being held in conjunction with Eduardo's case . . . anything that would help them find Tess. So far, they had nothing.

He punched in Carlos's number, praying the detective had an update for him.

Mason heard the noisy precinct in the background as Carlos picked up. "Mason, hey. I was just getting ready to call you."

"I'm looking at a bunch of dead ends here. I need something."

"We might have a lead," Carlos said, "but first the bad news. We struck out on the messages sent to Emily and her father. No way to trace them, but I can tell you it was a different phone from the one that called Rafael and his mother this morning."

"What about the guy from the funeral home you dragged in?"

"His name's Juan Carter. When we told him we could tie him to a string of recent kidnappings and murders, he confessed to kidnapping Eduardo, but nothing more. We've tied him to a local gang—Griffin is running that angle down right now—but while he admits Eduardo's kidnapping had to do with a dispute over a drug debt, he swears he doesn't know anything about Tess or Mrs. Cerda's disappearance."

"And Jacobs?"

"Still not wanting to cooperate and insists he doesn't know anything about the kidnappings. I think he's telling the truth."

Mason ran his fingers through his hair and paced the sidewalk in front of the school. Even if they could tie the kidnappings to one of the local gangs, something wasn't right. He still believed that Rafael had somehow been manipulated. That his mother had been used as leverage. That implied that someone else was involved. "So what's the lead?"

"You remember about six months ago, when someone broke into the department's evidence locker?" Carlos asked.

"Yeah. They stole a couple weapons, some jewelry, cash, and fifty-thousand dollars' worth of heroin."

"Exactly," Carlos said. "Here's the kicker. The gun Rafael used is a match to one of those stolen weapons. Unregistered and impossible to trace back to the original owner."

"Which makes it the perfect weapon."

Mason's mind spun as he ran through the timeline in his head. Eduardo had been taken early Sunday morning. Mrs. Cerda disappeared Monday morning just after seven. Rafael walked into the school with the gun around eight. Emily had been convinced someone was manipulating Rafael, but the only motivation that made sense was that whoever had taken Eduardo in the first place had grabbed Mrs. Cerda as an extra guarantee that they got their money. But a ransom situation in a school wasn't the normal cartel MO. Unless . . . unless someone else had kidnapped Mrs. Cerda and given Rafael a gun and enough incentive to walk into a school with a weapon.

"Whoever was behind the thefts at the precinct knew what they were doing, which points to an inside job," Mason said. "So what if we're looking at two separate cases?"

"Two kidnappers?" Carlos asked.

"What if someone found out about the first kidnapping and decided they wanted a piece of the cash?"

"It's possible, but who else besides you knew about Eduardo's kidnapping?" Carlos asked.

The department mole.

It was the one thing that made sense. It wasn't as common as accepting bribes or falsifying reports, but he'd heard of officers who had participated in organized crime themselves. What if someone else had known about Eduardo's kidnapping, had the stolen gun, and decided to play it to their advantage.

The pictures had never been out of his possession. The door to Avery's office had been shut, because he hadn't wanted anyone listening in. He brushed a patch of snow that had fallen on his neck, barely feeling the stinging cold. He might be grasping at straws, but what if someone *had* overheard their conversation?

"Mason . . . what are you thinking?"

He shifted his thoughts to Carlos's question and tried to formulate them into something coherent. "What if we're looking at a second kidnapper? Someone who had nothing to do with Eduardo's kidnapping? Someone who took Tess and maybe Mrs. Cerda as well."

Someone who thought they could take advantage of the situation. Someone who thought they could walk away with two million dollars if they played their cards right.

"I don't know, but it's worth looking at. Who else knew about your meeting with Rafael?"

"According to Rafael, he didn't tell anyone else. The people who took his brother made it clear they didn't want anyone to know—especially the police. He was taking a chance contacting me."

"So let's assume he didn't tell anyone else. Who did you talk to?"

"After talking with Rafael, I took the photos straight to Avery. I knew she was involved in the Torres investigation, and I thought there might be a connection."

"Was anyone else in the room with you while you were talking?"

"No one. I felt the situation needed to be kept under the radar." There was another possibility. "What if there's a bug in Avery's office?"

"You seriously think someone might have bugged her office?"

He understood the incredulity in Carlos's voice. His first thought was that it wasn't possible, but on the other hand, it would explain how someone inside the department had been able to access sensitive information over the past few months. "Where are you right now?" Mason asked.

"I'm heading for her office now. Give me a minute."

Snow crunched beneath his shoes as Mason started pacing the sidewalk in front of the school. A second kidnapper meant that the dynamics had just shifted from a clear-cut ransom case with a list of possible suspects to not knowing who the players were.

Two million dollars was a lot of motivation. An open opportunity for someone ready to take a risk.

"Anything?" Mason asked.

"Not yet."

The snow was falling harder. He stepped under the awning that ran along the front of the main building. Most of the parents had left hours ago with their children, leaving the parking lot empty except for a couple of reporters and the team of law enforcement officers searching for Tess.

He drummed his free hand against his leg. They both knew

what to look for. Something small, compact, and not easy to find. If they had more time, they could bring someone in to sweep the room, but time wasn't on their side.

"Mason . . . I've just stepped back outside her office, but I found something. A listening device mounted beneath her desk with a magnet."

So he'd been right. Someone had been listening in, had found out about the kidnapping, and decided to take advantage of the situation.

"What did it look like?" Mason asked.

"It's a small, silver canister, about the size of a dime. Maybe a bit smaller."

He'd used similar devices before. Had met a guy who sold electronic surveillance devices and had learned everything he could from him. While working undercover, he'd bought and sold illegal drugs, catching suppliers in the process by using the same kind of electronic surveillance as Carlos described. But that equipment wasn't supposed to be used inside the department.

"Were there any serial numbers, dates, or any kind of markings?"

"Not that I could see, but I'm leaving it intact for evidence."

"Good."

Mason worked through their options. If someone on the force was involved, they'd probably been at the school all day. Which meant there was a good chance that there was a partner involved who had done the actual communicating with Rafael. And had possibly taken Tess. There had to be a connection between the two cases.

"I'll call you back as soon as I can, Carlos. I need to find the captain."

CHAPTER
20

Emily's vision blurred as she stared at the school's surveillance footage on the computer screen. She'd spent the last thirty minutes sitting next to Detective Rogers, going frame by frame through the video that had been taken from the time Tess left for her father's car until Emily received the text. After seeing nothing out of the ordinary, they'd expanded the search—and the timeframe—to look for anyone who seemed out of place. But whoever had taken Tess had managed to avoid getting caught on camera.

And Tess was still missing.

Emily scooted back her chair before addressing the detective. "I need to take a short break. My eyes are crossed and my head is killing me."

"Of course." He nodded, his eyes still fixed on the monitor. "Take as long as you need."

She dug a bottle of ibuprofen from her bag, then reached for her water that sat on the edge of the desk where she'd been working. Fifteen minutes ago, she'd called Jackson for an update on her sister. Avery's blood pressure had dropped on the way to the hospital, and she was groggy from painkillers, but the doctors expected her to make a complete recovery—as long as she rested the next few days.

Emily washed down two of the capsules with a swig of water, unable to stop her smile when she thought of Jackson's disclaimer. Convincing Avery to rest was like convincing the moon to stop rotating around the earth. She had, though, advised him not to tell Avery about Tess—not yet anyway. She knew her sister. She might be furious for initially being kept in the dark, but what she didn't need was the added stress of knowing her daughter was in danger when there was nothing she could do about it.

"Emily?"

She looked up at Mason, who had just stepped into the front office, his leather jacket covered with a dusting of snowflakes, his expression reflecting how she felt. Cold, tired, and frustrated.

Emily bridged the distance between them, hesitant to ask the obvious question. "Did you find Tess?"

He shook his head. "Not yet, but there are some things we need to talk about."

She caught the edge in his voice and felt her blood pressure spike. "What's wrong?"

"I've just finished talking to the captain."

"And . . ."

He glanced around the office, still filled with a half-dozen law enforcement officers and school staff tracking down leads on Tess's disappearance from their makeshift command post. "Let's go outside. It's more private."

He waited for her to grab her purse before taking her hand and leading her out the front door of the school. It would be dark in a few hours, which meant it would be harder to find Tess. She might not be a cop, but even she knew that in missing person cases, time was the enemy. And at the moment, the enemy was winning.

Outside, the wind caught the edge of her coat, sweeping the afternoon chill straight through her. She shivered. She'd been able to change out of her blood-stained outfit from when Philip had been shot, but the knee-length charcoal sweater dress and tights she'd had stashed in her room in case of emergency weren't nearly warm enough. "You're scaring me, Mason. What's happened?"

"There's a lot more involved with Tess's abduction than we originally thought. I know you're scared, but I need you to trust me. I need to get you somewhere safe."

Somewhere safe? At the moment, she wasn't sure such a place existed.

"Why? Where's my father?"

"He's with the captain."

I need you to trust Mason.

She tried to squelch the unsettled feeling spreading through her. Her father had told her to trust Mason. She felt Mason's hands press gently against her shoulders to steady her, but the school and the grounds still swirled in the background.

"Emily, I need you to come with me."

Trust Mason.

She was trying to, but she needed answers first. "Why?"

"We believe your life could also be in danger."

"Who believes that?"

"The captain. Your father. Me."

She tugged on the edges of her coat sleeves, feeling frustrated and vulnerable. "What does Tess's disappearance have to do with me?"

"We don't believe Eduardo's kidnappers are behind Tess's abduction."

"Wait a minute." She stopped and looked up at him. "Are you trying to tell me you think there's another kidnapper?"

"Yes. Maybe it's nothing more than a string of coincidences, but we can't take any chances until we know exactly what's going on. And I don't want anything to happen to you."

She tried to read his expression, wanting to ask him if this had become personal to him. If his concern and desire to protect her was more than the fact that he wore a badge.

"What about Tess? There has to be something we're missing. Someone who saw something. Who walks away with a thirteen-year-old, from a crime scene with half the city's police force in the vicinity?"

"That's what we have to find out, but in the meantime, I promised your father I'd take you somewhere safe. Come with me, and I'll tell you everything I know on the way."

"I need to talk to my father." She pulled out her phone and dialed his cell.

"You won't get ahold of him. He's interrogating a suspect with the captain. That's why he sent me."

She let it ring, but Mason was right. After three rings, her father's phone switched to voice mail. The truth was, she was too tired to fight. She trusted her father. She was going to trust Mason as well.

He escorted her toward his unmarked vehicle on the edge of the parking lot. Right now, she should be getting ready to go home from school. A couple hours of Christmas shopping with Grace. A quiet night grading papers. Normal. Ordinary. Except nothing about today was normal.

Mason's black, older-model Chevy pickup fit his personality. Rough around the edges. Solid. Reliable. He opened the passenger door and let her climb in. On any other day, she'd have been impressed by the chivalrous act, along with the fact that there were no fast-food wrappers lining the dashboard and no junk mail littering the floorboards. Add to that, the truck smelled like cinnamon and not Chinese takeout. She remembered Michael teasing Mason for being so clean. He'd countered that after dozens of undercover jobs and all-nighters with messy partners, having a clean car had become an obsession.

She stared out the window as they drove away from the school and squinted. Gray clouds, swirls of white snow, tree-lined streets . . . Everything seemed out of focus.

"Tell me what's going on, Mason."

"First of all, the officer sent to stay with Tess while your father spoke with the captain is missing."

Emily felt a sick feeling sweep through her. "What else?"

"Tory found video footage of Mrs. Cerda being shoved into a van this morning, a half a mile from the hotel where she works."

"Which proves what? That she was kidnapped? That Rafael really was innocent? If someone had been manipulating him, using his mother as a way to control him, then Rafael shouldn't have died."

"Emily—"

"They killed him, Mason. How could that have happened?" A sick feeling flooded through her. "He was being manipulated, they knew it, but still put him in a position where he was forced to defend himself."

"The situation's complicated." Mason's hands gripped the steering wheel as he made a left turn on a green light. "After talking to the captain, I believe that the person who manipulated Rafael—and is behind Tess's abduction—is someone inside the department."

"Wait a minute." His answer took her by surprise. "You're telling me a dirty cop has taken my niece?"

"We found a bug in Avery's office. There's a good chance that whoever planted the bug overheard my conversation with your sister this morning. Someone is sweeping her house for a second bug right now as well."

Emily trembled. Four months ago, someone had broken into Avery's house. How many nights had she spent time with her sister sharing from her heart since then? To think that some stranger had been listening in sickened her.

Mason stopped at a red light and flipped on his blinker.

"While I was in the classroom with you, they were able to track down the radio transmitter on the ear bug Rafael was wearing. They found that same van two blocks east of the school. Someone *was* telling Rafael what to say. And that isn't all they found."

He paused, as if he were trying to give her time to process everything he was telling her.

"What else did they find?"

"Mrs. Cerda was in the van. She was bound and blindfolded so she can't identify the man who had been in the van with her."

"What happened to him?"

"He managed to slip away."

Silence swept between them as he turned off onto a winding residential street where the branches of the trees met in the middle of the road. She glanced at the street sign, her frustration growing, as he pulled in parallel to the curb, turned off the motor, and turned toward her.

"Where are we?" she asked.

"It's a safe house. This is where your father wanted you to go, but first there is one more thing you need to know. Rafael . . . he isn't dead, Emily. He's inside with two FBI agents."

"What?" Emily tried to blink back the confusion. "Wait a minute. I heard the captain shoot him. Saw them carry him out in a body bag . . ."

"They faked his death for his own protection."

"What?"

"I promise you I didn't know anything about this while I was in the classroom with you, but the captain received information that convinced him that, one, Rafael was being manipulated, and two, if they let him walk out of that school alive, they would likely have been killed."

She tried to let his words sink in. "So you've been lying to me this whole time."

"I didn't know about any of this until right before I came to get you. And the problem is, we still don't know who all the key players are in this, which means the fewer people who know, the better. The captain agreed that you needed to know."

She looked at him, wanting to beat her fists against his chest. "Who knows about all of this?"

"The captain. Your father. Jackson, Charlie, and one or two other officers."

"It was a crazy plan."

"I convinced the captain to let me tell you the truth."

"And that's supposed to help me feel better?" She regretted the bitterness in her voice, but the emotional roller coaster she'd been on the past few hours had spun her nerves on edge. She pressed her fingers against her temple. "I'm sorry."

"Forget it. You've been through a lot today."

"Which still doesn't give me the excuse to be snippy."

"You have every excuse to be snippy." His smile helped break down some of her defenses. "But for the moment, I need your help."

"How?"

"The captain is hoping we can get some information from Rafael. They thought your being with me when I talk to him would help since you're close to him. And you'd be safe."

"Why did they choose Tess?"

"We don't know yet, beyond the two-million-dollar ransom they didn't get the first time."

Emily closed her eyes. The back of her head throbbed. She would do anything to help find Tess, but she couldn't simply dismiss her skepticism. "Can I be honest?"

"Of course."

"I keep reminding myself that Michael trusted you. Rafael trusted you, my father and even I trust you, but none of this makes sense. Why should they trust you? My sister has a paper trail of evidence that she intends to use to put you behind bars, and she's never kept any of it a secret."

"The captain has had me investigating Michael's death since the funeral."

"But Avery doesn't know?"

He shook his head. "We have proof that someone has been feeding her false evidence—presumably our mole. If that person finds out we're looking for him, we could lose any advantage we currently have."

"But you don't know who the mole is?"

"No, but for him to have risked such a payoff, I have to believe we're getting close."

"So he—or she—needs that ransom money before they can disappear?"

"I believe so. Yes."

Which would make them desperate. "What can I do?"

"We need to find out what Rafael knows."

She tried to push aside the lingering slivers of fear that kept resurfacing. This was why she'd chosen the career path she had. She had no desire to get caught up in a game with such dangerous stakes. But neither could she turn away and do nothing.

She felt Mason's hand close around hers, looked up at him, and caught his gaze, wishing he could promise her everything would be okay. That they would find Tess and all of this would be over.

"Will you help?"

"Yeah." She nodded. "Let's go talk to Rafael."

CHAPTER
21

Emily walked up the paved sidewalk toward the single-story house in one of the city's quieter neighborhoods and tried to wrap her mind around everything Mason had just told her. She studied the mixed brick and siding on the exterior of the house, but all she could see was Rafael being carried out of the school in a body bag.

And none of it had been real.

"How do you think Rafael is?" she asked.

"Scared. Confused. Here you've got this quiet, straight-A student suddenly thrown into a situation he doesn't know how to handle with some pretty serious consequences."

She tightened her grip on her bag. "I'm happy he's alive, but also so angry at whoever tried to manipulate him."

"I'd say being angry is right on par. I know I'm angry."

"Especially knowing all of this happened over the love of money." Emily stopped to face him along the sidewalk, winter chill slicing through her coat as she tugged at the top button. "And beyond what happened today, there will be emotional scars that linger long after all of this is over."

"It's one of the things I've had to deal with head-on over the past few months."

"What do you mean?"

"I've come to believe that God hears our prayers and wants what is best for us, but I've seen enough to know that man's choices often go against God. He doesn't always stop people from making stupid choices that affect those around them."

Like Rafael. Like Tess.

Mason stopped at the front door. "You know I can't make any promises about the outcome, but I can promise you this: We're going to do everything we can to find Tess. We're going to take this one step at a time. And step one is talking with Rafael."

Emily drew in a deep breath, then nodded and walked into the entryway of the house in front of Mason. The room smelled musty, as if no one had been living here recently.

"Emily, this is Agent Bradley and Agent Pierce, with the FBI. They've been brought in to help."

Emily nodded at the officers and wondered who'd assigned them to the case. Knowing who to trust wasn't going to be easy. "It's nice to meet you both."

"We've gone through some preliminary debriefing with Rafael," Agent Pierce said, "but waited for you to get here, as the captain requested, for the official interview."

"Thank you, Agent Pierce."

Emily followed Mason into the living room and saw Rafael standing in the middle of the room, the normal smile on his face gone, his eyes vacant. Today had changed him forever. She threw aside any teacher-student protocol, crossed the room, and gave him a hug. "I can't believe you're alive."

"I'm sorry . . . so sorry," he began. "I never wanted to hurt anyone. I just . . . I didn't know what to do."

"I'm just glad to see you're alive."

"I am too." Mason shot him a smile.

Rafael turned to Mason. "I told you about the threats to kill my brother this morning, but then they called and told me that they had my mother as well. They said I was taking too much time and they were convinced they weren't going to get their money."

"I know. She's safe now."

"And my brother?"

"The doctors still aren't sure if he's going to make it. The bullet did a lot of damage."

"When can I see them?"

"I promise we'll arrange something soon. At least for you to see your mother."

Rafael leaned against the back of an overstuffed armchair and dropped his gaze. "Where were they keeping Eduardo?"

"Emily's sister and her team found him in a funeral home not far from here. That's where he was shot."

"Has he been able to talk to someone? Explained that all of this was a mistake? He's not involved in the cartel and selling drugs."

"Not yet." Mason motioned for Rafael to sit down in the chair while he took the couch beside Emily. "But our police dogs found drugs in your house hidden under the carpet in your room."

"No." Rafael shook his head. "That's not possible."

"And there was also a large amount of cash."

"I don't believe that." Rafael's voice rose a notch. "He had to have been set up somehow."

"I know you care a lot about your brother, but you have to know that not only do we believe he was involved in selling, more than likely it was on a big scale."

"No . . . not Eduardo." Rafael chewed on his thumbnail. "I've worked hard to keep my family together. To make sure that my brother stayed off the streets . . . stayed off drugs."

"No one's blaming you, Rafael."

"But they should." Rafael pressed his fingers against his temples. "I keep thinking of all the things I said while I was in the classroom. I was so scared and didn't know what to do. He kept telling me what to say. Telling me that they were going to kill Eduardo and my mother if I didn't do what they wanted. And the whole time I heard my mother crying in the background."

"I promise you'll be able to see her, but in the meantime we need your help. Tess is missing."

"Tess? I don't understand."

"We believe there's a connection to what happened this morning with whoever is behind Tess's disappearance. Someone didn't get the ransom money, so they're hoping for another way to collect."

"So they took Tess?"

"Yes. Now I know you've already given your statement," Mason continued, "but I want to walk through this morning's timeline again and see if we're missing something. Hopefully, we'll find a clue that will help us find Tess."

Rafael nodded. "You know I'll do anything."

Mason pulled a notebook from his pocket. "Some of these questions I've already asked you, but start with yesterday morning when they took Eduardo."

"I was up late studying for a calculus test when they barged in through the front door. It all happened so fast."

"Did you get a good look at the men who took him?"

"No. There were three of them, but they wore black masks."

"Did you tell anyone about his abduction?"

"Only you." Rafael shook his head. "They threatened to kill him if I said anything."

"What happened this morning?"

"I couldn't stop thinking about Eduardo. I searched our home and didn't find anything. Maybe I only wanted to believe he was innocent, but Eduardo is smart and stays out of trouble. I thought everything was okay."

Mason scribbled down a few notes before asking his next question. "Where did you go after you spoke to me this morning?"

"I took my mother to work. I drive her there every morning before school because we only have one car. Today I told her she should stay home. She was exhausted from not sleeping and worried about Eduardo, but she told me if she missed work she would lose her job, so I went ahead and took her. After that, I got the phone call that they had her too."

"Did you talk to anyone else after that?"

"No."

"Tell me about the phone call."

"It was a blocked call, no number, and one of those . . . those garbled voices. They told me that they had my mother too. That plans had changed. That they no longer were interested in just two hundred and fifty thousand dollars. If I wanted my family to live, I had to do what they said." His eyes filled with tears as he looked away. "I didn't want to do it. You have to believe me. I didn't know what to do. It was . . . is . . . like some awful nightmare."

"I know." Mason leaned forward. "Tell me what they told you to do."

"They told me to go to the park across from our apartment building. There would be a blue backpack in the southeast trash with an ear bug, a hat, and a gun. I was to take what was inside and leave the bag in the trash."

"Any markings on the bag, any identification?" He'd make sure officers searched the area, but more than likely it would just be another dead end.

Rafael shook his head. "No. Nothing."

"Did you see anyone at the park? Maybe a car following you, or someone acting strange?"

"I don't remember." Rafael's foot tapped against the carpet. "I was so scared. I knew I should call you back, but they told me they would be watching my every move, and if I didn't do what they said they would kill my mother. I didn't know what else to do. And shooting Philip . . . it was an accident. You gotta believe me. He came at me, grabbed the gun, and it went off."

"No one is blaming you for what happened, Rafael." The compassion in Emily's voice was evident. "I'm not sure I would have made a different choice, given the same circumstances."

"They kept putting my mother on the line. She was crying. They swore they were going to kill her if I didn't say what they told me to say."

Rafael's love for his mother and brother struck a chord with Mason. Whether or not the boy had made the right decision to walk into a school with a weapon was a question a judge would have to answer at some point, but even with the extenuating circumstances, one fact remained clear: Rafael had been willing to sacrifice everything to ensure his family's safety.

He couldn't say that about his relationship with his own father.

"So while you were in the classroom, someone watched what you were seeing via the video camera in the hat, and talked to you through the ear bug."

"Yes sir."

"Did he ever use a name? Anything to identify who the other person might be?"

"No. He would just tell me how to respond, and if I didn't do it right, he'd threaten my mother's life."

Mason leaned against the back of the couch. He'd prayed that Rafael could give them their next lead, but so far nothing he'd told them was particularly helpful. Before he finished, he did have one more question.

"You did well, Rafael. Mentioning the scholarship to Penn State was a clever move that convinced Miss Hunt you weren't behind this."

Mason's phone rang. He checked the caller ID. It was his brother. He glanced at Rafael and Emily, wondering if it were possible that his day could get any more complicated. He should be here helping Rafael. He should be helping Emily find Tess. He should be halfway across the country with his brothers and father.

He excused himself and moved across the room to take the call. "Craig? Hey. How's Dad?"

"Mason . . . Listen, I know you have a lot going on, but Dad's going downhill fast. He's running out of time."

He'd checked the flights. The last one out tonight left for Denver at six forty. He'd never make it.

"There's a five forty-five flight out in the morning," Mason offered. "I'll try to be on it."

"And if that's too late?"

He hated the guilt. Hated the bitterness that stood in the way of forgiving. "I'm doing the best I can."

He didn't want to be the one who put job before family, but that's exactly what he was doing.

CHAPTER
22

Emily watched as Mason pushed the button to end the call, clearly upset. He excused himself, then walked into the adjoining kitchen. Something was wrong. *God, if something's happened to Tess, I'm going to need you now more than ever, and Avery . . .*

Whatever it was, waiting was only going to prolong the inevitable. She had to know the truth. Mason stood in the kitchen, hands braced against the tiled countertop.

Jaw tensed, Emily felt her heart pounding. "Mason . . . what happened? Did they find Tess?"

He turned to her and shook his head. "No. It's something . . . something personal."

"Something wrong?"

"It's nothing."

She shouldn't push, but whatever had happened was clearly something. "I might still be in a state of shock over everything that has happened today, but your 'it's nothing' doesn't sound like nothing to me."

She watched his expression change as if he were trying to decide whether or not to tell her. He grabbed a mug from the counter and poured steamy hot liquid from the coffeepot.

"I'm sorry. It's none of my business. I shouldn't have asked."

"No. It's okay. I'm just having a hard time separating work and my personal life."

"And you're surprised it doesn't always work?" She raised her brow and shot him a grin. "They're both a part of who you are. There's hardly a day when I don't come home worrying about one of my students. I worry about my mom while I'm at school . . . sometimes putting either side behind is impossible."

"It's my father." He traced the rim of the cup with his finger, paused, then reached for a packet of sugar. "I just got a call from my brother. My father's dying. He's at his home in Denver. Hospice has come in. They don't expect him to make it much longer."

"Wow. I'm sorry." She reached up to brush her fingers against his arm, then pulled back. Not enough had passed between them for her to feel familiar. Not enough to feel as if she'd known him forever and somehow understood the pain of what he was feeling, and yet that was how she felt. "I don't remember your talking about your father."

Unlike her large extended family that celebrated yearly family reunions with first and second cousins, she didn't remember Mason ever speaking about family beyond his brothers and his aunt.

"My father's been out of the picture for a dozen or so years, until my brother called me this past weekend. Told me my father had been diagnosed with terminal cancer six months ago and only has a short time left to live."

"Why just tell you now?"

"Like I said, there really hasn't been any contact for years. I guess things change when you're on your deathbed. You want to suddenly make up for things you've neglected over the years."

"That makes sense. But it still hurts, I'm sure."

"Yeah." He looked up at her, the pain evident in his eyes. "I didn't expect to feel anything, which I know sounds cold, but he isn't a part of my life anymore."

"I'd say your response is normal."

"Normal, maybe, but conflicting as well. Have you ever had something you thought you dealt with? Thought it was behind you and then, wham . . . you get hit up the back side of your head."

"Every once in a while I have those feelings about Michael's death. I don't have anyone to blame, which sometimes makes it even harder."

"That's exactly what I mean."

"What about your father? Are you planning to go see him?"

"I was scheduled to fly to Denver this morning. It was one of his deathbed wishes, to have his three boys together again. But when Rafael came to me this morning, I knew I couldn't just walk away from him. And then . . . well . . . you know the rest of my day."

"So you've been having to choose between two crises all day today."

"Yeah."

"How long has it been since all of you were together?"

"I see my brothers as often as I can, but with our work schedules it only works out to be once or twice a year. We talk on the phone and Skype, but it's not as much as I'd like."

"And your father?"

"He walked out of our lives a long time ago. Remarried. Twice. Moved away. It was a relationship that over the years I learned to accept I would never have."

"Do you want to see him again?"

"I don't know. In some ways it was easier when I was seven and didn't have a choice as to who walked in and out. The choice was never up to me. But now . . . to be honest, I don't know what I want."

"What happens if you go?" She'd always been one to analyze the problem. Fix it if she could. To try to let it go if she couldn't. Not that life always fell into that simple of a package, but it was a place to start.

"If I go? I see my brothers and my father. I find out why it was so important that I show up. And then . . . and then I guess it'll be over."

"What happens if you don't go?"

"If I don't go?" He paused. "Not going and dealing with my father would be the easy way out, but . . ."

She waited for him to continue.

"Honestly, if I don't go, I know I'll regret it. Regret not being there for my brothers. Maybe one day regret that I didn't give my father one last chance."

"Maybe you have your answer then."

He chuckled. "You make it seem so simple."

"It's not simple, it's just important to look at things both ways. To try to temporarily look past the emotion of the moment that can blind us. My father always made me do that when I had a choice to make. Some situations really were simple. And others . . . like yours . . . not so much."

Her gaze flicked past Mason to the window overlooking the backyard, where another inch of snow had fallen in the past hour. She'd had to ask herself the same questions before calling off her wedding with Charlie, and had discovered that the price to marry him was far greater than she was willing to pay. Life's choices were rarely completely black and white, and it wasn't always easy to follow through once a decision was made.

"Did your father teach you how to forgive as well?" he asked.

"That's another issue I struggle with at times."

"I think my not being able to—or wanting to—forgive my dad is the real barrier to my going. It's something I've had to face since giving my life to Christ. I know I've been forgiven, but learning to forgive someone who spent his entire life ignoring me . . . that's tough."

"What kind of memories do you have of him?"

"Most are better off forgotten. The last good memory I have is of him taking me and my brothers to a baseball game when I was seven. I was so excited. He'd just gotten a good-paying job—jobs were few and far between—so he bought hot dogs, popcorn, cotton candy . . . anything we wanted."

"That's why saving Rafael was so important to you."

His eyes narrowed. "Yeah. Rafael grew up a lot like I did. Single parent, few options to get ahead."

He was giving her a chance to understand him on a deeper level. Allowing her to see a side of him she'd missed all these years. "What happened today wasn't your fault. You did everything you could to stop it."

"But what about the next Rafael? Sons need their fathers. They need that relationship with them."

Emily mulled over his question. There simply weren't any easy answers. "I'm not the cop here, but I know with my own job it didn't take me long to figure out that I can't save them all. No matter how hard I try, no matter what I do, there are going to be some who walk away and leave me feeling as if I've failed to make the impact I wanted to make."

"Maybe that's why I was always a bit envious of Michael's relationship with your father."

"Trust me, our family is far from perfect, but I hope I never take for granted what I have, because I know it's becoming more and more of a rare thing."

"To come from a two-parent family was almost unheard of when I was growing up. You grew up fast. Learned to make it on your own." He leaned back against the kitchen counter, hands in his jacket pockets. "I'm not sure I can forgive him."

"I think you underestimate yourself."

"What do you mean?"

"Not having a father has allowed you to minister to boys like Rafael. You know what it's like to lose a father, to grow up in a single-parent home, to have to grow up fast, take the responsibility of a family before you're really ready. And in the end, not forgiving only hurts yourself."

"You sound like your father now."

"Usually any advice I hand out is advice I need to hear as well."

"So what is your advice this time, Counselor?"

His smile brought with it that unexpected flutter in her stomach. "I have a feeling you've already made your decision."

"The next flight I can catch is in the morning."

His phone rang, reminding her once again why they were there.

"Did they find her?" she asked as soon as he'd hung up.

"Not yet, but that was the captain. He needs me to go to the station. Ben Jacobs, the man who broke into both your sister's house and Rafael's apartment, has apparently had a change of heart. He's ready to talk."

CHAPTER
23

Emily watched Mason leave through the front door of the safe house. Somehow, he'd become the anchor in today's storm. But while she couldn't dismiss the attraction brewing between them, at the moment there was something far more serious to consider. Her niece's life was still in danger, and her sitting here in the house while the rest of them tracked down her abductor wasn't going to help.

"Mason . . . wait." She followed him out onto the front porch, her insides brimming with frustration. She needed to do something or she was going to go crazy.

He turned to face her at the top of the porch stairs while she paused, suddenly unsure of what she wanted to say. She resisted the urge to reach out and smooth his unruly lock of hair back into place, wishing he could stay with her.

She pressed her lips together and tried to shake off the distraction of his nearness. "I need to be out there doing something to find Tess, not cooped up here in this house being babysat by some government official."

He shot her a smile. "You sound like your sister. It must run in the family. That stubborn streak, and always needing to be in the middle of things."

"I'm serious, Mason. Let me come to the precinct with you. I'll do anything."

His smile faded. "I need you to stay. Please. Primarily because it's my job to make sure you're safe. I promised your father I would look after you, and I can't do that if you're not somewhere safe."

"But—"

He took a step forward and pressed his index finger lightly against her lips. "Second of all, Rafael knows you. He's scared and needs someone familiar with him. You can be that for him."

Emily tried to ignore what his touch was doing to her, while feeling a stab of disappointment at his reasoning.

There had to be something more. "It's not that I don't believe what you're saying is true, but I'm not buying that this is all about Rafael. He doesn't really need me here. What haven't you told me?"

He looked away as if he had something to hide.

"Mason, what is it?"

"I've already told you that the captain and your father are afraid that Tess's abduction has something to do with your family. That it wasn't just a random abduction, but that they're targeting your family specifically."

"You don't really think that's true, do you?"

"There's no way to know at this point, but until we know what's going on, it makes sense to take extra precautions. Your father made me promise that I would have you stay here, just in case."

"What about my mother?"

"She's safe. She's at the hospital with your sister where there are two uniforms right outside the door. Your minister's wife is there as well."

Emily closed her eyes for a moment, trying to sort through her feelings. She knew her father wanted what was best for her . . .

that both he and Mason wanted what was best for her, but all this did was make it more important that she help find her niece. "So I sit here and do nothing, while you're out trying to find Tess."

"Trust me. You won't be doing nothing. I still believe there's a chance that Rafael knows something about whoever took Tess—even if it isn't something he's consciously aware of. If you can, help him remember something. Anything. Sometimes even the smallest details are all we need to close a case."

"And if you don't find her in time?"

"We're not going to go there. Not now. Not ever." He took her hands and rubbed his thumbs across the back of them. "Listen, I know you're scared. This entire situation has been extremely personal for you, from Rafael's involvement this morning to everything that's happened since then. But I really do need you to trust me on this one. Your father's right. Stay here, see if you can help Rafael remember something, and stay safe."

"What about you?"

"Are you worried about me?" He shot her a broad smile that shouldn't make her stomach dive, but it did.

"From what I know about you, you can take care of yourself, but . . . yeah. I'm worried about you."

He drew her against him and wrapped his arms around her. The gesture was surprising and unexpected. Just like her reaction. She melted into his embrace. He made her feel secure. Protected.

He pulled back and caught her gaze. "I want to make sure you're safe as well."

"I understand, but just because I'm not a cop doesn't mean that I can't do something. I really do want to be out there looking for Tess."

"And I truly believe that one of the keys for ending this lies with Rafael. He was set up by whoever is behind all of this. Anything you discover could help us find Tess."

"I still think you're trying to placate me."

He let his hands rest on her shoulders, then pushed her hair back. "No . . . well . . . maybe a little. I really do want to make sure you're okay. Since we don't know who is behind this, I'm simply not willing to take any chances. Just promise you'll stay here."

"Fine." She shot him a half smile. "But note that I'm a conscientious objector."

"Your complaints are duly noted, Miss Hunt."

She laughed softly, wishing he didn't make her heart race so quickly. There were a million reasons why she couldn't fall for him. It was too much like a rebound. She was too emotional after everything that had happened today. And then there was her "no cops" rule . . .

"Emily?"

Despite her shaky resolve, she couldn't help but smile up at him, wondering if he was feeling the same, crazy, jumbled, and unexpected feelings she was.

She swallowed hard. "I'll be fine as soon as we find Tess and all of this is over."

What would happen then? The only thing she knew at this moment was that she didn't want him to simply walk out of her life.

He tilted her chin up and looked into her eyes. Intense . . . safe . . . mesmerizing. He wasn't playing fair. And the fact that he was a cop wasn't helping either. That thought alone terrified her. Her fears were based on reality. Avery had lost her husband. They'd both lost Michael. Taking a chance on an adrenaline junkie wasn't something she intended to sign up for. Even Charlie had made her realize that. She might not have lost him, but the demands of his job had always come before her and her needs. It hadn't taken too long to figure that out. But Mason wasn't Charlie.

Mason's face hovered above hers.

Her chest heaved as she breathed in the combination of tangy citrus and sandalwood. "Is this how you treat all the females in your protective custody?"

"Only ones with bright eyes who manage to make my heart race."

She felt her cheeks blush. She shouldn't be standing here, lingering with him. There was too much to do. But her heart had gone from pure terror to somehow feeling safe. Today had changed her in ways she wasn't even sure of at this point. And Mason Taylor was the one person helping her hold it all together.

Until she was certain he was going to kiss her.

She tried not to panic. She wasn't ready for this. Not today. Not when her heart was about to explode with pent-up emotions. Distraction or not, she needed to protect her heart. She'd been down this road before with Charlie, the irresistible charmer who'd swept her off her feet until she'd realized she was about to make a mistake. She wasn't going to do that again.

She took a step back. "I'm sorry."

"No, I'm sorry." Mason cleared his throat and fished his car keys out of his jacket pocket. "You're right. I'm taking advantage of the situation. We're both barely hanging on to our emotions after today."

Which meant what? That tomorrow morning when she woke up with Tess safe and her sister home from the hospital, she was going to forget Mason Taylor and how he'd managed to break down the walls around her heart.

Except she wasn't sure that was true.

"What happens when this is over and our emotions are back to normal?" She asked the question before she had time to think about the consequences. Didn't she already know the answer? When all of this was over and things were back to normal, she'd go back to lectures on early modern Europe and American history, and he'd go back to chasing down the bad guys. They lived in two different worlds and there was no reason they ever had to cross again. "I'm sorry. I don't know why I asked that."

His smile was back. "I'm not opposed to waiting and finding out."

She looked up at him, regretting for a moment she hadn't given in to his kiss.

He smiled, then took the steps two at a time as he headed toward his car in the driveway.

"Mason?"

He turned around and looked back at her.

"Be careful, and find Tess for me."

CHAPTER
24

Emily watched Mason pull away from the curb and head toward the precinct. The neighborhood was quiet other than the wind blowing through the tree-lined street. She hated the fact that she'd panicked. Hated that she'd let fear overwhelm her. Because a part of her—a very big part of her—wanted him to kiss her. It was a vulnerable part of her that needed to run as far away as she could from everything that had happened today. And that included Mason Taylor. Which made no sense.

This morning, she'd confessed to Grace she was embracing the fact that she was single. Until Mason walked back into her life. He'd managed to step into her life, dig up a bunch of old emotions, and revive them like a breath of fresh air blowing across a dying fire. But even she wasn't sure what had happened between those moments when she'd first caught him looking into her eyes, realized he wanted to kiss her, felt herself respond . . .

She'd already made one exception to not getting involved with a police officer when she'd started dating Charlie. And everyone knew how that one had ended. On the other hand, when it came to Mason there was definitely that unqualified spark between them.

Either way, she'd been right about one thing. The one thing that had stopped her from kissing him. That fragile string of emotions she was feeling was close to pushing her over the edge.

Fear over Tess's disappearance. Fear over the fact that Avery had been shot. Even fear over the fact that her life could still be in danger.

She stepped back into the safe house, locked the door behind her, and started digging up every memory verse she could remember about trusting and not being afraid. But even that didn't slow down the rapid beating of her heart. It was easy to trust when things were going okay. Today, she felt as if she were walking on a tightrope with no safety net to catch her.

Emily pressed her fingernails into her palms and let her gaze wander. There were no homey touches in this room. A couch, two chairs, and a couple of end tables. A framed print of a cluster of dogwood flowers probably picked up at a garage sale hung crooked on the wall. A stack of outdated magazines on the coffee table. A set of "Made in Atlanta" coasters lay beside them.

Emily glanced up at Rafael, who stood in the living room, pacing like a caged animal. Whatever feelings she needed to figure out would have to be dealt with later. Mason was right. Rafael looked lost. Confused.

The two FBI agents behind him in the living room reminded her of a scene out of prime-time television. This wasn't her world. But like it or not it was a reality she was going to have to face head-on today.

She stepped in front of Rafael. "This is all going to be over soon. Eduardo's been found. Your mother's safe. And they will find Tess."

"You're wrong." Rafael shook his head, his hands fisted beside him. "This will never be over. If my brother lives, he's going to prison. Which means my mother's lost another child . . . And as for me? Tell me how I'm supposed to walk back into that school after holding a class at gunpoint . . . And that's assuming that I don't end up in prison with my brother."

Emily's shoulders drooped. That feeling of vulnerability was back. He was right, and she had no idea what to say. No idea how to fix things. No idea how to fit what had happened today into her normally orderly world where rote facts didn't change and two plus two always equaled four.

"You're right. I don't have all the answers, and I'm just as scared as you are right now. My sister is in the hospital, and they can't find my niece . . . But Mason was right. We need to talk. To see if you can remember something that will help them find Tess, and the man who is behind this."

He pressed his lips together, his hands shaking at his sides. "I've gone over everything again and again. Whoever they are, they're smart."

His chest heaved with a raspy breath. He needed a distraction.

"Let's forget all of this for a while and go get some hot chocolate. I think I saw some packets with tiny marshmallows in the kitchen. I don't know about you, but I love those."

Agent Pierce looked up from his computer. "There's also some sandwich fixings in the fridge if you're hungry."

"Can I fix something for either of you?"

Both agents shook their heads. "We ate before coming here, but thanks."

"What do you say?" Emily turned back to Rafael. "We need to keep up our strength. And I don't know about you, but breakfast was a long, long time ago."

Rafael's eyes narrowed, then he nodded.

Inside the kitchen, Emily set her cell phone on the counter, dug into the fridge, pulling out a package of ham, cheese slices, and a small, unopened jar of mayonnaise. She found a loaf of white bread on the counter. Ingredients were sparse, but they'd do. At least until she was able to sit down for a meal of Mama's homemade stew and biscuits.

"Why don't you heat up some water for the cocoa, while I make the sandwiches. Ham on white with mayo okay?"

"Sure." Rafael stared at matching yellow coffee mugs she'd placed in front of him. "I don't think I'll ever get past the thought that all of this is my fault."

"The way I look at it, if it wasn't for you, this situation could have ended a whole lot worse." She started covering the bread slices with mayonnaise. "You found a way to let me know what was going on, enabling us to get you out alive. Your brother and mother are alive, not to mention every student in that classroom . . . You're a hero, Rafael."

"A hero?" He knocked the mug he was holding under the faucet against the sink, cracking its side. "I'm sorry."

"Forget it." She dropped the mug into the trash can and let the lid swish closed.

"A hero would have known what was going on in the life of his brother. Gone to Mason and let him handle things. A hero wouldn't have given in to fear and walked into that classroom with a gun."

Emily ripped open the package of ham, praying for the right words. "I can't say what I would have done if I was in your place, which means I can't even begin to judge what you did. It's easy to think I would have simply gone to the police and let them handle everything, but with my family's lives on the line . . . I don't know. You weren't left with an easy choice. They had the leverage they needed and used it."

"Do they know yet who's behind this?" he asked.

She pressed her palms against the counter. "Mason believes it's tied to a case my sister's working on. Ransom kidnappings, just like your brother's, except at least four of the victims have been found murdered. We know that the men arrested at the funeral home were part of a local gang, and there is a good chance that not only is the cartel involved but also a possible mole within the police department. Specifically who's behind it, though, I don't know. I don't think anyone knows at this point."

"So there's no doubt anymore?" Rafael looked up and caught her gaze. "No doubt that Eduardo was selling."

"No."

"I just can't believe he could deceive me like that, and I believed him. I wanted to believe him."

"Mason and his team will find out who was behind this."

Rafael grabbed another mug from the cupboard, filled them up with water, then set them in the microwave. "But I should have known what Eduardo was involved in. Should have found a way to stop him."

"Rafael." Emily turned to him, hands on her hips, and softened her expression. "We can go through this all day, wondering a multitude of what-ifs, but going there won't change anything. Let's focus instead on finding the men behind this."

He pulled two paper plates from the package while the microwave timer continued counting down for the hot chocolate. "Okay."

"Think about everything that has happened since the night Eduardo was abducted. Anything that stands out, from your apartment that night, what you might have seen in the park."

He shook his head. "Reliving things over and over isn't working. I don't know who was behind this."

Emily dropped pieces of cheese onto the sandwiches, then put the tops on them. "This is no different than taking a test. Think about the test-taking skills we've worked on together. The information is there, in your mind, Rafael. When you're stressed, the information is harder to recall. But you're safe now."

His jaw tensed as he shook his head. "I can't see it."

"I want you to close your eyes and take a few deep breaths. Remember how we've talked about making mental pictures about what you've read or heard?"

Rafael nodded.

"I want you to think of why this is important. For you . . . your mother . . . your brother. You can do this."

Rafael nodded.

Emily leaned back against the counter, the sandwiches forgotten for the moment. "I want you to picture the friends your brother hangs out with. Do any of them stand out? Strike you as someone who could be involved with one of the local gangs?"

"No."

"Okay. Good."

She continued going slowly through the past two days with him. What he might have seen when the masked men broke into the house. Their mannerisms, voices, anything that would set them apart.

"Tell me what you saw at the park when you went to pick up the backpack."

Rafael squeezed his eyes shut. "A couple cars passed on the side street. There was a runner coming toward me. A woman. I . . . I picked up the pack, shaking . . ."

"Did the runner follow you?"

He shook his head. "She ran past. I don't think she really looked at me."

"Was anyone else there?"

"No . . . Wait." He looked up at her. "There was this man. He was leaning against a car across the street. I remember feeling like he was watching me, but I thought I was just being paranoid."

Emily felt her heart pound. Maybe it was nothing, but it fit. There was a department mole. Weapons had been stolen. Avery's office and house bugged. If he—or she—were involved, they might have been at that park making sure Rafael picked up the pack.

"Could you recognize him?"

Rafael shrugged a shoulder. "I could try."

"It might not be anything more than a coincidence that he

was there, but we need to let the agents know." She turned and picked up the knife to cut the sandwiches.

A crash sounded from the front of the house. Wood splintered. The knife slipped from her fingers and onto the tile as fear ripped through her. A shot rang out. Someone shouted. Two . . . three shots.

It took Emily a second to react. Mason had been right. Someone had come after them and found them. Heart pounding, she shoved Rafael toward the back door.

Emily fumbled with the lock. Where were the FBI agents? If they were alive, they would have been in here already. If they were dead, she and Rafael were on their own. She was still trying to open the door when a man walked into the kitchen, wearing a hoodie, baggy jeans, and a ski mask.

The back door finally swung open.

"Run, Rafael!"

He was right behind them. Limping. Had the agents shot him? She pulled the door shut, praying that the extra seconds would be enough.

They ran past a pile of firewood and a shovel, through the side gate into the front yard. She glanced down the street. It was quiet . . . cold without her coat. The row of driveways in either direction sat empty, which meant she had no idea where to go. All she knew was that they couldn't stop running.

A light snow was falling. She slipped on the grass, then struggled to catch her balance. He was gaining on them. She could hear him behind them. Rafael yelled at him to stop. Fingers gripped her shoulder as he slammed her into the ground. Warm, moist breath tickled her skin. She could feel the gun pressed against her temple.

He was going to kill her.

His voice was raspy as he whispered into her ear. "Good night, sunshine."

CHAPTER
25

Mason made his way to the interrogation room where Carlos was waiting for him and glanced at his watch. Two and a half hours had passed since they'd received the first text that Tess had been taken. Two and a half hours with no progress in finding her. Which meant that Ben Jacobs better be ready to talk. And he better have the answers they needed.

His stomach growled as he passed the row of vending machines. Breakfast had consisted of leftover Chinese takeout from the night before. Lunch was long forgotten. He stopped in front of one of the machines, dug out a crisp bill from his wallet, and punched the buttons for a Snickers. Chocolate might not be at the top of the food pyramid, but it should help keep him focused.

Lack of food, though, wasn't the only thing messing with his focus. Emily Hunt had managed to do that without even trying. He'd watched the way she related to her students earlier today, refusing to panic in a difficult situation, and putting their needs above her own. Now, every feeling toward her he thought he'd long since buried had resurrected full force and was trying to completely throw off his equilibrium.

He ripped off the end of the wrapper and took a bite. He still wasn't sure what he'd been thinking when he'd almost kissed her. All he knew was that she'd managed to work her way straight into his heart. That wasn't supposed to happen to this undercover cop who tended to put his job before anything—or anyone—else, and was used to the long hours with no one to come home to.

She made him want to change all of that. Made him wonder what it would be like to come home after a tiring stakeout to a woman who loved him.

He took another bite and headed down the hallway to the interrogation room. Whatever he was feeling toward her would have to be analyzed another day. For now, he'd made a promise to her, and he intended to keep it. They needed to find Tess.

Carlos was waiting for him in the hallway.

"Any updates on Avery?" Mason asked.

"The last update we received was that they'd had a few issues again with her blood pressure dropping, but she should be okay."

"Does she know about Tess yet?"

"I don't think so."

Mason let out a low whistle. "I'd hate to be the one to tell her."

"You and me both."

Mason nodded toward the room where Jacobs sat waiting for them. "I've looked through his file. Are you sure he has something worth our time?"

"It's the best lead we've got at the moment. If someone was behind his breaking into both Avery's house and the Cerdas' apartment today, we need to know who."

"Then let's do this."

Mason stepped into the room behind Carlos and tossed his empty candy wrapper into the trash can before sliding into a chair. He studied the wiry man across the table from him. He looked older than his forty-seven years. Fingers drummed against the table. His foot tapped against the floor. The last interview had pretty much amounted to nothing more than a demand to see his lawyer. Something had changed his mind. At least that's what they were hoping.

Mason folded his arms. "We understand you've decided to talk?"

"Yes, but before I say anything, I'm going to need protection." Jacobs's eyes pleaded with them as he leaned forward, elbows on the table. Something—or someone—had him terrified. "And you have to promise me no jail time."

Mason's brow rose at the man's last demand. He looked at Carlos and let out a low chuckle. "Let's see. He's just been arrested for a burglary that included a stash of drug money that can be tied to kidnapping and ransom demands. But he wants us to promise him no jail time. Am I missing something here?"

"Wait a minute, you need the information I have. I just need guarantees."

Carlos stood up, bracing his arms against the table. "What kind of guarantees? We don't even know if the information you have is worth a get-out-of-jail-free card."

"First of all, I didn't have anything to do with any kidnapping or ransom demands."

Carlos laughed. "And you expect us to believe that? You don't exactly have a pristine past." He tapped on the Jacobs file sitting on the table. "In fact, you're a repeat offender looking at prison time. With this arrest, I can ensure you go away for a very, very long time."

Jacobs looked panicked. "No."

"So you think if you cooperate with us today, all of this will, what? Simply disappear?" Mason asked.

"That's the deal."

"What do you think, Mason? We've already got him for drug possession, robbery, intent to distribute." Carlos glanced back at Jacobs. "Do you want me to continue?"

The man turned away, jaw tight, lips pinched.

"I'm not sure you really understand the seriousness of your situation, Jacobs. You're looking at serving the maximum sentence without the possibility of parole. And I haven't talked to the DA yet, but I'm pretty sure that if convicted of another felony, you're facing a very, very long time in prison."

"That's why I'm agreeing to make a deal." Jacobs slammed his palms against the table. "I won't go back there."

Mason folded his arms and leaned back. "Start at the beginning then. Why did you break into the Cerda home?"

"I had an arrangement with someone."

"What kind of arrangement?"

Jacobs's gaze dropped. "Do we have a deal?"

"You give me something I can use, and I'll do what I can to influence the DA in your favor. What kind of arrangement?"

"I started doing odd jobs on the side for someone."

Mason frowned. They were going to have to take things one step at a time. "What kind of odd jobs?"

"I received a call the first time about . . . four months ago. He told me to search that other cop's house and leave a bug."

"What were you looking for?"

"He told me he needed a file and that I could find it in the basement on a desk."

"What was in the file?"

"It was a case file on . . . I think his name was Michael. Michael Hunt."

"How many times has your contact called you?"

"Six . . . maybe seven times."

"And today?"

"The same thing. I received a phone call."

"Blackmail?"

"I'd call it more of a . . . mutual agreement. He needed things done . . . I needed certain . . . activities to go unreported."

Another cop. Mason suppressed a smile. Maybe they were actually getting somewhere.

"What kind of activities?"

"That's not on the table today."

Mason glanced up at Carlos. They'd drop that line of questioning . . . for now anyway. "What did he tell you to look for in the house this morning?"

"He said I'd find either drugs or money hidden somewhere."

"You took a risk. We found out this morning that Eduardo was kidnapped. Didn't you think that the police would show up at the house to search?"

"I didn't know what was going on, or about any kidnapping victim. He just told me that the family would be out all morning and that I needed to hurry. I was almost done searching the house when I heard the landlord's voice and realized that you guys were coming in. I hid in one of the back closets while they swept the house. Heard them in the other bedroom and thought I could get out clean." Jacobs looked up at Mason. "At first this arrangement seemed advantageous to both of us, but he knew things, and made it clear that he was going to get what he wanted."

"So he threatened you. With what? Prison?"

"Yes. He told me if I didn't do what he said that he'd have me thrown back into prison, and this time for life. He said it would be my word against his, and you know where that would go. I'm a convicted felon, and he . . . he's a decorated officer."

They were making progress, but Mason didn't like where this was going. Dirty cops accepted bribes in exchange for not reporting organized drug and prostitution rings, and possibly even participated in the crimes themselves.

"Why not just tell him no? Why take the chance of getting caught?"

"Like I said, he knew things." Fear was in Jacobs's eyes. "I knew if I got arrested, I would go to prison. He has the connections to make that happen."

"So your contact is on the force," Carlos said.

"Promise you'll protect me."

Mason shook his head. They were wasting time. "Enough running around in circles, Jacobs. Who is it? Who are you working for?"

Jacobs's hands clasped in front of him. Sweat glistened on his forehead.

"Without a name, I can't do anything."

"You still haven't promised me protection."

Jacobs stared at the table, clasping and unclasping his hands in front of him.

"Listen to me, there's a girl's life at stake. You help me, and I'll convince the DA to give you a break." Mason rubbed his forehead. He needed some Tylenol before his headache got worse. "Just tell me his name."

Jacobs drummed his fingers on the table. "His name is Charlie. Charlie Bains."

CHAPTER
26

Charlie Bains was their mole?

Mason felt a heavy weight tug at him as he stepped out of the interrogation room, struggling to accept what Jacobs had just told them. He had a hard enough time believing that one of the men sworn to protect their country had betrayed them, but Charlie had never been on his radar in regard to the department mole. The man might come across as a bit full of himself at times, but a traitor? No way.

Carlos joined him on the other side of the one-way glass with Tory and Griffin, arms folded across his chest, clearly facing the same skepticism. "Do any of you believe him?"

"No, but on the other hand, why lie at this point?" Mason asked. "The man's clearly scared, but apparently jail scares him more than the repercussions from ratting out his source."

In the adjoining room, Jacobs drummed his fingers against the table. Brow beaded with sweat. Foot tapped beneath the table. Nerves had taken over.

"I've been checking into Jacobs's history." Tory held up a thick folder. "So far, everything he's said has checked out."

"What about the text message regarding Tess?" Griffin asked. "It came while Charlie was talking with Emily."

"An attempt to make her his alibi?" Mason said.

"Texts can easily be scheduled," Tory said. "No matter what any of us think about Charlie on a personal level, until we have hard evidence saying otherwise, we can't ignore the possible consequences of him being behind this."

Mason didn't like where the conversation was headed, but Tory was right. Whether or not Jacobs's admission was true, at this point they couldn't ignore the possibility. "Charlie has been involved in every aspect of this case, which means if he's behind what has happened today, he knows everything we do."

"Do we know where he is?" Carlo asked.

"I'll call the captain, give him a quick briefing, and find out." Mason punched in the captain's number, spoke for a minute, then hung up. "Charlie left the school ten minutes ago. Told the captain he was following up on a lead with an old informant of his."

Carlos shook his head. "That doesn't look good."

"No, it doesn't." Mason turned to Tory and Griffin. "Captain wants you to track Charlie's phone. He's smart, but if he's running, he might not be thinking clearly. We need to find him. Then start looking for a connection between Jacobs and Bains. An arrest, testimony, anything that ties them together."

"On it."

"Carlos, we'll meet back up at the safe house. Backup is already on its way, but Captain wants us to go by the assumption that if Charlie is the mole—and involved in what happened today—not only does he know where Tess is but where the safe house is as well."

Which meant Emily and Rafael's lives were in danger. And until all the pieces of the puzzle came together, they were going to have to take every precaution they could, including moving Rafael and Emily to a new, secure location.

He and Carlos headed out the door as he punched in FBI Agent Bradley's number, his heart aching for Emily. If Charlie was behind this, she needed to know the truth. She might not love him anymore, but even that wouldn't ease the sting of betrayal.

He let it ring a dozen times, frowning as he hung up the call.

"The agents aren't answering."

He tried Emily's phone next.

Nothing.

"He's gone after them."

Mason spoke his fear out loud. Panic wasn't a word he liked to use, but today was markedly different. No matter how hard he tried to ignore his feelings, he'd fallen for Emily, and if anything happened to her . . .

"We don't know that they're in danger," Carlos said. "Not yet."

Accurate or not, the detective's assurances fell short.

Ten minutes later, they pulled onto the quiet road leading to the safe house, Mason's nerves stretched to the breaking point. He'd been right when he'd told her he was taking advantage of both of their emotions in this situation, but even that admission had done little to tone down his feelings toward her . . . or his own fears.

Because he had no doubt that even when all of this was over—and she was safe—he'd still feel the same way. Which was why he was willing to wait if that's what it took. And willing to do whatever it took to ensure she and Rafael were alive. And that they stayed alive.

Two patrol cars were already in front of the nondescript safe house.

"What would you do if you were Charlie?" Mason broke the silence that had settled in between him and Carlos.

"If he's the mole, afraid that he's about to get caught, he's going to have to run."

"If he isn't already running."

"He needs the ransom money in order to disappear, and a place to hide out until he gets the money."

Which was why he'd taken Tess.

Mason took the porch steps two at a time, pausing at the front door that had been kicked open. His jaw tensed. It didn't make sense. Why break down the door?

"Charlie could have walked in with few if any questions asked," Mason began.

"Could mean someone else is involved."

Mason nodded. "The man in the van."

The officers met them at the door with quick introductions. "We got here five minutes ago. We were told to secure the scene, then hand it over to you at your arrival."

"What have you got?"

"House is clear, but both agents are dead."

A sick feeling spread through the pit of Mason's stomach as he stepped into the safe house. Agent Pierce had a gunshot to the back of his head. The man probably hadn't even known what hit him. Agent Bradley lay on the floor against the red-stained carpet, eyes open, staring blankly at the ceiling.

"They were guarding two people. Where are they?" Mason's anger mounted. He hated the fact that they'd lost two good agents who hadn't deserved this. Hated the fact that they might not be the only ones dead.

"I don't know, sir. We searched the house. It's empty. Looks as if they might have escaped out the back."

"Start searching the neighborhood and find me a witness."

"Yes, sir."

More officers would be here in the next few minutes to help with the search. In the meantime, they needed to piece together what had happened. "So what do we know?"

Carlos stopped beside the overstuffed chair as he took in the details of the scene. "Shooter burst through the front door, stepped into the living room, quickly executing both agents."

"He knew they were here," Mason added. "Knew what to look for."

They glanced around the simply furnished living room. Nothing more than a couch, a couple chairs and end tables. Emily's coat and bag had been left on the couch. It was cold outside, which meant she'd left in a hurry. Voluntarily or against her will? That was what he needed to find out.

A file of papers lay strewn on the floor beside Agent Pierce's body; an empty bag of miniature chocolate bars forgotten beside a computer on top of one of the end tables.

"If it wasn't Charlie?" Mason began.

"Charlie must have told someone."

Mason stepped into the kitchen. Bread and sandwich fixings on the counter . . . Sandwiches on two plates beside Emily's phone . . . Knife on the tile floor . . . The back door open.

"The shooter caught them by surprise. Emily and Rafael were here . . . fixing lunch . . . heard the front door burst open and the shots—"

"—and ran." Carlos finished his sentence for him.

Mason nodded. Either they were looking at another kidnapping . . . or somehow Emily and Rafael had gotten away.

God, please, let it be the latter.

They stepped outside. The backyard was landscaped with nothing more than a small patio, a few bare bushes, and a pile of wood, enclosed by a six-foot fence. The side gate leading to the front was open.

"Looks like at least three sets of prints." Carlos pointed toward the soft ground where today's rain and light snow had helped capture the footprints near the gate leading into the front yard.

Mason squatted down beside the pile of wood, looking toward the street where the footprints led. "You think they got away?"

"It's possible. Looks like one of them fell over here."

Mason followed Carlos through the gate into the front yard

where a shovel lay on the ground. He'd have the lab process it for fingerprints and traces of blood.

"Maybe they were able to knock out the attacker with the shovel," Carlos threw out.

"Assuming they got away, where would they have gone?" Mason was asking his questions out loud. Questions neither of them had answers to at the moment.

God, please . . . let her have gotten away.

Mason looked for details the same way he attacked every case he worked. Examine the big picture, then hone in on the details. The nondescript street. Houses that fell in the middle-of-the-road price range. Nothing fancy, well-kept yards. The row of empty driveways implied most worked during the day. Nothing called attention to the fact that this house was being used as a safe house.

He stopped at the edge of the sidewalk and turned to Carlos. "Neighborhood's quiet."

"Finding witnesses is going to take time."

Time was something they didn't have.

"Let's assume Emily and Rafael got away," Carlos said as they searched the side yard for another clue. "She's out there with no phone or money. He'd try to follow them. Where would she go?"

Mason felt his chest constrict. She wouldn't know whom to trust. She might not know that Charlie was the mole, but she knew Avery's house and office had been bugged. That someone had been listening. Which more than likely would make her leery of going to the police.

And he had no way to warn her about Charlie.

"She'd go to a neighbor."

He looked down the street. No cars in the driveways for as far as he could see. "Maybe. But in the middle of the day it might be hard to find anyone at home, and if someone was after her, she wouldn't have time to go door-to-door waiting for someone to answer. She needs to disappear."

"Found some blood."

Mason's heart plummeted. He knelt down beside Carlos three feet away from the marred grass where one of the three had fallen. "Either one of the agents got a slug into our shooter, or the shooter . . ."

Mason's gut clenched. Or the shooter hit Rafael or Emily.

He looked up. One of the officers was escorting an older woman. Midfifties, short, gray hair, wearing jeans and a sweat-shirt. "I've got someone here who saw a couple running down the street. Says she also called 911."

Mason introduced himself to the woman who identified her-self as Nicky Sanders. "Can you tell me where you live, ma'am?"

"Across the street." Ms. Sanders nodded east up the road. "Three doors down."

Mason eyed the one-story bungalow with a couple of crape myrtles and dozens of smaller shrubs. From the front window, she'd have been able to see the front yard, but not the gate lead-ing to the backyard.

"I'm normally at work this time of day, but I came down with this nasty cold I can't shake so I decided to stay home." The woman dragged a tissue from her pocket and blew her nose. "I was heating up some soup, when I heard something that sounded like a gunshot. With all the crazy stuff you hear about on the news, I didn't want to take any chances. I immediately called 911."

"Did you see anyone?"

"I went to the window, still on the phone with 911. I saw a woman and a young man run across the yard and down the street. Honestly, I'm not even sure who lives there. I've never really noticed anyone there except for a regular lawn service."

"Was there a car out front?"

Ms. Sanders nodded. "A black, four-door something. I don't really know cars."

"Okay. What else did you see?"

"They ran down the street, the opposite direction of my house, then disappeared."

"What about the car?" Mason asked.

"A man stumbled across the front yard from the far side, one . . . maybe two minutes later. He looked as if he'd been injured. He limped to the car and drove off. "

"So the other two didn't get into the car with him."

"No."

Mason felt a sliver of relief shoot through him. If Emily and Rafael had made it out of the house alive, there was a good chance they were safe.

"Could you recognize the man who drove off?" Carlos asked.

"No." Ms. Sanders sniffed as she shook her head. "He was wearing some kind of mask . . . like a ski mask."

"Tall? Short?"

"It was hard to tell, but definitely short. Maybe five seven or eight?"

Charlie was at least six feet. Mason's cell went off, and he pulled it out of his back pocket. He excused himself and took the call from Tory. "What have you got?"

"I was able to track Charlie's phone. He's still got it on."

"Good." He hadn't turned it off, which meant he was either running scared and not thinking, or felt cocky. Either could be a recipe for disaster. "Where is he?"

"Four blocks away, at the North Ridge Mall."

Bingo.

"Call for backup to meet us there. Carlos and I are on our way."

CHAPTER
27

Emily pushed her way through a steady stream of shoppers with Rafael. For a Monday afternoon, the place was packed. Hip-looking teenagers hung out in packs, while moms juggled strollers, toddlers, and overstuffed diaper bags. Retired couples and plump middle-aged women walked laps—all in addition to the extra crowd of Christmas shoppers. Which was exactly what she'd wanted. Getting lost in a crowd was the safest place she could think of until she could figure out what to do. At least that was what she hoped.

"Jingle Bells" played over the loudspeaker . . . colored lights twinkled on dozens of holiday storefront displays . . . kids waited in line to see Santa . . . pushy kiosk venders vied for her attention . . . Emily tried to block out the noisy confusion surrounding them. All she could think was that it was a miracle they were still alive. And that she had to find a way to get them to safety.

But how, when she didn't know who to trust.

The last thirty minutes replayed through her mind. Their attacker's first mistake was wanting to take them alive. At least that was what she assumed. Otherwise she had no doubt that both she and Rafael would be dead. His second mistake had been not anticipating Rafael's courage to save her. Rafael had come down hard on their assailant with a shovel, stunning him for the few crucial moments that had given them time to escape.

But he was still looking for them. She was sure of that. Which meant he could be anywhere. If he was here—without his mask—he'd be able to blend in with the crowds. And she had no idea what he looked like.

A uniformed officer walked toward them. Emily grabbed Rafael's arm and hesitated. She was being overly paranoid, and she knew it. Security was always high this time of year, but mall security had nothing to do with her, or the man who was after them. She glanced behind her, then started walking again. The only problem was that the often-called "mall cops" were in communication with local police. Which meant possible communication with the department mole.

Emily couldn't shake the doubts. He was bridging the gap between them. Emily pulled Rafael to the other side of the walkway. She'd always trusted the police. Been proud of what her father and siblings did. But not today.

"You still think it's a dirty cop behind this?"

"It's a possibility, which means we have to be careful until we can get ahold of my father or Mason."

What she did know for sure was that she had no phone, no money, and no idea who to trust.

The food court was ahead of them. There was another exit at the far end where they could try to get a taxi to take them to the police station, or even better, to the hospital where her father was.

"Faster."

They picked up their pace, hoping they didn't look out of place. The last thing she wanted was to attract attention.

Another man in uniform came toward them.

Emily grabbed Rafael's arm and pulled him into the nearest store, pretending to look interested in a row of spiked accessories, tattoos, and piercings options.

The officer greeted someone outside the store. They laughed about something she couldn't understand. They weren't talking about her . . . or were they? She couldn't take a chance.

"Looking at getting a tattoo or maybe another piercing?"

"A tattoo?" Emily turned to the salesgirl who didn't look a day over seventeen or eighteen with tattoos up her arms and at least a dozen piercings. "No . . . I'm just . . . looking."

Looking? Right. If the situation weren't so serious, she'd have laughed. Mama would pitch a conniption fit if she came home with a tattoo no matter what her age. The only good thing was that no one would ever think to look for Emily Hunt in a tattoo shop. But even so, at some point, she was going to have to trust someone.

"I'm sorry, but . . ." Emily hesitated, glancing at the people passing the shop. There was no sign of either officer. "Can I use your phone? I lost mine and I really need to make an important call."

The salesgirl shoved a strand of midnight-colored hair behind her ear, clearly unconvinced Emily was legit.

"Please." There was no way to explain why she couldn't go to the police. Why she was even afraid to call 911. Or why she looked so bedraggled. "It's very important."

She chomped on her gum like she was trying to decide what to do, then finally nodded and handed Emily her cell phone.

"Thank you."

Emily punched in her father's number, then waited for the call to go through.

No answer.

Panic bubbled inside her. Where was he? Her heart pounded. His lawyer was getting Tess's ransom together, while he'd probably gone to the hospital room to see Avery . . . with no cell phone coverage. He wouldn't be worried about her. She was supposed to be tucked away in the safe house.

She didn't know Mason's number, and her sister wouldn't get her call. So much for the ease of speed dial. She didn't even know Grace's number by heart, and in fact couldn't remember the last time she'd actually memorized someone's number.

She hung up and handed the phone back to the salesgirl. "I couldn't get through, but I appreciate your letting me try."

"What about a taxi?" Rafael wasn't ready to give up. Maybe he was right.

Emily nodded. At least they'd be doing something instead of just running. "We could meet my father at the hospital."

"I've got the number of a taxi service programmed into my phone." The salesgirl pressed a speed dial number, then handed Emily the phone. "Just in case I ever need a designated driver."

"You're a lifesaver."

A minute later, Emily hung up the phone. A cab would meet them in ten minutes outside the main entrance.

Please, God, keep us safe as we walk out of here . . .

"Thank you. I really appreciate your help." Emily handed the phone back to the salesgirl. "Rafael, we need to go."

All they had to do was get to the main entrance and into the cab. Her father would know what to do once they found him, and they'd be safe. They started down the crowded promenade. Someone caught her eye. She blinked, knowing she had to be wrong. Charlie hated malls . . . Unless the shooter had been spotted here. Or maybe he was looking for her in the neighborhood.

Even if the shooter were here, Charlie would know what she should do.

Emily steered Rafael around the opposite direction. "Where are we going now?"

"I just saw Charlie Bains. He's my . . . my ex-fiancé."

"You trust him?"

"He's not exactly the person I'd like to see right now, but yes, we can trust him."

Funny how the only man she wanted with her right now—besides her father—was Mason. She bit her lip, trying to hold back the tears and waves of fear that threatened to smother her. Maybe wanting to kiss her had been nothing more than an emotional reaction based on the situation, but she knew if he walked up to her right now, she'd feel completely safe.

A woman blocked her way. Emily tried to maneuver around a double stroller piled high with shopping bags. She strained to find him again in the crowd. He had to be right in front of them. The background music vibrated in her head, along with all the noise from the shoppers.

"Excuse me. Please."

She found him again. "Charlie?"

"Emily?" He turned around and looked at her, confusion in his expression, followed by relief. "What are you doing here? I've been so worried. Everyone's looking for you."

"You heard what happened?"

"Yes." He slipped his arm around her waist. "Which is why we need to get you out of here."

She nodded her agreement while fighting back the tears threatening to erupt. "Someone came into the safe house. Busted down the door. There were gunshots. Charlie, I—"

"I know, baby. I know."

Emily hiccupped. She couldn't fight the fear any longer.

He pulled her against his chest. "It's going to be okay, Em. I promise. You're safe now."

Emily hiccupped again, then nodded. She wanted to believe him, but it was going to take a long time for the fear seeping through her to completely vanish. "What happened to the agents?"

"I'm sorry, but both agents . . . both agents were shot. They're dead. Which means everyone has been worrying, because we didn't know where you were."

Emily took in the news about the agents. She'd known something terrible had happened, but hearing it from Charlie only confirmed that reality. If she and Rafael had been in that living room, things might have turned out different.

"He ran out of the house after us. I didn't know where to go."

"Hey . . . hey. You did the right thing. It's going to be okay." He stopped in front of a thirty-foot Christmas tree where a miniature train buzzed around the tracks and pulled her into a hug. "I'm so sorry, babe. So, so sorry."

For a moment she let herself breathe in the familiar smell of his woodsy citrus cologne. The feel of his suit jacket and silk tie against her cheek. Bing Crosby crooned in the background. She closed her eyes, wishing Charlie could make the situation disappear. But there wasn't time for daydreams. Their attacker could be here stalking them. The next time they encountered him, they might not be so lucky.

"Did you see who broke into the safe house?"

She shook her head. "He wore a mask. All I know is that he was short and bulky. I think he might have been shot in the leg by one of the agents."

"Do you think he followed you here?"

"I don't know." She was frustrated with all the questions. Frustrated because she didn't have answers. "And I don't know what he wants."

"We'll find him, but first we need to get you out of here. The safe house clearly isn't an option anymore, but I can drive you to the station."

"I don't want to go there. If there's a dirty cop behind this—"

"Trust me. You'll be safe there. We're going to catch whoever is behind this. I promise." He leaned toward her and tilted up her chin. "You know you can trust me, Emily. You know that, don't you?"

She nodded.

"I need to let the captain know you've been found, then we'll get you out of here."

She waited until he finished his call before asking another question. "Why are you here?"

She didn't remember ever going to the mall with Charlie. She preferred local shops and boutiques, while Charlie tried to avoid shopping completely, choosing instead to buy everything online.

"I'm here to meet a contact from one of the local gangs, trying to find out who's behind this. But he can wait." Charlie wrapped his arm around her waist and pulled her against him. "Let's get you both out of here. You don't have anything to worry about anymore, Em. You're safe now. Both of you."

CHAPTER
28

The cold wind sucked Emily's breath away as she hurried with Charlie across the parking lot that was decorated with candy canes and stars for the holiday season. Clouds hung above them, partially blocking the sun that would be setting in the next hour. Someone's car alarm wailed. A handful of holiday shoppers headed for their cars while juggling armfuls of packages.

Emily barely noticed any of it.

"My car's parked at the far end," Charlie said. "It's impossible to find anything close this time of year."

She nodded. His arm was still around her, warm and protective. Any feelings of attraction had long sense evaporated, but that didn't mask the relief that she felt safe again.

She shivered without her coat. The temperature had continued to drop, and a light snow fell. Charlie must have felt her shiver, because he stopped to shed his suit jacket and set it across her shoulders.

She glanced up at him. "I'm okay."

"No, you're not. You're freezing."

She nodded her thanks, but she was shaking as much from fear as she was from the temperature. She grasped Rafael's hand to be certain that he kept up with them, her mind was spinning. She needed to call her father. Needed to call Mason, but first she just wanted to get away from here. Just because she finally felt safe didn't mean her questions had all been answered.

"Do they know who's behind all of this?"

Charlie shook his head. "Not yet."

"And Tess?"

"We're still looking, but we will find her. We think the man in the van—the one who more than likely also snatched Tess—works with the cartel. We just don't know his identity yet."

"Why take Tess?"

"Presumably because he didn't get his money."

She'd almost been killed, Tess was missing, her sister shot, Eduardo kidnapped . . . and it all came down to money.

"What about the men they caught at the funeral home or Eduardo? Someone has to know something."

"If they know something, they're not talking. Most of these guys have family back in Mexico. They know if they talk, the cartel will kill them. They are more afraid of what might happen back home than of the local authorities here."

He stopped behind his silver Impala and unlocked the vehicle. "Stop worrying. We're going to find out who's behind this, and more importantly, we're going to find Tess."

Emily rounded to the passenger side of the car, praying he was right.

Someone shouted behind her.

Emily spun around and felt her heart jerk into her throat. Mason stood a dozen feet away, gun drawn at Charlie. A woman who'd been heading for her car screamed and ran toward the entrance.

Charlie pulled out his own gun from the other side of the car and aimed it back at Mason.

"Put your weapon down, Charlie."

Emily shook her head, confused. "Mason, what are you doing?"

"Charlie's the department leak. Rafael, I want you to move away from him."

"Wait a minute." Charlie grasped Rafael's arm. "You can't be serious about this."

"I'm very serious. I want you to put your weapon on the ground and put your hands in the air. A dozen officers will be here any minute."

Emily shook her head. She didn't believe him. Couldn't believe him. This had to be some sort of mistake. "Charlie can't be the leak."

"Trust me. He is." Mason spoke to her, his gaze never leaving Charlie.

"He's lying to you, Em."

Emily looked at Charlie, then back to Mason. "I don't understand. The agents at the safe house were murdered. Rafael and I ran. Charlie found me here. He's taking me somewhere safe."

"He's not here to rescue you."

"Em . . . You know me. You know I would never hurt you."

"Which is why this has to be a mistake." The only person she completely trusted was her father. But he'd told her to trust Mason. She took a step away from the vehicle, feeling torn. She might not love Charlie, but she knew him. Knew he wasn't capable of betraying the department. Knew he wasn't capable of betraying her.

Or was he?

Finding Charlie was supposed to have been her escape from the nightmares of today. Hers, apparently, were far from over.

She moved slowly toward the back of the car. "Tell me he's wrong, Charlie."

"Of course he's wrong. You know me, Em."

"He's lying," Mason said. "We have proof."

Charlie laughed. "You actually believe this guy. You and I both know it's just a matter of time before the truth comes out.

Mason's the one who is behind Michael's death. The one who has been working with the cartel. Avery has a stack of evidence against him."

"I'm not going to argue with you, Bains. Put your weapon down."

"You know what your sister would say," Charlie said. "She's got enough evidence to bury Mason."

Trust Mason.

"He's the department mole, Emily," Mason said. "He planted a bug in your sister's office. Overheard my conversation about Eduardo with her this morning, and thought he'd found his ticket out of town, because he's desperate. The truth is that Avery was closing in on you, wasn't she, Charlie? She has been collecting evidence, but it wasn't about me. You knew it and realized that time was running out."

"All lies."

"The only problem was you didn't have enough money to run. So you thought you'd try this morning's ransom scenario—which brought about another set of problems, because nothing went your way. You ended up panicking and taking Tess. But the bottom line is, it's over, Charlie. You can't win this one."

Emily pressed her hand against the car window and looked at Charlie. "Do you know where Tess is?"

"You always did ask too many questions, Em."

"Just tell me the truth, Charlie."

"I'm not sure the truth matters anymore."

"The truth always matters." She caught something in his eyes as he looked away. "You really are the leak."

Charlie tightened his grip on Rafael's arm and laughed. "I always figured you'd find out eventually, though this wasn't exactly how I'd pictured it."

Snow was falling faster now, leaving a white covering across the parking lot. Even in Charlie's jacket she was freezing. She felt her lungs constrict. Struggled to take in a breath of air. How could she have been so wrong about someone? Breaking off their engagement had been difficult enough to face. If he was the department mole, that meant he'd never loved her. He'd only been using her.

And on top of that, he'd walked her out of the mall, told her he was rescuing her, all while knowing he was the one who'd set up Tess's kidnapping. Manipulated Rafael. Never really called the captain to tell him she was safe. The thought made her want to vomit. She might not love Charlie anymore, but knowing she'd been nothing but a pawn in some sick game . . .

Emily's mind struggled to acknowledge what was happening. "I don't understand why you would do something like this. I trusted you, Charlie."

His smile held a hint of disdain. "You've always been gullible."

She tried to ignore the stinging jab. "So this is all about money?"

"Two million dollars—along with the money I've already got stashed away—is enough to disappear for a very long time. Hopefully, the rest of my life."

"And you think this is the way to do it?"

"It would have been simpler if you'd have just come with me."

"Emily's a lot smarter than you give her credit for, Charlie."

Charlie shook his head. "And you, Taylor. You just couldn't leave things alone either, could you? You always have to play the role of hero. Like today. Taking over the negotiations, showing up with Emily while playing the valiant knight who rides in and saves the day. Except this time, it's not going to end well for you."

"It's over, Charlie, and you know it. Put the gun down and let Rafael go."

"And then what? You'll arrest me, and they lock me away for the rest of my life? I don't think so."

"That's exactly what's going to happen. Put the gun down on the ground and your hands behind your head."

"Forget it. Until I get my money, you'll never find Tess."

"You can't do this, Charlie." There was no way to stop the panic now. "She looks up to you like an older brother."

"Tell us where Tess is," Mason said.

"Get me my money and I might."

"And then what?" Mason asked. "Even you know there's no way out of this."

"There's always a way out. And as for you, Mason, you're wrong. I still plan on winning this round." Charlie fired a round of shots at Mason.

Emily screamed as the bullets struck Mason in the chest. He dropped to the ground, his gun skittering across the pavement.

"What are you doing?" She hurried to Mason's side, torn between Mason's safety and the safety of Rafael.

Mason groaned. She crouched down to check on him. His breath came in short spurts, as he tried to sit up. "I probably have a couple cracked ribs, but I'll be okay. Bullets hit my vest. Just need to catch my breath, but you . . . you and Rafael need to get out of here."

"I'm not leaving you. He'll kill you."

She glanced down the row of cars toward the mall, empty of shoppers this far out on the perimeter of the lot. She needed someone to call 911. Needed Mason's backup team to arrive.

"Where's your team?"

"They're coming, but we split up trying to find you."

She stood up and turned back to Charlie. "Please . . . put the gun down and let Rafael go before someone else gets hurt."

Charlie laughed, his gun still aimed at Mason. "I'm sorry, Emily. Really I am, but how does the saying go? Every good thing must come to an end. You were good for me, Emily. Made me forget sometimes who I really was. But for now, I want you to get into my car, because you're coming with me. When your father finds out that both of his girls are in danger, he'll realize he doesn't have a choice but to give over the money."

"Forget it." Emily scooped up Mason's fallen gun, then pointed the barrel at Charlie, still trying to steady her trembling hands. "Where's Tess?"

Charlie laughed, his gun still aimed at Mason. "What are you doing, Emily? Put the gun down before you shoot someone."

"No. Tell me where she is." Emily tried to steady her hands as she held up the gun. She might not be a cop, might not feel courageous, but Charlie had hurt enough people. This had to end right here. Right now.

"How about this." He avoided her question. "If you don't get into the car now, and come with me, I'll shoot your boyfriend, and this time I'll aim for his head."

"No."

"Or what? You'll shoot me? You couldn't shoot a fly."

Mason started to get up, but Charlie shifted the gun toward him. "Don't even think about getting up. I'll shoot her if you move another inch, Taylor."

Emily struggled to breathe. This wasn't the Charlie she'd known. "I might not be a cop, but you of all people know that Daddy made sure I can shoot."

"Maybe, but shooting a person is different. Look at your boyfriend still lying there on the ground. Backup might find him here, but by then you and I will already be long gone."

Charlie looked away from Mason and caught her gaze. This time his expression was completely void of any compassion she'd seen earlier. Something smacked against the hood of Charlie's car. Emily turned as Rafael's shoe bounced across the vehicle. The diversion was enough to catch Charlie off guard. He looked away for a moment, loosening his grip on Rafael, who took advantage of the situation and dropped to the ground.

Charlie swung his arm back toward Mason, but this time the bullet he shot pinged off one of the cars, missing Mason.

She had no other choice. Emily let all the air out of her lungs, steadied her hands, aimed the weapon at Charlie, and pulled the trigger.

CHAPTER
29

E mily's entire body shook. Nausea spread through her. She'd never wanted to shoot anyone. Never wanted to be a cop. Never wanted to marry a cop. So many nevers.

And now she'd shot—maybe killed—someone.

Charlie lay crumpled on the ground, blood pooling beneath his torso. She tried to stop shaking so she could figure out what to do next, but she couldn't. Instead she stood, unable to move. Sirens wailed in the distance. Snowflakes landed on her face. What had she just done?

Someone gripped the gun clenched between her fingers.

"Give me the weapon, Emily." Carlos moved in beside her.

She let him take the gun, her hands still shaking. "I didn't want to shoot him. He shot Mason. Said he was going to kill him."

"I know, Emily. It's over now."

Her gaze shifted from Carlos to Rafael. He stood next to a uniformed officer who'd just arrived on the scene. He was okay. She was okay. And Mason?

"Where's Mason?"

"He's a bit banged up," Carlos said, "but he'll be fine. The bullet struck his vest."

She searched for him among the arriving officers before spotting him. Someone was helping him to the back of one of the squad cars where he could sit down. The vest might have saved his life, but he'd still feel as if he'd been struck by a freight train.

Emily blew out a sigh of relief, but Carlos was wrong. This wasn't over. She looked back to Charlie. Officers were on the ground beside him, trying to stop the bleeding until the ambulance arrived. She wanted to see Mason, but she needed to talk to Charlie.

She started walking toward Charlie, heart pulsing in her throat, body trembling . . . How long would it take for the image of him lying on the ground—knowing it had been her fault—begin to fade?

"Emily, wait." Carlos grasped her arm. "You're in shock. I need you to come with me and sit down until one of the paramedics can check you out."

She shook her head. Only one thing really mattered right now. "I have to talk to him. He knows where Tess is."

"I'll make sure someone talks with him—"

"No." She turned to Carlos. "Please, I know Charlie. I can get him to talk to me."

Carlos let go of her arm and nodded. She crossed the pavement to where he'd fallen when she'd shot him. How had their relationship ended this way? He'd betrayed her, and she'd never even realized it. Never known who he really was. Had he ever loved her?

"Charlie?" She knelt down beside him, out of the officers' way. Sirens screamed in the background. He was breathing, but the pain was clear in his expression.

God, please, don't let him die.

Just because she didn't love him—just because he'd betrayed her—didn't mean she wanted him to die. Not this way.

"Charlie." She fought back the tears. "Tell me where Tess is."

He grabbed her arm, surprising her with his grip. "You could have come with me, Em. We would have been free. Just you and me."

Emily fought roiling emotions threatening to smother her. Had he really thought she would go with him? This wasn't the man she'd once promised to marry. The man she'd believed had stood for justice and integrity. "What you're talking about isn't freedom. It's running."

His breathing was shallow. Raspy. "But we would have been together."

She'd wanted that. Once. They'd planned to build north of town. She envisioned a two-story with a big yard and room for children, an exercise room, and an organic garden in the back. No matter what he said now, he'd never intended to go through with any of it. Even today, when he'd told her he wanted her back . . . it had been nothing more than a way to create an alibi and find out information.

"I found this beautiful secluded island," he continued. "It's paradise, Em. All you have to do is sit . . . sit and watch the waves all day long. You and me with nothing . . . with nothing but time on our hands."

A cold shiver shot through her. She didn't want to think about how he'd sold out the department. Presented the lies as truth, and deceived everyone they knew. Didn't want to be reminded how close she'd come to making the biggest mistake in her life by marrying him.

She shook her head, ignoring his ramblings. "Just tell me where Tess is."

"I needed . . . needed the money . . ." His eyes rolled back, limbs shaking.

"Where is she, Charlie? Where is Tess?"

He was losing consciousness. If he died, she'd be the one to blame. And they might not find Tess.

"No . . . Charlie, where is she?"

The paramedics took over. "We're going to have to ask you to move back, ma'am."

Red lights from the ambulance flashed as the paramedics worked to stabilize him. Darkness began to settle in around them. Someone shouted. They lifted him onto the stretcher, IV in his arm, oxygen mask helping him breathe . . . a moment later the back doors of the ambulance closed, and Charlie was gone.

A strange numbness settled over her as the ambulance drove away. She felt disconnected. Lost. She needed to find Mason. Tell him that they still didn't know where Tess was. If they could locate the man in the van, maybe they could locate Tess. He had to know where she was.

Someone's cell phone rang, pulling her from her thoughts. Otis Redding sang "Sitting on the Dock of the Bay." Charlie had loved that song . . . She ducked down at the edge of his car where the music was coming from. Charlie's black smartphone lay on the ground beneath his car. Emily picked up the phone. A text message had come through.

Emily stared at the screen. He'd told her his password once. If he hadn't changed it . . .

She typed in his old password and the message appeared on the screen.

Where are you?

She froze, her mind scrambling to put together the pieces. Charlie hadn't come to the mall looking for her. He'd come to the mall to meet someone. What if it was him? The man in the van.

She wrote back without stopping to think about what she was doing.

Tied up. Can't make it.

She held her breath and pushed Send.

You owe me. Meet me @ BT @ 7.

Mason walked up to her, wincing as he took off his leather jacket and slipped it around her shoulders. She hadn't noticed she'd lost Charlie's suit coat. She needed to focus. Needed to find a way to shake off the horror of what she'd just witnessed.

"Thank you." She touched the hole where the bullet had ripped through his shirt and lodged in his bulletproof jacket, then looked up at him. "How are you feeling?"

"Like I've been shot." His expression softened. "But you're the one I'm worried about."

She shook her head. "You need to see a doctor to make sure nothing is broken."

"We both do. You might not have been injured, but you can't ignore the emotional trauma of what's happened today."

She glanced down the row of cars now covered with a light dusting of snow. She kept seeing the same images over and over again. Charlie shooting Mason. Charlie dropping to the ground. The officers fighting to stop the bleeding. She knew enough psychology to recognize the basics. Traumatic events often triggered emotions that left the victim feeling stunned or dazed. Feelings became intense and irrational followed by repeated flashbacks, rapid heartbeat, confusion . . .

She wanted to believe that none of those symptoms fit her. That she couldn't still feel the gun between her fingers, see Charlie bleeding out in the parking lot, or hear the pulsing wail of the ambulance.

"Is that your cell?" he asked.

She looked down at her hands, still clutching Charlie's phone.

She shook her head. "It's Charlie's. Someone sent a message and I responded."

"Who was it?"

"The man Charlie was meeting here. It could be him, Mason. The man in the van. He has to know where Tess is."

"What did he say?"

She struggled to clear her mind. To disconnect herself from a reality she still wasn't able to face. "He wanted Charlie to meet him at : . . . at the BT."

Mason flipped through the messages. "I'll have Tory see if she can trace the number and figure out what BT stands for."

He pushed back a strand of hair that had fallen across her eyes, then pressed his fingers against her wrist. She knew her pulse was racing. Her skin hot and clammy.

"You're going into shock, Emily."

"Of course I'm in shock. I just shot someone." She shook her head, feeling frustrated and helpless. "I'm sorry, but if Charlie dies, we might not find Tess and I . . . I will have killed someone."

He cupped her chin with his fingers and caught her gaze. "None of this is your fault either, Emily. Don't ever believe that. He left you no choice. You saved my life."

She fought back the tears because she knew he was right. She'd seen it in Charlie's eyes. He would have killed Mason. She took a step forward and leaned gently against him, careful not to press against his injured side. He was the only thing that felt familiar and safe. He wrapped his arm around her waist, giving her that security she craved.

"Tell me how this could happen. I know Charlie. He wasn't perfect, but this . . . department mole . . . manipulating Rafael . . . kidnapping Tess . . . I don't understand how things could end this way."

"I don't know what was going on in Charlie's head, but it probably happened slowly, over a matter of months, before he realized he was in too deep to get out."

"And I missed all of the signs." Everyone loved Charlie, charming and attentive. She searched her mind for a memory, a clue she'd ignored that would have told her he wasn't the man she'd always believed him to be.

Mason pulled back slightly and caught her gaze. "I'll make sure someone follows up on this message, but in the meantime, you and I are going to the hospital."

She nodded. She was too emotional, and too tired, to argue.

"What about Avery? I need to see her."

"I'll make sure you can." His arm around her tightened as he pulled her against him. "We're going to get through this. I promise."

CHAPTER
30

As soon as she'd been released by one of the physicians, Emily met her father at the doorway of her sister's hospital room where he gathered her into a hug. She pressed her head against his shoulder. He'd always been her safety net. A place she could go to for advice and unconditional love. But today her world had toppled on end and she wasn't sure even Daddy could fix everything.

"I'm so sorry about Charlie," he began.

"Me too." She glanced past him at her sister, who was propped up in the bed talking with one of the nurses. It was going to take a long time for all of them to deal with what had happened today.

"If it helps," he said, "none of us had any idea Charlie was capable of doing what he did."

"But I should have known." It was a detail that refused to stop nagging at her. "I knew him better than anyone else. I should have sensed something."

Her father tilted up her chin and caught her gaze. "You can't blame yourself for anything that happened today. You aren't responsible for Charlie's decisions."

She knew he was right, but that didn't stop her from believing that if she'd realized what he was doing, she might have been able to stop what was happening today.

She nodded her head toward Avery. "How is she?"

"Her blood pressure has finally stabilized and the bullet wound on her thigh has been sutured, but I think she's ready to rip out her IV. She wants to be out there looking for Tess, but there's no way she's ready to walk out of this hospital."

"Sounds just like Avery."

Her father wrapped his arm around her shoulder. "Maybe you can talk some sense into her as soon as the nurse is finished changing her IV. Remind her that the most important thing she can do right now is get better."

"What about Jackson? Has he been here yet?"

"He came as soon as he heard about the shooting, but he just got called back to work. Something to do with this case."

"And Mama?" She'd felt guilty the whole way over here that she'd hardly had time to think about what Mama was going through today. When Michael died, Mama had lost a part of herself. The thought of losing one of her girls would dig deep and resurrect those raw emotions.

"She doesn't know about Charlie," her father said. "But she's not handling Tess's disappearance well or the fact that Avery was shot. Nancy Stuart drove her home about thirty minutes ago with some medicine prescribed by the doctor to help her sleep. I'm hoping—praying—she'll rest. As soon as Jackson gets back, I'll return to the house to be with her."

"What about Tess?"

"Nothing yet."

"And if Charlie is the only person who knows where she is?"

It was the question they were all thinking. Temperatures were dropping, and with few if any leads on Tess's whereabouts, time was quickly running out.

"We're going to find her. Because there aren't any other acceptable options."

Emily moved aside to let the nurse leave the room.

Her father squeezed her hand. "Sit here while I go make a couple phone calls. Cell phone reception in here is impossible."

Emily kissed her father on the cheek, then crossed the room to sit down beside Avery. Her sister braced her hands against the bed and tried to sit up.

"Hey, you don't have to get up for me. How are you feeling?"

"My daughter's been kidnapped, and they've got me strapped to an IV. I should be out there looking for Tess."

"No you shouldn't." Emily grabbed her sister's hand as she lay back on the pillow. "Half the force is out there right now looking for Tess—the captain, your team, and every available uniformed officer. Your role is to stay here and recover so you can take care of Tess once they find her."

"And if they don't find her?"

"They will."

Avery had always been the protective older sister. The strong one who'd found a reason to keep going when she lost her husband. Who'd come up fighting when Michael had died. She'd somehow manage to make it through today as well.

Her sister's normally pink cheeks looked pale in the incandescent lighting. "I know today has been just as hard for you. First Rafael and then Charlie. I still can't believe that he is the one behind all of this. But Daddy told me you did good today in that classroom."

"I'm not sure any of that matters. I shot Charlie." Emily caught the understanding in her sister's gaze. "Does the guilt ever go away?"

"It will lessen. I remember people calling me a hero and hating that word. It didn't matter that I really hadn't had a choice in the shooting. I wouldn't be here today if I hadn't pulled that trigger, but that doesn't always make living with the decision easier. People see what I do as a detective as black and white.

They think a justified shooting shouldn't impact me, because I did what I had to do. Did what was right."

Emily nodded, still too numb to fully feel the effects she knew would eventually hit her. "Today simply confirmed that all I want right now is to go back to my normal, boring life."

"I'm not sure I want to go back to mine," Avery said. "Every day I go out on the streets and try to clean up someone else's mess. Sometimes I get tired of digging inside a person's mind so I can see why they did what they did."

Emily waited for her sister to continue.

"Tess and I fought this morning, and I never had the chance to tell her I'm sorry. I think that is what's killing me the most. If anything happens to her . . . if I lose her without the chance to tell her how much I love her—"

"You're going to have that chance, Avery. Don't ever stop believing that."

"And if I don't?" She looked up at Emily. "I'm sorry. I just feel so out of control. I couldn't lead the investigation. I couldn't fix the situation. And now I've got a bullet hole in my leg and I'm tied to a stupid IV. All I can do is pray and trust that someone out there finds my baby, because I'm terrified. I can't lose her, Emily."

Emily pulled her sister to her, no longer able to stop her own tears. "We're not going to lose her, Avery. We're not going to lose her."

Mason eased his shirt back on after the doctor finished examining his side. They'd confirmed that there were no cracked ribs, only a few nasty bruises and the 9mm souvenir bullets he'd pulled out of his vest. A few inches another direction, and he'd be lying on an operating table right now.

God, so many things have gone wrong. So many people hurt.

Today reminded him of how sin had come into the world with Adam. But everything that happened today wasn't a reflection on God, but instead on man's decision to turn away from their Creator. And how turning away from his will affected everyone. Which was why he was worried about Emily. Today her world had been shaken to the core, and it wasn't something that any of them could fix or erase.

"You got lucky out there today, son." The older doctor's words pulled him out of his thoughts. "But even though the bullets didn't do any real damage, I'd still suggest you take it easy the next few days. You're going to be sore."

Tell me about it.

A moment later, he thanked the doctor, then headed for the third floor where Emily was. He wanted—needed—to see her. To make sure she was going to be okay, and to somehow try to help her through this. His phone rang as he stepped out of the elevator. He stopped at the edge of the waiting room where the reception was decent and took the call. It was the captain.

"Officers just found another body dumped," the captain began. "Same MO. Slit throat. Same ransom note stuck to the door of the victim's house. They're interviewing the family now."

The news hit like a punch to the gut. "They're sending us a message."

If they didn't get the money, Tess could be next.

"I think you're right, and Charlie's not going to be any help anytime soon. Doctors are giving him a fifty/fifty chance of pulling through. Our only other lead is to track down whoever was in the van with Mrs. Cerda, and we don't even know what he looks like." There was a short pause on the line, before the captain continued. "Which is why I want you to bring Emily in to the station for an official interview."

"I don't know if she's ready for that after what happened

today." Even though his first reaction was to protect her, he knew the captain was right.

"Emily knows Charlie better than anyone. She had to have seen something, met someone . . . anything that will give us another lead. Because all we've got right now is an unidentifiable suspect who's supposed to meet Charlie tonight."

Mason hung up, then found Avery's room. Emily was sitting beside her, their conversation intense.

She looked up after a minute, then joined him outside the room. Her expression mirrored his own fatigue, but there was still a tiny spark of determination in her eyes.

"What did the doctor say?" she asked.

"That today was my lucky day."

"I don't think luck had anything to do with it."

"I don't either."

He stood in front of her. Close enough for him to breathe in the subtle scent of her perfume, while trying to give her the space she needed.

"Any word on Charlie?"

"I just spoke with the captain." He hated having to be the one to tell her. "The doctors . . . they're not sure if he's going to make it, Emily."

He recognized the fear in her eyes because he understood what she was feeling. He remembered his own flashbacks, the guilt, and the constant second-guessing of what had happened the moment he pulled the trigger. He still had the occasional nightmare. It didn't matter that she'd had no choice, or that Charlie probably would have ended up killing all of them. There were always consequences when your moral beliefs clashed with reality.

"And there is something else," he said. "The captain asked that I bring you down to the station for an interview. You knew Charlie better than anyone else, and we still need answers."

"I don't know if I can."

Debriefing might be a part of the process, but he'd trained for this. She hadn't. She was only going to want to forget.

"You're not in any kind of trouble, Emily. I promise."

"I know, I just feel like I'm barely able to think right now, and to delve into everything again . . . Will you be there?"

"If you'd like me to."

She nodded.

"You understand that this is simply to try and find Tess. You've been through so much today, but you're strong. And even more importantly, there are people praying for you and your family. You're not in this alone, Emily."

Her faith was what would keep her going in the days to come when the numbness left and reality hit full force.

"Okay." She drew in a deep breath and looked up at him. "I'll do it. For Tess."

CHAPTER
31

Emily sat down on the offered metal chair in the interrogation room and gripped the seat with her fingers. Seeing her sister had brought home further the reality of today. The numbness had spread through her, though apparently not enough to completely mask the pain.

She slid off her coat that someone had brought from the safe house. The room seemed warm. Too warm. Maybe she was coming down with something. Or maybe it was just the combined stress from today . . . and knowing today's stress was far from over. She wished she could go back to this morning and start over again. Before Rafael had decided to walk into her classroom with a gun. Before Tess had vanished. Before she'd shot Charlie.

Mason reached for her coat, hung it on a hook on the wall behind him, then handed her one of the bottles of cold water he'd been carrying. "Can I get you anything else? If you're hungry—"

"No. I'm fine. Thank you."

He was feeling guilty. She could see it in his eyes. But while part of her wanted to escape, she knew she had to do this.

He sat down across from her. "You're not in any trouble over what happened today in the parking lot. You understand that, don't you?"

She nodded, thankful he was here. Surprised at how her

thoughts kept flipping back to the moment he'd tried to kiss her. Maybe it was just her mind looking for a diversion from the nightmare unfolding around her, but her heart told her it was more than that. Her gaze shifted to his chest. She was so grateful he was alive. It was a miracle the bullets hadn't caused more damage. Now she was praying for another miracle.

"You know why we're here." Mason sat down across from her. "We need to ask you some questions about Charlie so we can find your niece, because we believe he's connected not only to the man who was in the van manipulating Rafael but to Tess's disappearance. We can't question Charlie until he wakes up—and time is running out."

She nodded. If he woke up. The last report twenty minutes ago hadn't been good. Complications had sent Charlie back to the operating table.

"What about the man who texted Charlie in the parking lot? Can they find him?"

"He used a burn phone, so the call can't be traced."

"And the van?" she asked. There had to be a connection.

"The CSI team found fingerprints, but we still don't know who they belong to."

Panic was setting in. Tess was missing, time slipping away, and all they had were a bunch of dead ends. She put her elbows on the table and started rubbing her pounding temples, digging for any remaining threads of strength.

"Can I get you some Tylenol?"

She shook her head. "They gave me something at the hospital."

She'd refused the offer to take something stronger that would help her sleep. As much as she'd prefer not to face what was happening, giving in to sleep at this point would only delay the inevitable. Except at the moment, she felt like she'd just walked into Rafael's shoes. Everyone demanding information out of her she didn't have. She didn't want to relive her past with Charlie, but if finding Tess meant stepping back into the past, she would have to find a way to cope.

I need you to help me through this, Jesus. Help me cope. Help me remember.

She grabbed a package of tissues from her purse, blew her nose, and then nodded. "What do you need to know?"

Carlos cleared his throat across from her. Apparently she wasn't the only person in this room feeling uncomfortable. "You're here because you probably knew Charlie better than anyone else."

She'd thought that . . . until today. "Charlie was the kind of guy who knew everyone, but you're right. He didn't have a lot of close friends. Work always came first."

"Did you ever sense that something wasn't right? That he could have been involved in something illegal?"

"Never."

"So your breakup didn't have anything to do with your doubting his integrity?" Carlos asked.

"No." Emily shifted in her chair, wishing Carlos's questions weren't so straightforward. Clinical. "I didn't call off the wedding because I thought he was a dirty cop, or involved in some kind of illegal activity, if that is what you mean. I loved him, but in the end, it came down to the fact that I felt that something was missing from our relationship. And it wasn't just him." It was that something that couldn't be marked off on a checklist. She looked down, avoiding Mason's gaze. "I realized I'd said yes to his proposal for the wrong reasons."

Carlos scribbled on the paper in front of him, even though every word she said was being recorded. "Can you explain?"

Emily tapped her nails against the table. Two of her nails were chipped. She had an appointment to have them redone Saturday morning. Somehow it didn't seem important anymore. "Charlie was—is—a charmer. He came in and swept me off my feet. It's still hard for me to pin down my reason, but I've learned that sometimes the desire to get married can become more important than the person you're marrying. My friend Grace was planning her wedding at the time, and I got caught up in the idea of being married, instead of making sure our relationship was grounded in the right things."

"And his reaction when you called off the wedding?"

"He was . . . upset." Emily picked at one of the chipped nails, feeling exposed and vulnerable at the question. "I tried to make him understand, but I'm not sure he ever did."

"When you say upset, was he ever resentful, vindictive, or angry after your breakup?"

"I . . ."

An unexpected wave of panic washed over her. She could still see him so clearly. Lying in the parking lot. Snow falling. Blood pooling beneath him. She'd caught the fear in his eyes. Felt his hand gripping her arm when she'd tried to ask him about Tess.

I don't know what to do here, Jesus. I thought I was a good judge of character.

"I know this is hard." Mason leaned forward, the concern in his eyes obvious. "We just need to consider every angle."

"No. He never seemed angry. Just quiet. Hurt."

"What about his family?"

"His mother lives in an assisted-living complex in northern Florida near his sister."

"Are they close?"

"He flew down to see them a couple times a year. His father died about five years ago."

"What does his sister do?"

"She works for a real estate company."

"Did you ever meet her?"

"Once. She had a second trip planned, but canceled when the wedding was called off."

Carlos jotted down another note before looking back up at her. "Did Charlie ever talk to you about going away? Disappearing?"

You could have come with me, Em. We would have been free. Just you and me.

"In the parking lot today . . . when the officers were trying to get the bleeding to stop . . . he started babbling about how we could have gone away together with the money."

Another memory resurfaced. Charlie had taken her out to dinner at one of her favorite restaurants for her birthday. She'd been wearing a pink vintage cocktail dress she'd impulsively bought online. "There was another time." Had the signs been there all along? "He asked me if I'd ever thought of getting away from it all and moving overseas to some exotic locale like Argentina or Madagascar. I laughed, dismissing the idea as nothing more than idle talk. I reminded him that I was a southern girl, through and through, and while I enjoyed traveling, living overseas wasn't on my bucket list. At the time, I didn't take his comments seriously."

Emily wrapped her fingers around the water bottle. Questioning people might work for their line of work, but she needed to see things from a different angle. "Can I ask a couple questions?"

Carlos glanced at Mason. "Of course."

"You said Avery's office and possibly her home was bugged?"

"Ben Jacobs confirmed he put a bug in her house."

"My sister was determined to prove Michael wasn't the department mole. What if he realized she was about to figure out the truth? That Charlie was the leak, not Michael."

Mason nodded. "Charlie feared he was going to get caught, knew he needed to disappear, and saw the ransom opportunity as his last chance to cash in."

"Except from the very beginning things didn't go as planned." Her mind organized the situation like the World History timeline hanging on her classroom wall. "Charlie was the department negotiator and assumed he would be in control of the situation. And he would have been until you told the captain you knew Rafael and believed you could get through to him. Things continued to go wrong when I told you I believed Rafael was being controlled."

"He panics, realizing that his plans are falling apart."

Carlos tapped his pen against the desk. "Faking Rafael's death was Charlie's idea. He convinced the captain it was the only way to keep him safe."

"Why?" Emily asked.

"I'm assuming he saw Rafael as a loose end and thought he'd have more control at a safe house than the station."

"Rafael told me he saw a man watching him when he picked up the gun at the park," Emily said. "Said he thought he could identify him, which wasn't proof of involvement, but it might have brought up questions."

"Or," Mason added, "he might have thought Rafael knew where the rest of Eduardo's drug money was. He'd already sent Ben Jacobs to search for it in the Cerda apartment, so he believed the boy had it."

Emily drew in a slow, deep breath. If Charlie died, they might never know.

"Looks like another kink in Charlie's plan was the safe house." Mason leaned back in his chair, arms folded across his chest. "Since I knew Rafael, the captain assigned me to take you to the safe house and question him, which cut his access to Rafael. He realized he wasn't going to get his money. His partner was on the run—either about to get caught or had been caught—but he still had his eye on that two million, and he wasn't going to let it slip away. So he took a chance and grabbed Tess."

"Which brings us back to the man in the van," Emily said. "We can hope he knows where Tess is, because right now, besides Charlie, he's our only connection."

But they had no idea where the man was. Which meant no matter how they looked at the situation, they were still going in circles.

"Let's go back to the attack at the safe house," Carlos said. "If he was an associate of Charlie, there's a chance you've seen him before. Was there anything familiar about him?"

"I don't know. He wore a ski mask and long sleeves."

Emily closed her eyes. She didn't want to relive the feel of his grip on her shoulder. His warm breath against her skin. There had been something familiar about him, but she couldn't place him. All she did know was that if it hadn't been for Rafael, he would have killed her.

She felt her pulse speed up and she reached for the water bottle Mason had given her, trying to relax. She twisted open the cap and took a couple gulps.

"Think, Emily. He's our only link to Tess right now." Mason reached out and grasped her hand. "Did he have any identifying features? Anything—"

She jerked her hand away and shook her head. "I'm sorry, but I can't do this anymore, because I don't know. I just don't know."

Mason signaled to Carlos. "Give us ten minutes alone."

CHAPTER 32

Emily's gaze dropped. Guilt surfaced. She thought she could do this. She thought she could walk in, tell them everything she knew about Charlie, and in turn help them find Tess. She'd imagined herself in her sister's shoes, playing the role of the hero who swept in and saved the day. She'd just never imagined it would be emotional.

"I knew this would be hard, but—"

"You don't have anything to be sorry about. You just need a break. No recorders. No videos."

She fought back the tears, avoiding Mason's gaze. "I'm still trying to absorb everything. I trusted Charlie. Promised to marry him. I don't know how I didn't see the truth behind who he really was."

He sat patiently across from her, waiting for her to pull herself together. She wanted him to wake her up and tell her she'd been having a bad dream. That this was somehow just one big mistake. But life didn't work that way. Sometimes bad things happened and you had to stick around and pick up the pieces.

"I know this is hard, but I've watched you today." Mason reached across the table and took her hands. This time she didn't pull away. "You faced a tough situation and didn't panic. You held that classroom together today for those kids. They're safe largely because of you."

"Tess isn't."

"We're going to find her."

He held on to her hands, rubbing her palms with his thumbs. She'd come to look at him in a new light today. He'd become more than just the man who'd become a solid, secure presence in her life. More than a place of safety in the midst of a storm. He possessed that something she'd never been able to quantify on a checklist. Become the man she wanted to get to know. But he'd brought her here to help him figure things out. Not to let distractions tug on her or to fall apart because she'd been betrayed. She needed to focus. For Tess.

She drew in a deep breath and fought to hold on to her remaining reserve of strength. "I have more questions about what happened today."

"Okay."

"Who do they think was in that van manipulating Rafael?"

"The lab just confirmed that the fingerprints belong to a Mexican drug cartel agent."

She pressed her lips together, wishing she'd paid as much attention to work-related conversations between Avery and her father as she did to grading term papers. "So what did Charlie have to do with him?"

"The cartel pays millions every month for corrupt cops to look the other way, and unfortunately their bribes aren't limited to officials south of the border."

If she hadn't seen what Charlie had done in the mall parking lot, she never would have believed he was capable of this kind of betrayal. But those were feelings she'd have to deal with later.

"We're still trying to put all of the pieces together," Mason continued, "but we believe this agent was bribing Charlie in exchange for not reporting illegal cartel activities and helping to keep the department one step behind. The cartel agent is suspected to be involved in a string of unsolved murders your sister has been working on the past four months. He's new in the area, brutal and dangerous as he tries to gain more territory."

Emily worked to make sense of it all. "So he uses someone like Eduardo, who's been skimming money off the top of his profits, to teach a lesson—both to Eduardo and to those working for him."

"Exactly."

"This cartel agent. Why can't you bring him in?"

"We have a name and his fingerprints in at least three separate crimes, but we don't know what he looks like. We found the same fingerprints in the van, but there is no match in the system. These agents working for the cartel aren't US citizens, don't have visas, and are very good at going back and forth across the border undetected."

"What's his name?"

"He goes by a bunch of names. Scorpion, Fuego Rojo—or Red Fire—and Nerón."

Nerón.

A memory snapped to the forefront. "That name is familiar."

"Which one?"

"Nerón."

"What do you remember?"

Emily templed her hands in front of her, digging for the details. "It was a Saturday morning, a couple months before I called off the wedding, Charlie and I had arranged to meet for breakfast. I arrived thirty minutes early, thinking I'd order coffee and read, but Charlie was already there, talking with a man I'd never seen before."

"Was that strange?"

"Not really. Charlie was friends with half the community. What struck me as odd was the intensity of their conversation. I remember stopping halfway to their table, unsure of whether

I should interrupt or give them a few more minutes to talk, because I couldn't tell if they were fighting or just talking about something serious."

"What about the man? His build. Any distinguishing marks?"

"He was Hispanic. Short, but built solid, like he spent a lot of time working out. Five eight or nine. Broad shoulders. I heard Charlie call him Nerón. He left before I got to the table."

"Which makes him the same build and height as the man who attacked the safe house today."

"There was something else." Emily pressed her palms against the table and hesitated. "It's probably going to sound crazy, but I don't know that I would have even remembered him otherwise."

"Sometimes it's the smallest clue that ends up turning a case around."

"I don't know if I can explain it, because it was just a feeling. I even remember telling myself at the time that I was being silly. I knew Charlie had contacts—informants—who weren't exactly law-abiding citizens, but I also knew it was a part of his job. I figured this man was one of them. But as he left, he walked past me, and there was something about his eyes . . . It sounds stupid now."

"It's not stupid. What happened?"

"He looked at me as he walked past, and as he walked by, it was as if he could see right through me. I'll never forget his face. The restaurant temperature was set at seventy degrees plus, but I had chills running down my spine."

"Did you ever see him again?"

"No, and I never mentioned what happened to Charlie."

"So you don't know anything more about him."

Emily shook her head.

"But you could identify him if you saw him?"

"Definitely." Emily leaned forward, grasping on to the only lead they had at the moment. "It has to be him, Mason. The man in the van manipulating Rafael. The man who took Tess, then broke into the safe house. The man who's supposed to meet Charlie tonight. Have they figured out where he was planning to meet Charlie?"

"Tory thinks they were going to meet at the Black Tap. It's a neighborhood bar with suspected connections to the cartel. We're planning to take a team in there and try to find him."

Her mind was still spinning. "I could go there. Identify him."

"Whoa . . . slow down." Mason undid the lid to his water bottle and leaned back in his chair. "The Black Tap isn't a place you'd want to be, trust me."

"All I would have to do is sit in a corner and watch. I wouldn't have to come in contact with him."

"It's too risky. This man has already killed or ordered the deaths of four people we know of, which is probably just the tip of the iceberg."

She didn't feel brave or heroic, but if there was something she could do to help find Tess, she'd do it. "If the man I saw with Charlie is the same man, I can identify him, Mason. I can find who took Tess. No one else can do that."

He shook his head. "There is a problem. He would recognize you."

"Maybe, but you're an undercover cop. Don't you use disguises?"

"Sometimes, but—"

She shoved back the chair and headed for the door.

"Wait a minute, Emily. Where are you going?"

"I can't just sit around and do nothing." She turned back to him and caught his worried gaze. "We need to talk to Avery's team. I have an idea."

"Emily . . . wait."

Mason followed Emily into the bullpen where Avery's team was busy checking out leads on Tess's disappearance. The fear

he'd seen in Emily's eyes had been replaced with a stark determination, which scared him. She might come from a family of
cops, might be smart and capable, but taking on a man who
didn't think twice about torturing and dismembering an enemy
was a different thing altogether. And he was afraid he knew
exactly what her idea was.

"I believe I can ID your cartel agent."

Carlos leaned against his desk, arms folded across his chest,
his frown pronounced. "You've seen him?"

"Emily believes she saw him once while she was with Charlie," Mason said. "But we're not a hundred percent sure it's the
same person."

Carlos glanced at his watch. "We've already got a team planning to stake out the Black Tap tonight."

"But you can't identify him."

Mason shook his head. "You're not going in there, Emily.
It's too risky."

"It might be risky, but if I can identify him, it would be worth
it. He might know where Tess is, and as far as I know, he's our
only lead right now until Charlie gains consciousness." Emily
moved in front of Tory. "Avery once told me you were a genius
with disguises. If I go undercover, he'll never recognize me."

"It might work," Tory said. "We could change your hair
color, add a pair of glasses—"

"Undercover? Wait a minute." Mason frowned. This was not
going to happen. "No way. Maybe in a surveillance van, but she's
not going into that bar, Tory. She's a schoolteacher, and there's
a man out there who already tried to kill her. Let her pick him
out from a lineup, or from a video feed from the back of a van,
but she's not going into that bar."

"Excuse me." Emily held up her hand and turned back to
Mason. "In case you've forgotten, I'm standing right here. I want
to do this, and this is the easiest and quickest way."

"She has a point, Mason."

He still wasn't buying into this absurd idea and he knew the captain—and her father—would agree with him. "I know you're worried about your niece, but—"

"But what?" She folded her arms across her chest. "Do you have any other ideas to find Tess? I'm volunteering to go in there, with your team, sit down, and identify him. Nothing else."

Mason looked away, irritated over the fact that, absurd as it was, her logic was right. Time was running out and she was their only eyewitness at the moment. But he'd almost lost her today, and he didn't want to go there again.

His gut told him she could handle the situation. That she'd never be in direct contact with the man. Never be in danger. His heart told him otherwise. Told him to get her as far away from danger as possible. He caught the determination in her eyes and knew he wasn't going to win this round.

"We can't send you into the Black Tap dressed like that."

Emily looked down at her gray sweater dress and tights, still slightly damp from the snow. "Why not?"

"Have you ever been to the Black Tap?"

"No."

"It's not exactly located in the classiest part of town."

Carlos nodded. "He has a point. You'd stand out like a fish out of water."

"Which leads me back to my original protests of why I don't think you should go in there," Mason said.

"Avery was right, boys. You both forget that while I might be a white-collar crime expert, I have a few hidden talents from back in the day, and disguises are my specialty." Tory's smile broadened. "What do you say, Emily?"

"I say let's do it."

"Mason, clear it with the captain while I start working my magic."

———

Thirty minutes later, Emily glanced into the mirror, barely recognizing herself. The blonde wig, shoulder length and pulled back into a ponytail, completely covered her red hair. A pair of skinny jeans and a white tank top had been paired with a trendy jean jacket, cat-eye glasses, and leather boots. Definitely not her normal vintage look. Tory had even insisted on a fake flower tattoo running down the side of her neck to complete the look. Mama would cringe if she saw her like this.

"If you ever need a second career, you could make it in Hollywood." Emily spun around in front of the team. "My sister was right. You're good, Tory. Very good."

Mason put on an Atlanta Braves hat, then grabbed his leather jacket. "I have the go-ahead from the captain, but if you're really going to do this, there are a few rules."

"Fine." Emily tugged on the ponytail. Her own nerves were in a tight bundle, but this was something she knew she had to do. "You'll have my back. I'll be fine."

"You'll go in there with me as my date. As soon as you ID the man, I'm whisking you out of there. You don't make eye contact with him or speak to him. Nothing."

"I promise." Emily couldn't help but smile at his rules. There was something charming about the way he fretted over her. She could get used to his chivalry.

"One more thing. You'll be carrying a cell phone with a hidden audio transmitter . . . just in case."

She raised her brow, those bundled nerves trying to take over. "Just in case of what?"

"Think of it as an all-purpose safety net in case something goes wrong. It can be used like a tracking device in case we get separated, which we won't because you're not leaving my side."

"You don't think it will come to that, do you?"

"No, but there are never guarantees when dealing with criminals. I'll say this one last time. You don't have to do this. It's not too late to back out."

"I do have to do this. For Tess. For my sister . . . for myself."

He grabbed her hand and pulled her aside, giving them a measure of privacy. "I know what it's like to shoot someone. To feel guilty because you can never turn back the clock. Because you knew Charlie, that guilt will be multiplied. But you don't have anything to prove."

Emily dropped her gaze. She'd wanted to ignore it, but the guilt was there, trying to strangle her with its thick tentacles of doubt and fear.

"I mean it, Emily. I already see every one of those qualities within you. Determination, resolve, purpose . . . You don't have anything to prove."

"I know."

He put the cell phone in her hand and wrapped her fingers around it. "But I'm still not taking any chances."

"Okay."

He brushed back a strand of her wig. "In five minutes, we're meeting with the other officers involved to go over everything before leaving. I want you to know who's on the team, so you know who to run to if things go south."

Emily nodded, her stomach churning despite her proclaimed brave front.

"One more thing. I have my own set of rules."

"Your own set of rules?"

"My job is to keep you safe, so if you see him, remember—you will not make eye contact with him. You will not speak to him. If you end up needing the cavalry, the code word is 'snowman.' Because if anything happens to you—"

"Nothing's going to happen to me. I have you."

She smiled up at him, heart pounding, and it wasn't simply

because she was about to go on her first—and hopefully only—undercover gig.

He brushed his fingers across her hand. "Maybe when this is all over, you and I can go out . . . on a real date. I know this restaurant downtown I think you'd love. It's quiet and the food is fantastic."

"I'd like that."

"So would I."

Carlos cleared his throat, then handed Emily his phone, dragging her back to reality. "Your father wants to talk to you before we leave."

"Okay." Emily took a deep breath. "Daddy?"

"Hey, sweetie. I just received a briefing on what you're getting ready to do. You know you don't have to do this."

"I've already been told that at least a dozen times, but I need to do this. I'll be okay. How is Avery?"

"She's hoping to be released soon, but this has been rough on her. She's scared and can't do anything about it. Something she isn't handling well." There was a pause on the line. "As for you, be careful, Emily. If anything were to happen to you . . ."

"I'll be careful, and I know you'll be praying."

Emily hung up the phone. A minute later, Mason was making quick introductions to the team that would be there with them, instructing them about the plan. Carlos, Tory, Griffin, and three guys the captain had assigned to the stakeout—Gordon Britten, Russell Coates, and Randy Venetten.

Mason turned to Emily. "Are you ready?"

She drew in a deep breath and nodded. "Let's go."

CHAPTER
33

Emily drummed her fingers against the table, wondering how Mason could look so calm when her insides felt as if they were about to explode. Despite all of Tory's efforts, she was still convinced someone would notice she didn't blend in. Worried he would recognize her if he saw her.

She drew in a breath of heavy smoke. Someone was singing an off-key version of a Garth Brooks song, the music blasting so loud she could feel the pulse raging in her chest. Part of her wanted to run. The other part was still fighting to find the courage to stay and see this through. She took a sip of her lemonade and looked around the room, trying to look like her pasted-on smile was real because this was something she always did. Exposed brick walls held cockeyed photos and flashing neon signs. Waitresses served plates of food with little maneuvering room, over sticky floors. Customers played air hockey or threw darts between glasses of whatever local brew was being served. The Black Tap was a watering hole for the masses.

She turned back to Mason. "I hadn't expected it to be so . . . crowded."

Which had her worried. If she missed him, they'd be facing another dead end.

"Try Friday night when there's a live band onstage lighting up the scene."

She'd never considered herself snobby, but karaoke and cheap beer didn't exactly fall in the middle of her comfort zone. Besides that, the smell of stale booze, stale cigarette smoke, and greasy burgers was doing nothing to ease her growing headache. "Am I the only one who sees this entire situation as ironic?"

"Ironic how?" Mason dipped a fry into a pile of ketchup, then popped it into his mouth.

She leaned forward even though no one was paying attention to them or could overhear their conversation if they tried. Mason had warned her that even the surveillance they'd set up with the transmitter hidden in the cell phone in her jacket pocket was going to be tough, if not impossible, to follow due to the excessive noise around them.

"Ironic because I'm the daughter of a former police captain with zero desire to play the role of hero, who is now sitting in this ridiculous getup, at a somewhat disreputable local dive bar simply because I happen to be the only one who can recognize a wanted—and deadly, might I add—cartel agent."

"While you have a valid point, I have to disagree with at least one thing." He grabbed another fry, looking like he was on a date, not a stakeout. "I think you look rather hot in that getup, and that tattoo was definitely a nice touch."

"Hot?"

"Seriously, Tory did a good job with your makeover, though I'm having a bit of a hard time getting used to you as a blonde."

"You're not helping." She tried to shoot him a mean glare, but ended up laughing. "I was looking for sympathy, not encouragement."

"I don't know." He flashed her a smile. "Like I said, I think this look is good for you."

"You're awful."

He leaned forward. "Where would you rather be right now?"

She made another visual sweep of the room, trying to look relaxed. Never forgetting why she was here. The man's face was etched into her memory. "Sitting at home with a good book, dinner with a few close friends, shopping . . . pretty much anywhere but here. And you?"

"I guess over the years I've gotten used to having to go places out of my comfort zone, as well as learning how to blend in even when I don't feel comfortable."

"So why this?" She kept scanning the room, thankful that talking was helping to calm her fears. "Is it some kind of effort to save the world, or is it a sense of adventure you crave? The adrenaline rush?"

"Both, I suppose. I started out wanting to help kids like Rafael. Kids who were going down a similar route that I'd gone down. That, and I wanted to get drug dealers off the streets because I'd seen how it had affected my family." Mason popped the last fry into his mouth. "At first I thought I could rush in like Superman and save them all. Unfortunately, I found out quickly that it doesn't work that way."

"You've done that today."

"Today's not over. We still have someone else to save."

Tess.

Unlike him, she had no idea how to get rid of the fear. "What if I was wrong? What if I don't recognize him, or he doesn't show up? It's already past seven."

"Unless he found out about Charlie, he'll be here." He took her hand from across the table and laced his fingers between hers. "I know this isn't easy, but all you have to do is give the signal when you see him, then my team will whisk you away to safety. We're going to get him."

She nodded, but casting her burdens on the Lord always ended up being easier said than done.

Movement caught her eye near the front of the bar. Two men walked in, their gazes sweeping the room as if they were looking for someone. Nervous? Angry? She gulped in a breath of air. The one on the left was the same build, same ethnicity as the man she remembered. She just needed him to turn so she could see his face . . .

She let out the breath she'd been holding as he stared past her, nodded, then proceeded to a crowded table toward the back.

"Is that him?" Mason asked.

"No."

"Stakeouts are all about building your patience. He'll be here."

"I don't get it. How do you get rid of the fear—real or simply perceived—in a situation like this? I feel as if I'm drowning in it."

His hand squeezed her drumming fingers. "I'm not sure it's possible to always get rid of the fear. Not completely anyway. But you focus on what you're doing and hopefully the lives that will be saved because of it."

Emily could still feel the pressure of his fingers against the back of her hand as he pulled away to take a sip of his Coke. "I'm sure you've been through dozens of high-adrenaline situations, but the most nerve-racking my life ever gets is during a football game with our school's rival or final exams. I'm not used to having my life on the line."

Mason laughed. "Don't be so hard on yourself. Even seasoned cops can get flustered when they find themselves in a situation they shouldn't be in."

"I keep looking around the room, afraid even if he's here that I've missed him."

"Maybe you need a distraction."

Emily raised her brow in question. No matter what her sister believed about Mason, she liked him. He was attentive, strong, compassionate . . .

"What kind of distraction?" she asked.

"How about this. What's your favorite ice cream?"

"My favorite ice cream?"

He lowered his head, but his smile had broadened. "Go with me on this."

"Okay . . ." The man never failed to intrigue her. Once she found the time to step back from the situation, she wanted to contemplate how he'd managed to steal more than a corner of her heart throughout the course of the day. And she wasn't sure she wanted to take it back. "Favorite ice cream is cookie dough."

"Favorite kind of food?"

"Italian."

"Place to travel?"

"New York City."

"Interesting. I would have thought you were more of a country girl."

She couldn't help but smile. "Not at all."

"Favorite holiday?"

"Thanksgiving."

She felt her shoulders relax as she answered. Whatever he was doing was working. She caught the glimmer in his eye, alert to what was going on around them, yet seemingly relaxed at the same time.

"Movies?"

"Anything that ends with happily ever after."

"Biggest phobia?"

"I thought we were talking about happily ever after." She shot him a half smile. "Heights."

He wrinkled his nose. That dimple was back again. "So no sky diving?"

"Never." Her breathing had deepened, her pulse slowed. The distraction was working. "Now it's your turn."

"Okay."

"What's your biggest phobia?" she asked.

"Spiders."

She laughed. "You'll face a bullet, but you're afraid of a little spider?"

"I was bit by a black widow when I was six and ended up in ICU. I've hated anything with eight legs ever since."

"Ouch. Can't blame you for that. Okay, what's your favorite sport?"

"Basketball."

"Movie genre?"

"Action."

"Pet?"

"German shepherd. We had one growing up, but had to give it away when we moved. Someday I plan to get another one."

"Really? I found one online this past weekend that I'm planning to adopt once I find a house." She drew in a deep breath, then let it out slowly as he caught her gaze. She liked getting to know him. Liked him. Liked the fact that they had things in common and how comfortable she felt with him no matter what happened to be raging around them.

"See." He nudged her with his elbow. "It worked."

"Yeah, I'm as relaxed as I can be while sitting in a rowdy pub as the only one who can ID a murderer." She laughed and felt her cheeks flush. Her response had nothing to do with the situation they were facing and everything to do with the man sitting across from her. "But you're right. I feel better."

"How about some dessert?"

"You're kidding, aren't you?"

"No. One thing I've learned in my job is to eat when you can.

You never know when you might get stuck with nothing more than a stale power bar and a lukewarm water bottle."

"I'll pass." She managed to finish another lemonade, but her stomach couldn't handle any more food. "Somehow I don't think I'm going to go hungry in the next couple hours."

She eyed the now empty plate sitting in front of him—some kind of five-alarm burger packed with chilies and jalapeños. He'd devoured that after a plate of nachos, while she'd barely managed to eat more than a couple bites of her shrimp platter. Unlike Mason, stakeouts and food weren't a good combination in her book. And from the looks of it, she should have brought a bottle of antacids for him.

He grabbed one of her fried shrimps. "They've got chocolate brownies and ice cream. Come on. I'll split one with you."

"Go ahead. I'll pass. Besides, I need to go to the bathroom." The laughter in his eyes faded. "Can't you wait?"

"No." She shrugged a shoulder. "I drink a lot when I'm nervous, and tonight I'm very nervous."

"Looks like you should have stopped at the third jumbo glass." He glanced toward the back of the smoky room where a narrow hallway led to the restrooms and frowned. "I'm not sure that's the best idea."

"You have this place surrounded. I don't think I have anything to worry about." She caught the hesitation in his expression. "I'm the one who's supposed to be worried tonight, remember? I'll be fine."

"I'll come with you."

Now he was getting ridiculous. "You're not coming with me—"

"It's a decision not up for debate. It's a single-stall bathroom. You go in, lock the door behind you, and I'll be waiting outside."

He signaled at their waiter to bring them a plate of brownies and ice cream, then took her hand as they made their way through the restaurant.

She studied people as they walked past crowded tables, trying to appear uninterested. Couples sat at cozy tables or hovered around the bar. She stepped back into the darkened hall where the restrooms were located, suddenly grateful for his presence.

He squeezed her hand, then let go, before checking to ensure the bathroom was empty. "This will all be over soon. I promise."

CHAPTER
34

Emily locked the door of the one-stall bathroom behind
her, then braced both arms against the sink. She closed
her eyes for a moment and drew in a slow breath. She'd hoped
it would be quieter in here so she could think, but instead a
speaker blasted music from the bar. Not that she really wanted
to think. Or remember. The sick feeling in the pit of her stomach
had yet to disappear.

She hadn't wanted to tell Mason that her escape from their
table had been more than just drinking too much lemonade.
Despite his efforts to calm her, she still struggled to breathe.
Struggled to stop her heart from pounding in her throat.

She splashed water onto her face. All she really wanted right
now was to identify the man they were after so she could leave.
And he would come. He had to come. Because he was their only
lead to Tess. Which was why she needed to pull herself together
so she could go back out there and find the man behind all of
this. She grabbed a paper towel to blot her face, then looked
back into the mirror.

Emily felt her stomach drop. Felt the sharp surge of adrena-
line hit. He stood behind her, his image reflected in the mirror.
Hat, black-rimmed glasses, deep shadow across his jaw . . .
But it was the eyes she recognized. His arm snaked around her

shoulders, knife pressed against her throat. All before she'd had a chance to react.

He shook his head, warning her.

"Don't make a sound." The blade of the knife glinted in the mirror's reflection. "I don't know about you, but I've always liked knives better than guns. They're quiet, while just as deadly."

Panic swallowed her. This was no random mugging. He recognized her. Had come for her. She could tell in the slight curl of his lips. The satisfaction in his eyes. The same eyes that were still able to look straight through her. A chill ripped down her spine. Mason had been right to be concerned about her safety. She never should have left that table.

The window behind the stall banged in the wind where he'd entered the room. This wasn't supposed to happen.

Mason's right outside the door, Emily. A few more minutes and he'll come busting in here to save you . . .

Nerón pulled her phone from her jacket pocket, shut the sink drain, and turned on the faucet. Emily watched the lifeline disappear under the water. So much for the distress word. The officer listening would simply think she was standing too close to the faucet.

Which left her with one other option. To scream. But if she did that, it would still take Mason seconds to break down the door. She caught the intent in Nerón's eyes. She'd be dead before she hit the tiled floor.

"Your boyfriend thinks he's smart. Another uppity cop trying to save the world. Thinks he out there protecting you. That you're safe." Nerón's smoky breath against her face made her want to vomit. "At least he lets you get out and play." *Oh God, please . . . don't let me die this way.*

She stood perfectly still. Needing to keep him talking. Needing time to think. "You were at the safe house."

"Yes."

The man shifted his weight. Lowering her eyes, she could just see the patch of blood seeping through his pant leg. He'd been shot and patched up. Which might prove to be her one and only advantage. Because this was no simulation. Her father had insisted she take self-defense classes. There she'd learned that no matter what they showed on television, escaping without injury from a determined attacker with a knife pressed against your throat was virtually impossible. Add to that, he had at least thirty pounds on her, and he'd killed before.

"You play hard." He pressed his mouth closer to her ear. "You and your friend who gave me the nasty bump on my head."

He slid the side of the blade against her skin. Her chest heaved, lungs ready to burst. This wasn't Rafael, trying to save his mother's life by holding a class hostage. This man was an agent for the cartel, who hadn't thought twice about murdering two agents earlier today. Who would have no qualms about killing her.

She swallowed the bile rising in her throat. "Nerón . . . or should I call you by one of your aliases. Scorpion or Rojo Fuego?"

He caught her gaze in the mirror. "They're good names, aren't they. Shows the fear people have in regard to me."

"Maybe that's true . . . Nerón . . . but it's over."

His laugh pierced through her. "Apparently, you've forgotten one thing."

"What?"

"That I clearly hold the advantage. Though, I almost missed you with this blonde wig and glasses. Clever. Thought you could slip in safely, identify me, and be home for supper."

"How did you know I was going to be here?"

"Charlie might be currently indisposed, but he isn't the only one in my pocket. And I can't exactly leave alive my only witness."

Emily's jaw tensed. "What do you want?"

His lips curled into a smile. "To watch you die."

"Emily?" Mason's voice sounded from outside the room.

Nerón pressed the knife into her flesh, allowing a trickle of blood to run down her neck. "Tell him just a minute, and he better wait, because if he comes in, you're dead."

She was as good as dead anyway.

Emily forced herself to ignore the pain and the rising panic. "Just a minute, Mason. My stomach's upset."

Emily stared at her reflection. He was enjoying toying with her. The trail of blood running down her neck dripped onto her white tank top. After everything that had happened today, she was about to die by the hands of the man who started all of this. A silent killing. Easy escape out the bathroom window. He'd been behind the kidnappings and murders. Behind the distribution of drugs that leaked poison into its users. Young men like Eduardo. She might not be able to stop them all, but she had to find a way to stop this one.

Show me the way out, Jesus . . .

She had to keep it together. To think straight. Mason was close. She had to find a way to communicate with him. But she still had one more question.

"Where's Tess?"

"Your niece?"

"You took her. Where is she?"

"Funny thing is, if you hadn't shot Charlie, I would have."

"Why?"

"Charlie was a fool. He thought he'd found a way to keep both shares of the money by taking her behind my back."

So he really didn't know?

She forced her mind to concentrate. If this was going to end, she needed to find an advantage. Something that would slow his response time. She stared at him in the mirror. He was cocky and wanted to savor her death, but he'd been shot. Beads of sweat glistened across his forehead. His hand shook. He was in pain. She had to find a way to take advantage of that pain.

Someone banged on the bathroom door.

Nerón glanced away. Emily reacted in that split second. She kicked his injured leg as hard as she could with her heel, while shoving his hand away from her throat. Nerón groaned and dropped to his knees. The bathroom door slammed against the wall behind them. Officers swarmed into the room, dragging him away from her. Mason threw him against the wall and handcuffed him.

Tory pulled her out of the bathroom and into the hallway, her eyes on Emily's neck. "Are you all right? Your transmitter went out so we decided to move in."

Emily could only nod. She wiped her hands against her neck, then looked down at the red stain on her fingers, terrified at how close she'd come to dying. Tory grabbed a square of gauze from a first-aid kit and pressed it gently against the cut. Someone shouted, music blared, incandescent lights above her flickered, but Emily could only think of one thing.

Charlie isn't the only one in my pocket.

"Wait." Emily stepped back into the bathroom where they were reading his rights to the man who'd almost killed her. He'd known she was going to be here. She reached into his jacket pocket, avoiding his piercing gaze, and pulled out a cheap burner phone. She redialed the last called number.

A phone rang behind her.

She looked to Mason, then to the source of the call. "Charlie wasn't the only mole."

Russell Coates started to run, but it was already too late. Officers had him handcuffed before he could even consider pulling his gun. Emily slid down the wall until she was sitting against the tile floor, as they led the two men out of the hallway. Numbness had completely set in.

Mason sat down beside her. "I don't think I've ever been so scared. I'm so sorry . . . so sorry I wasn't there. I never should have let you go in there."

She took his hand and looked up at him. "This wasn't your fault."

"I should have anticipated a second leak."

Her legs shook beneath their clasped hands. "He was going to kill me. Just like the others. Said I could recognize him. But that wasn't everything he told me."

"What else did he tell you?"

"He told me he doesn't know where Tess is. That Charlie took her on his own, intending to keep all the ransom money. I think he was telling the truth."

"Charlie's still unconscious."

"What now? The temperature outside is dropping. She might not make it till morning."

He wrapped his arm around her and pulled her against him. "They're still out there looking. They won't stop until they find her."

She drew in a slow breath. She felt like she was in a tunnel. Dark with no light. She paused and turned around to face Mason, her heart skittering within her chest.

The tunnels.

"What if Tess never left the school?"

"What do you mean?"

"I can't believe I didn't think of this before, but it was so long ago." Emily sat up straight. She had to be right. "Avery and I went to high school at Dogwood Academy. Charlie did too. He was three years ahead of me, so I didn't really know him back then."

"Okay . . ."

"There are tunnels beneath some of the buildings. Not many people know the story, but sections of the original buildings were once used as a mental health hospital."

"I remember hearing about the hospital, but the tunnels . . . what were they for?"

"The tunnels were used as a morgue during a yellow fever outbreak, and to hide runaway slaves during the Civil War."

"That's quite a story."

"It's not just a story. Those tunnels really exist."

She definitely had his attention now. "There wasn't anything mentioned about them on the blueprints."

"I'm not surprised. They've been closed for decades and most people think they're nothing but a ghost story, but I went in them once. Years ago. I took a stupid dare from a group of friends."

There was a hint of surprise in Mason's eyes. "Somehow you don't seem like the type to take a dare."

"Let's just say that I had nightmares for weeks after that, convinced I was going to come down with yellow fever—which probably would have been a better option than if my father had found out." Emily pressed down the memories. "The bottom line is that it's possible Tess never left the school grounds."

CHAPTER
35

Emily's heart felt as if it were about to explode. She led Mason and two uniformed officers down the familiar stone path toward Chalkley Music Hall, feet crunching on the snowy path while old memories forced their way to the surface. She'd been thirteen. Her best friend's brothers decided to amuse themselves that Friday night by daring Julia and her to spend thirty minutes inside the tunnels. She'd never been sure why she'd agreed to the dare, because she'd been forced to suppress the haunting memories ever since.

"Emily?"

She felt something rub against her and jumped. Mason stood beside her, his hand resting gently on her arm.

"I'm sorry."

"Don't be. We're going to find her."

"I know."

"You shouldn't be out here." He caught her gaze, worry clear in his expression. "Your heart is racing and you feel hot, even though it's barely thirty degrees out here."

"It's more than just today's ordeal." She swallowed hard, not wanting to remember.

"Tell me about the dare."

"It was stupid." She tried to catch her breath, hating the

waves of vulnerability wrapping themselves around her. Back then she'd thought it would prove she wasn't a coward. That she was more than the Goody Two-shoes daughter of the captain. "I've never been so terrified in my life."

"How long were you down there?"

"A couple hours. Michael found me. I was shaking from the cold and spouting off promises that I'd never do something so stupid again. I also realized that I'd never come up with the courage my father, sister, and brother carried with them."

"You've shown enough courage today to make up for a lifetime." Mason rubbed her arms. She was shivering again. "Emily, I want you to show us the entry, then go back to the school and wait for us. That's all you have to do—"

"No." She shook her head. "If Tess is down there, I want to be with you when you find her."

His hand wrapped around hers. "You don't have to go down there."

Emily drew in a deep breath. "Please let me. For Tess."

She shoved aside the memories and looked up at the second story of the Greek Revival–style house. Fifty years ago, under the supervision of a restoration architect who insisted on keeping the period lighting, pine flooring, and stained-glass windows, the building had been completely renovated. Even the long veranda was still framed by old shade trees. But today, instead of doctors and their dying patients, the hall was filled with a grand piano, violins, and other instruments—not the haunting voices of patients long since forgotten.

Emily led them around the side of the building. The snow had stopped falling, but in its place a gray, hazy fog hung amongst bare, ghostly trees. After her own experience in the tunnels, she'd read about their construction. The passageways had been constructed out of granite from a quarry started at Stone Mountain in the 1830s. Railroads had extended the granite's reach from Atlanta to the locks of the Panama Canal to Tokyo.

But it was what lay deep inside the tunnel walls that had her feeling panicked. At thirteen, she'd taken a wrong turn and gotten lost. Or maybe it had been nothing more than fear that had paralyzed her into believing she was lost. Either way, she hadn't been able to find her way out.

"Where's the opening?" Mason's question dragged her back to the present.

She walked along the side of the hall, around the veranda. It had to be there somewhere, but it had been so many years ago. So many years of suppressing the fear of that night.

But she wasn't thirteen anymore. And Mason was with her.

The rough edge of one of the stones caught her eye. "There."

"It looks as if it's been opened recently." Mason pushed on the stone, then aimed his flashlight down the hole as the slab creaked open. "You sure about this?"

She nodded.

The musty smell of mold greeted her as she stepped onto the narrow staircase behind Mason. Damp walls. Dark shadows. Air as thick as her memories. A rat scurried by. Emily pressed her lips together. If Tess was down here, she was going to be terrified.

Mason's flashlight flickered. He whacked it against his palm until the light brightened again. The night she'd been in the tunnels had been different. The battery on her flashlight had died, leaving her in pitch darkness. Julia had run. Emily had been too afraid to move.

"What do you remember about the tunnels?" Mason asked.

She forced herself to stay in the present. "They spread out under the building like a maze."

Plenty of corridors for dumping the dead bodies yellow fever had claimed.

"How many ways are there to get in?"

"As far as I know, only one, but I can't be certain. I've heard rumors that there's an entrance from one of the back rooms of the hall. There was also supposed to be one leading to the cottage located behind us, but that building was torn down a number of years ago, and from what I understand, no tunnels were ever found. I'm guessing if there once were tunnels linking the two buildings, they caved in years ago."

"Then we'll focus here for now, but we need to split up." He motioned to the other officers. "Stay in contact via your radios."

"Yes sir."

Emily took the first corridor to the left with Mason, lit only by the light of his flashlight against the stone walls. They took the next right. Past dusty piles of trash and scribbled writing on the wall.

Mason's radio crackled. "We just found Officer Reed, sir. She's dead."

Emily's chest heaved. For a moment, she was thirteen again. Terrified. And certain she'd never escape the darkness of the tunnels. "If he killed Tess too . . ."

"Don't go there, Emily. We're going to find her."

The beam of Mason's flashlight caught movement ahead.

"Tess?"

"Aunt Emily!"

She started running toward Tess, who sat on the ground at the end of one of the widened corridors, hands tied behind her.

Emily dropped onto her knees and cupped Tess's tear-streaked face before pulling her niece into her arms. "It's over, sweetie. It's finally over."

CHAPTER
36

Emily sat down on her mother's beige linen sofa beside her father, while Mason and Avery—who had finally been released from the hospital—took the matching wing chairs across from them. Her mother's tastes had always been too eccentric for her, as she'd taken her love for southern charm and spread it thicker than a buttered biscuit, preferring heavy furniture, damask wallpaper, and flashy chandeliers. Emily's preferences, on the other hand, ran more toward simple, natural wood and fabrics.

But Charlie was the main reason they were here. The thought of what he had done made her feel dizzy. Nauseated. She had watched Charlie shoot Mason. Had seen them slip Charlie into the back of the ambulance. But her mind still refused to believe the truth. Somehow Charlie had been behind everything that had happened today.

Her father took her hand. "I don't know how else to tell you, Emily, other than straight out. I received a briefing from the captain thirty minutes ago. Charlie didn't make it."

The air whooshed out of Emily's lungs. She grabbed one of her mother's damask throw pillows and pulled it hard against her chest. She shouldn't care Charlie was gone. Shouldn't feel the gut-wrenching pain that threatened to tear up her insides.

Her father squeezed her hand. "Emily?"

She drew in a deep breath. "I'll be okay."

The emotions of the day magnified her reaction, but it was more than that. He'd betrayed and used her. It felt strange that the death of someone she clearly hadn't known was affecting her. She couldn't help but wonder what might have been if things had been different. Wondering if she could have done something to stop what had happened today.

Emily's foot tapped against the bamboo flooring. "Did he ever say why?"

"I'm not sure we'll ever know all the reasons, " her father said, "but one of the officers was able to question him briefly before he went into surgery. He confessed he was the department leak and knew he was about to be caught, so he came up with the crazy idea of using Rafael in a hostage situation, then somehow managed to talk Nerón into pulling it off with him. When things started falling apart, he panicked and grabbed Tess. It will take us awhile to figure out all the details, including verifying that Russell was the only one working with him."

So Charlie had used her to get what he wanted, probably never intending to go through with the marriage. She'd been a love-struck fool who'd fallen for his charm, because in dating her, he'd been given access to the house, her dad's office, giving him the edge he needed.

"There is some good news," her father continued. "Doctors believe Eduardo will make it. Also, with the arrests of Nerón and several of his associates, agents were able to confiscate one and a half tons of drugs along with cash and weapons. It's just a matter of time before charges will be brought against him as well for the murders of James Torres, Ivan Cruz, Dante Ortiz, Adan Luna. Thanks, to a great degree, to Emily."

"I told you that you did well, Sis. You might not be a cop, but if you're ever up for the challenge, I'd hire you on my team in a second."

Emily chuckled at the thought. "Trust me, there's not a chance of that happening. Ever."

Avery smiled at her response, but her smile quickly faded as she shifted gingerly in her chair and turned to Mason. "While it doesn't seem adequate, I owe you an apology. I was so focused on finding out the truth behind Michael's death that I played right into Charlie's hand too. You deserved better than that. You were Michael's best friend. You'd saved his life more times than I can count. I should have trusted you no matter what the evidence said."

"You're trained to follow the evidence. There was no way for you to know."

"But I was still wrong. Charlie also confessed he planted false evidence, knowing I'd go after it, to take the pressure off himself."

"And Michael?" Emily asked. "What about his innocence?"

"I'm praying we'll finally be able to prove, once and for all, he wasn't involved."

Emily wanted to ask more questions, but the fatigue in her sister's eyes mirrored her own. "Tess needs you, and you need some sleep."

Avery nodded. "She's with Mama right now, but she's afraid to sleep. Being around family is helping, but I'm still worried about her."

Her father stood up and squeezed Avery's shoulder. "All my girls have been through a lot, but your sister's right. You need to be with your daughter *and* follow the doctor's orders to get some rest. We'll get through this together."

"I'm not going to argue. I'm exhausted." Avery got up slowly out of the chair, wincing at the movement. "We'll talk more tomorrow, Sis."

"And Emily . . ." Her father bent down and kissed her forehead. "You've always made me proud, but today you went beyond the call of duty. You put your life on the line and brought justice. I'm proud of you."

"Thank you."

Her father cleared his throat, then smiled at Mason. "I'm guessing the two of you have a few things to talk about. I'll see you both tomorrow."

Mason nodded. "Good night, sir."

"Good night, Daddy."

Mason moved to sit beside her on the couch. She wanted him with her, but her emotions still felt raw. To realize her relationship with Charlie had been based purely on lies pointed to her lack of judgment.

"I won't stay long, but what can I do?" he asked.

"I don't know." Her legs wouldn't stop shaking. She was still trying to take everything in. "Somehow the fact that I broke things off with him should mean it doesn't matter, but to realize he was simply using me . . . How is it possible that all of this wasn't real and I didn't see it?"

Mason mulled over Emily's question. He didn't want to believe that Charlie's death could affect what had happened between them today, but he knew it had. She'd trusted Charlie. Loved him. Finding out he betrayed her was going to take a long time to forget.

"I honestly don't have an answer for that, Emily."

"Like with you and your father, somehow I'm going to have to find a way to forgive what he did."

Her statement caught Mason off guard. It was easy to focus on Emily and her situation. To encourage her to let go so she could heal. Talking about his own issues was a whole other thing. He grappled with what he wanted to tell her.

Because he'd never forgiven his father.

Emily brushed away a tear and shot him a wry grin. "Come

on, it's your turn now. I'm sitting here with swollen red eyes and smeared makeup, allowing myself to be completely vulnerable with you. The least you can do is remind me I'm not the only person in the world struggling with this issue."

He laughed in spite of the somber mood between them. "Don't worry. You're not."

"So . . ."

He took a deep breath. "I've never forgiven my father, and I've worn that unforgiveness like a badge."

He cringed at how vulnerable his own words sounded. Besides his brothers, he'd never spoken to anyone about his father. But he knew if he was going to keep Emily, he was going to have to be honest.

She grabbed a tissue off the end table and blew her nose. "My father always told me that forgiveness is a choice. A conscious decision to let go."

They'd both faced their demons today, and getting past them was going to take time. But nothing that had happened over the past few hours had changed what he was feeling toward her. It was all he could do to stop himself from pulling her into his arms and kissing her long and hard.

Emily pulled away, seeming to sense his thoughts. "I'm going to need some time to figure things out. Between Charlie, Rafael, and Tess . . . I'm just not sure which way is up. I'm not sure how to trust my heart and move forward . . . Yet."

"It's okay." He reached up and brushed away a tear sliding down her cheek. "I understand. I'm leaving in a few hours anyway."

She looked up at him and caught his gaze. Was that regret he saw? Longing? "When?"

"I've got the flight out to Colorado first thing in the morning. My father isn't going to live much longer. I need to be there for him and for my brothers."

"I'm glad you're going. I know you said you aren't close to your father, but if he dies and you're not there . . . you'll always regret it."

"I'm still not sure I want to go, and forgiveness might be a conscious decision, but it's a hard one as well. For my brothers' sake, if nothing else, I'll go and be there with them."

"It's the right decision."

"Maybe when I get back we can talk. About us."

He needed to know if she was feeling the same things he was. If she was open at all to this unexpected relationship he never would have dreamed possible before today. He wasn't willing to walk away because the situation was clouded with emotion.

She nodded. "I'd like that."

"Me too." No promises or guarantees, but at least she'd left an open door. "Are you going to be okay by yourself?"

"Yeah. I need to spend some time praying, trying to figure out what I'm feeling, while probably devouring a couple pints of cookie dough ice cream in the process." She grabbed another tissue from the end table and blew her nose. "But I'll be okay. Eventually. I just need time to process everything. I don't love Charlie anymore—that isn't even an issue—but that doesn't mean his betrayal doesn't hurt. Everything I thought we had was a lie . . . It makes me wonder about myself and how I can ever hope to be able to read other people."

He wanted to tell her that she could trust him. That he'd never do anything to hurt her. But today wasn't the day to do that. After what she'd gone through, it was going to take time for him to show her she could trust him.

"You don't need to apologize. Trust doesn't come easy when you've been betrayed."

"You understand, don't you?"

"My father wasn't there for me. There was a lot of hurt and rejection. Seeing him again is going to be very hard." He had a lot to learn about forgiveness. A heavenly Father had forgiven him. Surely he could learn to do the same. "Can I ask you to promise me one thing?"

She nodded, her eyes still brimming with tears.

"I've had feelings toward you for a long time, but the timing was never right, and maybe it won't be right again this time. But . . . when you're ready, if you're ready, to give us a chance, call me. I'll be waiting."

She nodded, reached out, and ran her hand down his arm. "Thank you. For everything."

"You're welcome, but you did pretty good yourself. You might not be a police officer, but your sister was right. I'd trust you to watch my back anytime."

Mason started to stand, then leaned forward and brushed her lips gently with his. Forward, maybe, but he couldn't help it. Emily Hunt had completely captured his heart.

He turned around, leaving the Hunt home like he'd done dozens of times in the past, but the next time he came back, he'd be returning to see the woman he was falling in love with.

CHAPTER
37

Mason parked his rental car outside the brick, ranch-style home in south Denver, hands resting against the steering wheel as he stared out the window. It had snowed last night, leaving a dusting of white powder across the front lawn. According to the news report he'd just picked up on one of the local stations, six more inches were expected over the next twenty-four hours. Bringing much needed new powder to the surrounding slopes.

But skiing wasn't on his agenda today. His father was inside. Dying. He'd heard from him twice over the past fifteen years. A wedding invitation from wife number two, and a death notice regarding his third wife. He'd ignored the correspondence, clearly sent out by someone who didn't know the situation. Didn't know that Nathanial Taylor had been anything but a father to the boys who carried his name on their birth certificates.

Memories surfaced, unsolicited. The day he'd found his mother overdosed on the couch. His brother Sam's funeral. The day he'd finally found the courage to leave home. His father wasn't in any of those memories.

Over the years he'd managed to bury the anger, pain, and loss, but this morning there was no escaping the past and the wall that had built up between them. Somehow he was going to have to find a way over, under, or around it if he was going to walk through the front door.

Mason stepped out of the car, careful not to move too quickly. He looked up at the house and saw that his little brother had stepped out on the porch to greet him. He'd made the right decision, even if he didn't understand the regret, guilt, and fear tangled up in his gut.

"It's been too long." Mason wrapped his brother in a big, one-armed bear hug.

"How are you?" Calvin took a step back. He had their mom's blue eyes, their father's nose and stubborn streak. "Can't believe you got shot."

"All in a day's work. I've missed you."

"I've missed you too, but Tulsa's less than a two-hour flight from Atlanta."

"That goes for you as well. But once that baby comes, I think I plan on showing up. How's Sarah?"

"She wanted to be here, but the doctor won't let her travel."

Calvin and Sarah's first child was due next month. A little girl they planned to name Emma Rose after Sarah's grandmother. She was going to be their father's first grandchild. Their aunt would have been proud.

His brother's question broke the silence. "Are you ready for this?"

"I'm still not sure I want to go in there."

"You didn't fly all the way from Atlanta to back out now."

"I did have a little encouragement on that side." He'd wanted to pick up the phone a dozen times over the past twelve hours to check on Emily and see how she was. But he respected her need for space. Prayed that she'd have room for him in her life when he returned.

"A new girlfriend?"

"She's . . . she's just a friend." For now.

"Listen to her, then. Sounds like she might be worth keeping."

"She is."

Funny how bad he wished she were here. He wasn't sure how it was possible, but so much had changed. And while he had no idea what the future held, he was certain about one thing. He had no desire to move forward without her. He'd spent the entire trip in prayer over his new relationship with Emily. And over his lost relationship with his father. Years of lost time. Mountains of regrets. Wondering if there was even a way to bridge the gap between them. Knowing that it probably wouldn't have changed anything, but wondering anyway, if he'd tried harder . . .

Today was something he was going to have to face on his own. And no matter how badly he wanted to erase his past, lingering memories that had haunted him and the pain that came with them had become a part of who he was today. Emily had been right. It gave him the drive to help kids like Rafael and make a difference in the world. For that reason alone, he wouldn't change anything.

"You can do this. We all can. No matter what happened in the past, we're family."

"I know."

Only, his younger brothers didn't remember their dad passed out on the floor, the women who'd come and gone, or all the times he'd left them alone.

"He loves you, Mason. He always has."

Forgive him.

I don't know how, Jesus.

"Come on."

Mason followed Calvin through the front door. The living room had been set up with medical equipment against the back wall and a hospital bed in the middle of the remaining space.

Nathanial Taylor was smaller than Mason remembered. He

wasn't sure he'd even recognize him if he hadn't seen an updated photo. He'd been told his father wasn't going to live much longer, and by looking at him, he could see why. Face drawn, skin pale . . . this was the man he'd spent his life hating.

Mason and his father shared the same tall frame, thin nose, and cinnamon brown eyes, but beyond that they shared nothing. Not even the happy memories most children had of their fathers. On the flight, he'd worked to remember everything he could about his childhood when his father had been a part of it, but he couldn't remember more than half a dozen fleeting incidents. The only good one was the baseball game. Either he had a really bad memory or there simply weren't any other good memories to resurrect.

"You came." His father's voice was hoarse and unsteady.

Mason stopped at the side of the bed, not sure of what to say.

"I . . . I understand you're a cop."

"A detective. I work mostly undercover."

"Detective. I'm impressed, though not surprised. I saw a story on the news this morning about that ransom case you just led. Heard you took a bullet and saved a young girl's life."

Mason reached for his injured shoulder. "It was nothing."

"I bet it wasn't nothing to that girl and her family. I'm proud of you. Always knew you'd turn out to be a fine young man." He turned his face away and started coughing, the effort shaking his entire body.

Mason wanted to run out of the room. The smell of urine and antiseptics overpowered him. He hadn't come here to listen to his father talk about how proud he was of him. He wasn't sure why he'd come here.

Forgive him.

He shook his head. How could he forgive a man who walked out on his mother? Who'd drunk his paycheck week after week? Who'd left them with nothing?

God, I know what's right, but how can I forgive him for what he did to our family?

Craig walked into the room and gave Mason a big hug, along with the reprieve he needed before turning back to his father.

"I wanted you all to be here. Together."

Mason worked to curb the emotion as he stood between his two brothers at the side of their dying father.

"I . . . I lived my life regretting so many things," his father continued. "Leaving your mother and you boys. Not being there when Sam died. Missing out on soccer games and science projects and senior proms. My first grandchild is about to be born, and I'm not even going to get to hold her."

"There's still a chance, Dad," Calvin interrupted.

He shook his head. "I spent my life believing lies. Not anymore. I paid a lawyer to make out my will last month. I'm leaving the three of you everything I have. I figure you can sell this place and split the profits. It isn't much, but hopefully it will help."

Mason felt the lump of anger he'd been carrying swell. "You don't get it, do you? I don't want your money. There's only one thing I ever wanted from you. I just wanted you to be there."

"I'm sorry I wasn't, Son. I don't know what else to say."

Mason pressed his lips together and focused on a dark spot on the wall. He hadn't heard his father call him "Son" for twenty years. Any apology seemed inadequate when placed beside a lifetime of hurt.

An apology couldn't take away the look of pain on his mother's face when she found out about his mistress. It couldn't make up for all the birthday parties and soccer games missed, or bring back his brother Sam.

Sorry didn't change anything.

"Why now? What's changed to make you want to suddenly make up for all your failings as a father?" He knew the words would sting, but there was no sense not calling a spade a spade.

His father lowered his head. "Looking death in the eye can make you see things a lot more clearly."

"Is that all you have to say?"

"Mason—" Calvin began.

His father tried to hold up his hand. "It's okay. You deserve to be angry, and I deserve whatever you have to say. I know I wasn't much of a father to you and I would be the first to admit it. I never knew how to show you that I loved you."

He started coughing again. Mason took a step back. He'd thought that in coming, he'd somehow find a peace over his past. All he felt right now was a desire to run.

"I need to go." Mason walked toward the door. Built-up anger swept through him. He couldn't do this. Not now. Maybe not ever.

Forgive him.

Mason grabbed the handle of the front door, then stopped. *Forgive him.*

Mason paused, then let go of the handle and walked back across the room. He watched his father cough while trying to catch his breath. Helpless. Broken. He wouldn't want to die that way. He didn't want his father to die that way either.

He reached out and took his father's bony hand. "I forgive you. I want . . . I just need you to know that."

His father smiled and closed his eyes.

———

Mason was about to hang up when Emily finally answered the phone.

"Mason?"

"Emily . . . I . . . I'm sorry. I know I shouldn't have called, it's just that . . ."

"No, it's okay. I'm glad you did."

"I just wanted to make sure you are okay. Were you asleep?"

"Trying to. I couldn't sleep at all last night. Too much swimming through my head."

"You could take something. An over-the-counter sleeping pill."

"I probably should, but what about you? Have you seen your father?"

"Yes, but . . . he passed away this afternoon."

"I'm sorry."

"So am I. Funny how I didn't think it mattered, but now that he's gone, there's this huge aching hole inside me. I miss him."

"Did you get to talk to him?"

"Yes. I told him I forgave him."

There was a pause. "When are you coming back to Atlanta?"

"I need to stay a few days to help my brothers with the estate. I should be back by the weekend. Monday at the latest."

"Call me when you get back, okay?"

Mason smiled. "I'd like that."

CHAPTER
38

Emily dumped the rest of the ice cream into one of her mother's crystal bowls, then licked the spoon. She'd regret the indulgence tomorrow, but for tonight she was giving herself permission to feed her grieving heart. And her heart desperately needed a sugar overdose. Losing Charlie wasn't the issue. She was long past that. But knowing he'd used her had left her feeling vulnerable.

Tossing the empty container into the trash, she hopped up on the stool at the kitchen bar and looked around her mother's newly decorated kitchen. Maple cabinets with glass fronts. Slate flooring, painted brick on the walls. The details they'd agonized over seemed insignificant after all they'd gone through in the past week.

How could I have been so wrong about someone, God?

The furnace clicked on and Emily felt the blast of warm air against the back of her neck from the vent. She knew everyone was worried about her. Her mom, her dad. Avery . . . Grace had called to see how she was getting along. Had offered to stop by if she needed to talk. A dozen friends and teachers at school had left messages on her phone. Even their pastor had called to see if she needed any counseling. If she were honest with herself, she knew she did. Principal Farley had given her the week off, but she'd insisted she'd be back in school on Thursday. She couldn't expect her students to show up when she was at home hiding under the covers.

"Hey, Sis. Save any for me?"

Emily licked the back of the spoon and shot Avery a guilty look as she limped into the room with her cane. "I wasn't expecting to see you again today."

Avery picked up the empty carton of cookie dough ice cream. "I can tell."

"I think there might be another quart in the freezer, unless Daddy got to it before me."

"I'm fine, actually." Avery dropped her purse on the counter. "Jackson just took Tess and me out to dinner and I ate far too much. I knew Mama and Daddy were out as well, so I just stopped by on our way home to check on you and pick up Tess's schoolbag. They're waiting in the car so we could have a moment alone to chat."

Finding a moment alone had never been easy in this household. But Emily knew Avery well enough to know that brushing her away would only make her push more.

"You're not sleeping here tonight?"

"With all the animals, Tess and I decided it's easier to be at home."

"How's your leg?"

"Sore, but I'll live." Avery eased her jacket off and laid it on the bar chair. "How are you?"

"Well, let's see." Emily took a bite of the ice cream, wondering if she'd ever be able to push aside the haunting memories. "I was held hostage, saw someone killed—or so I thought. Found out that my ex-fiancé never loved me, ended up shooting him, *and* was held at knifepoint by a murderous cartel agent, so yeah . . . it's been quite a week so far, and it's only Tuesday."

Avery set her hands on her hips and shook her head. "So, I'll repeat my question. How are you? Sister to sister."

"Sister to sister? Tired. Relieved. Grateful for what I have. Wondering how you do what you do day after day. I've never been in a situation where I felt completely out of control like that." Recent memories surfaced as they'd been doing all day. It was going to take a long time for them to fade. "Like no matter what I did, I couldn't stop the inevitable from happening."

"I do the same thing you do. Take one day at a time. And pray that somehow, maybe I can make a difference in this crazy, mixed-up world." Avery caught Emily's gaze. "Just like you with your students."

Emily shook her head. "At least what I do doesn't involve criminals and flying bullets."

Avery's hand moved to her bandaged thigh. "There are days I could do without that part."

"What about Tess?" Emily caught the worry in her sister's eyes as she took another bite of ice cream. It was one thing to experience a terrifying situation, but for your child to have lived through it . . . "How is she handling things?"

Avery's brow furrowed. "She'll be going to counseling for a while to work through things—something she's nervous about—but I know it's important for her healing. She's had to deal with a lot over the past few years, and now I'm worried about how yesterday's trauma will impact her."

"What happened yesterday affected all of us. You. Jackson. Mama. Dad. Mason. I also think it made us—or at least me—realize that life is too short to squabble about things that don't matter. Have you talked any with Mama today?"

"We talked while you were taking a nap," Avery said. "She's battling with guilt over dropping Tess off late, convinced if she'd been on time, Tess would have been in her classroom and safe."

"We can't know that."

"I told her that." Avery reached out and squeezed her hand.

"I know you've been told this, but if you need someone to talk to about what happened, I'm always here for you."

"I know." Emily nodded, not wanting to take for granted the support being offered. "I just need some space to work through everything. As for you, I'm glad you have Jackson to help you through this."

"I can't imagine a better man for Tess and me, and while I realize the road ahead isn't going to be smooth at every turn, he's the best thing that's happened to me in a long, long time. He makes me happy, pushes me to be a better person, loves me . . ." Avery cocked her head. "What about you?"

"What about me?"

"I understand Mason left for Colorado to be with his family early this morning."

Emily knew where Avery was headed, but she wasn't sure she was ready to go there. "His father passed away this afternoon."

"I'm sorry to hear that. I knew he was going there to visit family, but I didn't know the situation was so serious."

"It's sad, actually. He hasn't had a relationship with his father since he was a kid."

"Is there something else you need to talk about?"

Leave it to Avery to pry. "Like?"

"You're not going to make this easy on me, are you?"

Emily smiled. "No."

"What's going on between you and Mason?"

Emily dug the spoon into the bowl and pulled out a gooey bite. Not sure what her sister's reaction was going to be. "You could tell?"

"The way he looked at you, the way you looked back. His hand on your back for support . . . Do you want me to go on?"

"No." Emily felt her cheeks flush. "I'm not sure exactly what happened, and I certainly have no idea what the future holds, but what if he's the one, Avery? The idea both excites and terrifies me."

"What did you tell him?"

Emily took the last bite of her ice cream, then headed for the sink to rinse the bowl. "That I needed time to think. Some space."

"Don't keep him at bay for too long. He's cared about you for a long time."

Emily turned around and leaned against the countertop. "You know that?"

"I know that Michael told me that he tried to ask you out once."

"That was years ago."

"I think it's sweet, actually," Avery said. "That his interest in you has never really waned."

"You wouldn't have thought it was sweet yesterday when you were convinced Mason was the department mole."

"A lot has changed since yesterday."

"Yeah, it has."

The lives of so many had been altered forever. Rafael. Eduardo. Charlie was gone. And Mason had somehow managed to steal a corner of her heart.

"I'm sorry about Charlie. I knew he wasn't the one for you, but I had no idea he was capable of such betrayal."

"We all read him wrong."

Avery touched her bandaged leg and shifted in her seat. "You have to understand that my investigation into Michael's death was never motivated by anything against Mason personally."

"Are you sure about that?"

"He was Michael's best friend, ate Thanksgiving dinner with us, and sat in the den more times than I could ever count watching Sunday afternoon football with Dad. I was simply following the trail of evidence, and I couldn't let personal feelings stop me from finding the truth. Charlie planted just enough evidence to throw me off."

How many people had Charlie hurt? "Apparently, he did a good job."

"I never thought I'd say this, but I actually think Mason's perfect for you."

"Really?"

"We could always plan a double wedding."

"Whoa, slow down." Emily held up her hands and shook her head. "It's not that simple. If, and I do mean if, things happen to work out between Mason and me, it's going to be a long, slow time of getting to know each other. Yesterday was simply the first step."

"Seems perfectly simple to me. I remember you talking to me about him once. It's about time your feelings were brought to the surface."

Emily moved to sit back down at the bar stool beside Avery. If she were honest, the feelings had been mutual. That's what was scaring her. Trusting her heart felt like jumping off the deep end.

"What happened with Charlie . . . ," she said. "It just scares me. I loved him, Avery, but despite his crazy babbling of us running away together, I'm not sure he even planned to marry me. Our relationship was a farce, and I didn't have a clue. I don't know how I missed something like that. Deciding to put my heart on the line again is scary."

"We all missed the clues, but not all men are like Charlie."

"I know Mason is different. I truly believe his heart is for God and now maybe even for me, but the whole thing has my head spinning. What if you'd been right about him? What if he was the mole?"

"He isn't."

"But what if he was? Would I be walking into another situation like I was in with Charlie?" Emily wrapped her fingers around the edges of the bar stool. She'd tried to give Mason counsel on making choices. Maybe it was time to listen to her own advice.

It's just important to look at things both ways. To try to temporarily look past the emotion of the moment that can blind us.

Emotion was blinding her. Making her want to give in to fear. But if she didn't give Mason a chance, she'd never know what could be between them.

"Trust is hard," Avery said. "I've had to struggle with some of the same fears with Jackson. Ethan died, leaving me alone. It's scary to think that could happen again."

"Is it worth it in the end?"

"Opening up your heart to loving someone? I'm learning that no matter how fast and how far you want to run, when you find that right person who can ground you, keep you focused in the right direction, challenge you spiritually . . . it's worth whatever the risk to your heart."

"So you're saying I should give Mason a chance?"

"What do you think?" Avery asked.

"I've spent all day deliberating between calling him and swearing off men forever, because opening up my heart to someone else feels like a huge leap of faith." Emily tried to put her thoughts into words. "But I think I'm ready to chuck my list of requirements. I've realized that I need to trust God and my own good sense. I know that Mason's heart is for God, and I believe that in the end, all those things combined is better than any checklist I could ever come up with."

"Good, because you can't let Charlie scar your heart so bad you end up missing out on someone worth taking a chance on. And I definitely think Mason's worth your taking that chance."

CHAPTER 39

Emily sat down beside Mason on the couch, feeling the odd combination of excitement that he was here and complete awkwardness. She uncrossed her legs, trying to find a comfortable position, but the row of Mama's decorative pillows propped up behind them forced her to sit up straight.

She eyed the neatly wrapped package sitting next to him. "You didn't have to bring anything."

He attempted to lean back against the pillow with the silk peacock appliqué and shot her an uncomfortable smile. "It's the Hunt family sweater."

"From last Christmas Eve." She'd almost forgotten the tradition.

Mason had gone home with the family gag gift. The sweater—made from eight skeins of bright green and red and crocheted by Daddy's now deceased older sister—had been passed back and forth among family members and close friends for over a decade.

"You need to make sure Jackson gets it this year."

"Not a bad idea." He jabbed at the offending pillow with his elbow and nodded. "I appreciate your parents inviting me over. They were always good to include me in your family holidays."

Or at least they had until Michael's death. Michael's death had changed so many things.

She clasped her hands around her knees. "They've been waiting for you to return from Colorado so they can thank you in person for everything you did."

Mason Taylor had accomplished the impossible and moved from enemy number one to a part of the family again.

She searched for something to say, hoping to avoid an uncomfortable silence. "Any updates on Rafael? I've tried to call several times, but I understand he went with his mother to see family in south Georgia for the holidays."

"He did, but I was able to speak with the DA yesterday. The case against him has been dismissed."

"Wow. That's fantastic news. And Eduardo?"

"Things aren't going to turn out quite so good for him. He's looking at a page full of charges, all dealing with drug trafficking. Even though he's a minor, as soon as he gets out of the hospital, he'll end up spending some time behind bars." Mason's fingers tapped against the red-and-white snowman wrapping paper beside him. "How's your sister?"

"She's doing well. Healing nicely. And your rib cage?"

"The bruising is pretty much gone."

"I'm glad." Emily recrossed her legs. "They should be back any minute. All of them. My parents took Avery and Tess to the mall for some last-minute Christmas shopping."

"I don't mind." He glanced at his watch. "I was early."

"I'm glad. It gives us time to . . . to talk."

Emily groaned inwardly. She'd spent the past few days anticipating Mason's return and imagining where their relationship might be heading. But now that he was here, she felt like a tongue-tied teenager who was worried she was going to say something stupid. Or maybe she'd simply been wrong about them. Maybe now that the danger had passed, things were just back to the way they used to be. Maybe Mason was never going to be anything more than a family friend to her. Except she no longer saw him as an old family friend, nor did she want him to see her that way.

Mason's laugh pulled her from her thoughts.

She looked up at him, confused. "What's so funny?"

He leaned forward. "Listen to us. We sound like two single misfits who've been set up by their best friends on a blind date only to discover they have nothing in common. What happened last week might have skewed our emotions some—but I'm hoping that my description doesn't fit us."

She blew out a breath of relief, thankful she wasn't the only one feeling the awkwardness of the situation. "Maybe we do need to start over, but first . . ." She pulled two of the frilly pillows from behind her, threw them onto the chair across from them, then sank back into the couch with a sigh of relief.

"Your mother won't mind?"

"If she does, you can blame me."

He smiled, grabbed the two pillows behind him, and chucked them onto the chair beside hers before settling back.

"Better?"

"Much."

She felt herself starting to relax. "Tell me about your time with your family."

His gaze dropped, but she didn't miss the peace in his expression that had been lacking before he left. "Funny how something I dreaded so much turned into such a blessing. With my father gone, we'll never have the relationship I always wanted, but I still feel a closure I never expected. Peace that when my dad died I was there, exactly where I needed to be."

"I'm glad. I know that being there couldn't have been easy, but now you can move on with no regrets."

"I owe you for pushing me in the right direction, but what about you? You've had a lot of emotions to work through over the past week as well."

She pressed her lips together. The nightmares had started that first night. She'd awakened drenched in sweat, terrified that Charlie was going to kill her. The dreams had come less frequently as the week progressed, but she knew it would take time for them to vanish completely.

"It's going to be impossible to forget some of the things I saw. Especially shooting Charlie . . ." She stared beyond him at the lit Christmas tree in the corner of the room. "But I've spent a lot of time talking with Avery, Grace, and my parents, which has helped, and hopefully one day, I'll be able to look past what happened."

"I've always found it ironic that cops shoot bad guys on TV every episode," he continued, "but in real life it's not that way. Killing someone will always haunt you to some degree."

"You know that from personal experience?"

He nodded. "Yeah."

She smiled up at him, realizing how remarkable it was that she'd found someone who not only cared about her, but who understood what she was going through as well. "I'm glad you're here."

"I am too, because I'm sitting beside one of the most beautiful women I know." Mason took her hand and ran his thumb across the back of her fingers. "Though I am worried about one thing. I've heard rumors at work that you've sworn off dating handsome officers in uniforms."

"Really?" She laughed. "I'm not sure that will be a problem since I didn't think you wore a uniform."

"Is that my escape clause?"

"It very well could be."

Emily's smile was back as she breathed in the scent of Christmas. Cinnamon. Evergreen. And Mason's tangy cologne. The fireplace crackled in the corner, casting shadows around the living room. The consequences of what had happened might not vanish overnight, but for now all she wanted was to capture a few moments alone with the man sitting beside her.

His shoulder brushed against hers. Emily looked up at him and felt her heart race in anticipation. It was like days back in high school, waiting for the boy she liked to make a move. Because the more she got to know Mason, the more she liked him. His sense of humor, his compassion, his faith . . . His arm slid around her, then he ran his fingers along the base of her neck.

"You know," she began, "this . . . attraction between us could be nothing more than reaction to the danger of facing a ransom situation. A kind of hero-victim syndrome."

"Trying to play the devil's advocate?"

She flashed him a smile. "I just want to make sure you realize what you're getting into."

"Oh, I've heard a lot of stories about the Hunt women. They're stubborn, feisty—"

"What?"

"—and beautiful, as I've already said. I'm willing to take a chance if you are." He raised her chin until she was looking into his eyes. "And I have an idea of where we could start."

"Are you always so forward?"

"Only with a woman sitting beside me that I'm falling for."

She felt her heart pound as he leaned in closer. The front door banged open, startling both of them as it blew in a gush of cold air and noisy laughter.

Emily pulled back. "Looks like everyone is back."

"Bad timing."

"Very bad timing."

Avery stepped into the living room as Emily and Mason stood up, a gleam in her eye as she pulled off her gloves. "What have the two of you been up to?"

Emily swallowed her disappointment of the missed kiss and

smiled innocently at her sister. "We've been waiting for you to get back so we can start the festivities."

Her father shut the door behind them, then shed his coat. "You know how it is shopping with three women who can't make up their minds about anything. It takes forever."

"Daddy."

He winked at Avery. "Which has me worried, considering all the wedding shopping ahead of us."

Emily caught the guarded look that passed between Avery and Jackson. "The wedding is still on . . . isn't it?"

"Oh yes." Avery hesitated, leaving Emily to wonder what was going on. "But there has been a slight change of plans."

"Avery?" Mama frowned. "What kind of change of plans?"

"Instead of a fall wedding, we've been talking about Valentine's Day."

"*This* Valentine's Day?" Mama handed her coat to Daddy, clearly not pleased with the announcement. "Do you realize that would give us less than two months to plan the wedding?"

Avery let Jackson help her out of her sweater, still careful about her injury. "If you want to talk about rushing things, we just walked in on your youngest daughter looking awfully cozy with a guy she's never even gone on an official date with."

"Wait a minute." Emily felt her cheeks flush. "Don't make this about me."

"We could have opted for New Year's, Mama," Avery threw out.

"Don't worry, Mrs. Hunt." Jackson wrapped his arms around Avery and Tess. "The three of us have been talking and we're planning to keep things simple. We're thinking about a small church wedding with just a few friends and family."

"It sounds perfect, doesn't it?" Avery asked.

"Now I'm not by any means trying to steal the spotlight from the happily engaged couple," Daddy said, "but I think a change of subject is in order, and we do have something else to celebrate tonight. I've been waiting to say it publicly. Mason, our family owes you a lot for what you did last week."

"I was just doing my duty, sir."

"Maybe, but you risked your life to save my daughter and my granddaughter, and for that I'll be forever grateful. I want you to know that you're always welcome in my house . . . as long as you realize that I'm not ready to walk my other daughter down the aisle anytime soon."

Emily's eyes widened. "Daddy!"

Perhaps getting to know each other in secret would have been a better alternative to having their first unofficial date at a family gathering on Christmas Eve.

"Daddy's right," Avery said. "And while it seems insignificant, I owe you a public apology, Mason. In the pursuit of justice, I went after the wrong man. The fact that Charlie framed you, and I didn't catch it—"

"Please, no apologies. Charlie always was good at what he did, but unfortunately, that proficiency crossed over to the other side of the law. I just wish things hadn't ended the way they did."

"At least we can celebrate the fact that my three girls are okay, though there is one person missing from the celebration this evening." Her father took her mother's hand and drew it against his chest. "It's been a long, hard year without Michael, but at least nothing can take away the memories we have of him."

"We'll have time to reminisce later." Emily didn't miss the tears in her mother's eyes as she spoke. "Dinner will be on the table in ten minutes. So everyone go wash up and meet us in the dining room."

A moment later, Emily was alone in the living room with Mason again. "Was this the reintroduction back into our family that you expected?"

"Considering I never expected the possibility of getting you with the package, no. It's even better. And I noticed something else." Mason grinned at her and looked up. "Mistletoe."

"Maybe we should try again, because we can't exactly break tradition, now can we?"

"That would definitely go against the holiday spirit."

He wrapped his arms around her waist and pulled her against him. Their first kiss was everything she'd imagined. Passionate. Deep. Intense . . . and laced with that unquantifiable spark that was now burning within her. After a long, drawn-out moment, he took a step back, leaving her to catch her breath.

Mason's smile widened. "I never thought I'd actually get to kiss Michael Hunt's little sister."

"I think he'd approve."

"Not that I would ever give him the satisfaction of asking for his approval if he were here." He ran his fingers across the turned-down collar of her vintage military jacket, sending shivers of delight down her spine. "I can't make any promises about what the future holds for us, but I'd like to discover it with you."

She smiled up at him. Maybe everything hadn't healed, but her heart was ready to take that chance. "I'd like that too."

He gripped the steering wheel with one hand, the coffee he'd bought down the street at a local convenience store with the other. He hadn't expected that seeing them all together would be so emotional. The Christmas tree sat in the corner of the living room with its dancing white lights and his grandmother's glass star on the top. He could hear strains of "Joy to the World" filling the cold night air. Christmas Eve had always been Mama's favorite day of year.

He missed them. Hated the fact that they'd been deceived. Unsure if he'd ever figure out a way to make things right.

If he stayed undercover, he'd end up with a contract hit on his head. If he tried to come home, he'd be arrested. His handler was right. Unless their plan worked, there would be no escape.

Please, God, just one more week to finish the job.

Coming
SPRING 2015

Book 3 in the
Southern Crimes series

Read an
EXCERPT

1

Michael Hunt staggered from the impact of the blow. His hand reached automatically for his bruised rib cage. He knew the techniques of ignoring pain. Bargain with self. Dissociate yourself from your body. Focus on the finish line. But focusing on the finish line wasn't easy when two years of undercover work was about to vanish.

His attacker, Tomas, shoved Michael into a chair and hovered over him. Topping six foot with a solid two hundred and fifty pounds of muscle, the man was clearly enjoying himself.

"I can do this all day." Tomas's smile displayed a gold tooth and far too much pleasure. "What's your real name?"

Michael struggled for a breath. "Michael Linley."

"Who are you working for? CIA? FBI? DEA?"

Michael groaned, then spit out the same name he'd repeated over and over the past twenty minutes. "Antonio Valez."

He could add his own list of jumbled abbreviations for Valez. CEO . . . CFO . . . CIO . . . After two years of working with the real estate mogul, the answers, both real and fake, surfaced automatically despite the thick fog clouding his brain brought on from the pain. Michael Linley . . . Liam Quinn. . . Michael Hunt. All layers of who he was and who he'd become.

"Try again," Tomas spat out.

Michael's jaw clinched as the man pulverized his side with his ironlike knuckles, knocking the breath out of him. He fought to concentrate on a water spot on the dingy wall, shaped like a rabbit. Tried to concentrate on anything but the pain. Anything besides the fact that today was Christmas and he might not ever see his family again. The best he could hope for—if he managed to survive—was a few cracked ribs and bruises.

But he wasn't betting on that.

"Last chance. Who are you working for?"

Michael groaned, tired of the relentless questions. The lines between fact and fiction had begun to fade months ago. All he'd ever wanted was to serve God and country. Now his family believed he was dead. His country believed he was a traitor. To live, he needed to convince Tomas he really was the man he'd claimed to be. A corrupt businessman, happy to insure Valez's dirty money came out clean. But while today wasn't the first time he'd faced death, something told him he'd run out of extra lives.

Michael lifted his head and caught Tomas's gaze. "I keep telling you. I work for Antonio Valez. You've known me for months. Nothing has changed." He forced a weak smile. "Besides, why would I betray any of you? I make too much money off of your boss."

"That's a question you're still going to have to answer to him, but in the meantime, I have something that should help jog your memory."

Michael looked up, his left eye swollen, vision blurred. Two of Valez's goons dragged a man into the cottage. It took Michael a few seconds to recognize Sam Kendall. The man's face was beaten. Blood crusted across his right cheek and his upper lip was split. They dumped Kendall onto the floor in front of Michael, then one of them shoved him over onto his back with his boot.

Kendall worked to brace his elbows against the floor in order to sit up. "I'm sorry, Michael."

Sorry?

The word shot through Michael like a stray bullet. Nothing—especially not sorry—would save either of them at this point. Neither could sorry make up for all those months of risking his life for the sake of justice. He never should have trusted the man. Never should have believed that having an inside man would save him.

Michael turned away, trying to mask any hint of recognition, but one look at Tomas's eyes and Michael knew everything he'd managed to accomplish had just been destroyed. He'd never be able to take down Valez and the men above him. His decision to meet with Kendall had been a mistake. Undercover work had always come natural to him, but he'd missed something today. Something that could end up costing both of them everything.

But despite the odds, he wasn't ready to give up. Not yet.

Michael shifted his gaze back to Tomas. "Wait until Antonio gets back. He knows I'd never betray him."

"Really? I find that hard to believe, because Antonio's the one who told me to take care of this problem. He's had some doubts regarding your loyalty, and this man proves it."

Michael drew in a breath and felt crushing pain sweep through his rib cage. Push too hard and Tomas *would* kill him. Push just hard enough and he might be able to save them both.

"Does Antonio really know what you're doing or is this your own personal witch hunt?" Michael kept talking, not giving Tomas a chance to answer. "I know how this works, and I even understand. Valez isn't easy to impress, and you need to climb the ranks. But what if you're wrong about me. Betraying one of the boss's trusted men isn't going to go over well when he finds out what you've done."

Michael caught the seed of doubt germinating in Tomas's gaze, but was another string of lies going to be enough?

"Untie me and I'll explain everything." Michael jutted his chin toward Kendall. "Including this man, because clearly someone is feeding you the wrong information."

"I don't think so." Tomas shook his head, clearly not ready to buy into Michael's attempt to talk his way out of an early grave. "We intercepted a message from your friend here to meet you. We know he's one of them. That the two of you have been communicating over the past few months, primarily phone conversations on burn phones and blocked email addresses, and that you were passing information on to him."

"No—"

"There's no need to defend yourself." Tomas laughed. "Your friend here's already confessed everything."

Michael studied Kendall's expression but couldn't read him. Tomas knew how to play the game as well as he did, but still, he had to be bluffing. They were both trained to withstand interrogation, which meant if Kendall had kept his wits, Tomas knew nothing. He was simply playing him. But if he were wrong and Tomas *had* stumbled upon the truth . . .

Michael felt his world slowly collapse around him. If they could tie him to the agent, they'd both end up with a bullet in their heads. Even if he did survive, killing Kendall would put him on the run, not just from the cartel, but the government as well.

The hesitation Michael had caught momentarily in Tomas's gaze vanished. "You do know what Valez does to people who betray him, don't you?"

It was a rhetorical question. Michael had seen firsthand what Valez and his men could do. The only reason he hadn't walked away months ago was because there were bigger fish to fry.

Taking down Valez would put a dent in the cartel's grip of the southern United States. Finding out the identity of La Sombra could cripple the entire organization.

He knew the stakes, just like he'd known the risks of staying undercover. There was no one to come to his rescue. No one beside Kendall who knew where he was. Or knew for certain, for that matter, that he was innocent.

Funny how life played out sometimes. This morning, despite Kendall's new reservations, he'd convinced the agent to give him another week before he walked away. Another week was going to be seven days too late.

"Can't answer?" Tomas's smile broadened, dragging Michael back to the present. "Valez has a dozen ways to silence people, but he prefers methods that are slow and painful. Whatever method he chooses, you'll both end up at the bottom of the Atlantic."

Michael's chest heaved, followed by another wave of searing pain through his torso. The authorities would never find either of them. All it would take was a trip out into the ocean, a weight, and their bodies would disappear. The chilly water surrounding the lengthy string of barrier islands off the coast of Georgia would become the perfect graveyard.

Tomas pointed his weapon at Kendall's head and pulled the trigger. Michael flinched at the explosion. Kendall's body jerked. A trickle of red trailed down his forehead as he stared lifelessly at the ceiling.

"You didn't have to do that!" Michael felt his heart rate accelerate, while his mind worked to absorb what had just happened. This wasn't how it was supposed to end.

I'm not ready to die, Lord. Not yet. You brought me here to help bring about justice, and this . . . this is pure evil.

Michael sat rigid, waiting for a bullet to stamp out his own life. Had he really thought he could outsmart the cartel? Believed they wouldn't find out what he was doing? His desire to bring them down might have numbed the sense of danger, but he'd never forgotten that death could—at any moment—become his reality. Just like he'd never stopped believing that integrity and truth could still prevail in a fallen world.

Tomas pressed the gun against Michael's forehead. The weapon clicked. Adrenaline soared. Nothing. Michael stared at the barrel of the gun, his heart racing as a wave of nausea swept over him. Russian roulette wasn't a game he wanted to play.

"Don't worry." Tomas pushed Michael's head back with the barrel of the gun and laughed. "The boss has something different planned for you. He's currently caught up with some unexpected business, but he'll arrive early tomorrow morning so he can take care of you himself. He told me he has something special in mind for you. Which gives you just over twelve hours to think about your final demise."

Tomas shoved the gun into the holster in his waistband, then exited the room with his two lackeys. Michael's gaze flicked toward Kendall's lifeless body, his open eyes still staring up at him.

It wasn't supposed to end this way, God . . .

A stab of pain shot through his throbbing rib cage as he weighed his options. It would be dark within the hour. His hands and feet were tied with zip ties, the windows of the cottage barred, and the nearest neighbor—a half-dozen miles away—would never hear him. Which meant he had twelve hours to find a way out. And even if he did manage to escape, finding a way off the island was only the beginning of his problems.

ACKNOWLEDGMENTS

Writing a book is always a team effort. I'm so grateful for my fabulous editors, Andrea, Barb, and Ellen, who are incredible at what they do. And to my family who gives me the time I need to meet my deadlines. Love you guys!

Lisa Harris is a Christy Award finalist and the winner of the Best Inspirational Suspense Novel for 2011 from *Romantic Times*. She has over twenty novels and novella collections in print. She and her family have spent the past ten years living as missionaries in Africa where she works with the women and runs a nonprofit organization that works alongside their church-planting ministry. The ECHO Project works in southern Africa promoting Education, Compassion, Health, and Opportunity and is a way for her to "*speak up for those who cannot speak for themselves . . . the poor and helpless, and see that they get justice*" (Prov. 31:8).

When she's not working, she loves hanging out with her family, cooking different ethnic dishes, photography, and heading into the African bush on safari. For more information about her books and life in Africa visit her website at www.lisaharriswrites.com or her blog at http://myblogintheheartofafrica.blogspot.com. For more information about The ECHO Project, please visit www.theECHOproject.org.

meet
LISA HARRIS

lisahawriswrites.com

AuthorLisaHarris

@heartofafrica

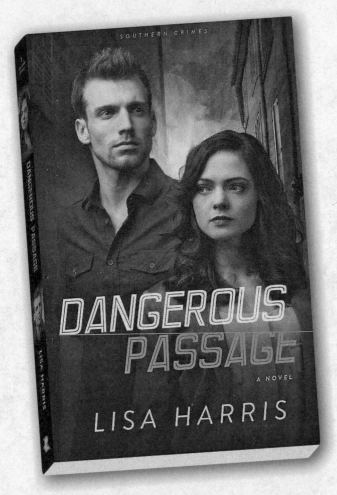